DEPRAVED

USA Today Bestselling Author

TRILINA PUCCI

PROLOGUE

DANTE

"Scusami." *Excuse me.*

The tailor interrupts me and my brothers, holding up another fitted tuxedo shirt for me to try on. I've been here for an hour being fitted for my goddamn wedding tuxedo. The things I do for this woman.

I shrug off the previous shirt I'd tried but couldn't button.

"You're so swole," Luca teases like the asshole he is.

"Who the fuck says that?" Dom chimes in as he adjusts his bow tie.

"Shut it, dick." I laugh, rolling my eyes at Luca. "He's just jealous because I can kick his ass... Need a reminder?"

Luca grumbles, undoing his collar.

"Fucking monkey suits. I've never enjoyed them."

I nod my agreement as our tailor, Sal, helps me into my shirt. I push my arm through the sleeve, but Sal stops, staring at me with concern. I pull my brows together, confused by his abrupt halt.

"Sal. Why are we stopping?"

"I apologize, signore. I didn't want to hurt you."

His old eyes drop down to where the nasty scar from my first and only gunshot wound mars my arm.

"It's fine, old man. Your eyes are tired. That's an old wound." I frown, the memory flitting through my mind.

He laughs and continues to help me on with my shirt, and my brothers look at me solemnly, knowing that I didn't just lose some skin and blood that day.

"If you don't mind me asking..." Sal coaxes, his curiosity getting the better of him.

"It's a gunshot wound."

The surprise on his face is evident by his wide eyes. "I hope they paid for that, Mr. Sovrano. Who would be stupid enough to shoot you?"

My face grows serious at the thought.

"My late wife."

CHAPTER ONE

DANTE

Life is crazy, wicked, and beautiful—but only if you fight hard enough to endure it.

Today I watched my brother marry the love of his life. Two years ago, I didn't even know Luca existed, Dominic either, but now I can't remember a time without them.

I stood next to Luca as a co-best man with Dominic and watched him look at the woman who loves him fiercely and promise to always protect her.

But Luca's not the only one who protects her now. Today, we all came together to make his same vow.

Gretchen's married in.

The mafia is our family. Our lifeline. Our legacy.

Me, Dominic, Luca—we're brothers by blood, created by our father. But Antonio, Nico, Vincenzo, and Matteo—they're brothers because of the blood we've spilled together.

All six of us stood at Luca's side knowing that what's precious to him has now become just as important to us.

That's our way.

More importantly, that's my way, as head of this family.

I tip my chin up, blowing a thick cloud of smoke from my lips where we're now seated outside around a table adorned with fancy flowers and candles, smoking our cigars and laughing about the night.

The sky is black, empty of even the stars, but the bulbs that hang outside over our heads reflect tiny halos of light that strike against the darkness. The halos seem misplaced—we're far from sainthood, but I guess even the devil was an angel once.

I look around the patio and through the glass wall that separates us from the party inside.

Luca had this bar decked out to the nines, not that much work was needed, seeing as Charlie's on First has the kind of sexy ambience that lends to jazz music and good scotch.

I wasn't surprised when Luca said he was using this joint for his reception. This place means something to him and Gretchen. Even though I thought this bar was a good venture for us, I'm pretty sure he bought this for her or at least because of her.

Because that's what men do.

We collect that which we don't want anyone else to touch. We're greedy by nature, making sure to possess all the things that elude us, the beautiful treasures we want. Whether it's money, power, or women, our nature tells us there's never enough.

And for men with flexible morals, that desire makes us dangerous. Because love is the only other emotion past hate that can ruin men like us and also give us purpose. Once we feel either down to our core, we'll never have enough.

I'm a man who bears a responsibility bigger than himself. For me, love is a myth, but hate...yeah, I got that shit in spades.

"Luca, your wife has some hot friends. I'm walking around

here with a permanent boner," Matteo throws out, adjusting himself at the table as we all laugh at him.

"Keep it in your pants—we're not at Church..." I warn then look over at Luca. "I still can't believe you blew off your own bachelor party."

He shrugs me off, uncaring, and takes a swig of his drink. My gaze drifts inside, back to where it's been fixed for most of the night: on Sarah London, the curvaceous, raven-haired vixen who manages Church, the exclusive sex club owned by me, Dominic, and Luca.

The moment I saw Sarah, I was attracted to her. It's impossible not to be. She's gorgeous, a pinup hiding behind a demure smile and unreadable eyes.

My thoughts begin to wander as I stare at her. Tilting my head and taking another puff of my cigar, I wonder whether she likes it rough or soft. If she likes to be held down, tied up... or maybe she likes to kneel.

The vision of her on her knees, waiting at my feet, makes my dick jump.

I see Luca nudge Dom to pay attention. Dom's face swings my way, and he smacks the back of my head.

"She's like our sister," he growls.

I bring my hand to my head and laugh. "Then I want to fuck our sister."

Antonio spits out his beer as we howl with laughter.

Luca pushes me, and I chuckle, puffing my cigar again. "She's smoking hot. I'm supposed to ignore that?" I jokingly complain to Matteo, who shrugs sympathetically, laughing again.

The glass door swings open and Blair, one of Gretchen's friends, pops her head out into our outdoor man cave.

"Fellas, the bride wants her groom. You have ten minutes to wrap it up."

Blair's hot in a sophisticated, cultured way. Not my type. I like 'em a little dirty. And the blue eyes I see behind Blair seem to call out to that part of me. Sarah may look sweet, but she's anything but. I can feel it.

"Oh, I'll wrap it up unless you prefer something else…" Matteo flirts with Blair, and we all throw napkins, ice, and whatever else is in our hands at him for his offense, but Blair just laughs.

"Stow it, pretty boy. What are you, twelve?" she chides as Sarah slips up next to her, eyes on me and a saucy smile growing on her lips.

"In inches?" Matteo raises his brows, and Vincenzo pushes his shoulder, but Blair grins sinfully.

Blair walks closer, grabbing him by the hair and pulling his head back roughly.

Bringing her lips dangerously close to his, skimming back and forth, barely touching, she purrs, "You can't handle me. Come see me when you have something to offer and bring your A game because I don't give second chances."

I raise my brows to Antonio, and he shakes with laughter.

Blair releases Matteo's head with a little jerk and walks back inside, but Sarah lingers for a moment at the door, looking back at me. I notice Antonio reach out, but she pulls back before he touches her hand, raising an eyebrow at him.

I can't hide the smirk that graces my face as I watch.

"Hey, beautiful, save me a dance?" Antonio asks as smoothly as he can.

My eyes stay trained on her for her answer, but when hers dart to mine, I bring my cigar to my lips, shaking my head minutely as I take in a few quick draws, watching her bite her bottom lip.

Sarah looks back to Antonio and nods her head. Fuck. She's a saucy little thing.

If that's how you want to play this...get ready, gorgeous.

Matteo turns to the group, interrupting my focus, and bites his fist.

"I think I just met the future Mrs. Prozzi."

The howls and laughter start again, but this time, I don't join. I'm too busy watching Sarah saunter across the room to the bar. That ass is trouble. Fuck me, I want to be in trouble. So fucking bad.

"Let's go before Gretchen kills us," Nico laughs out.

We all stand, buttoning our jackets to walk back inside, but before we get inside, I reach out for Antonio.

"Not her," I say, pointing a finger at Sarah. "She's nobody to you. We clear?" Antonio laughs. "Crystal," he says, chuckling, and walks ahead into the bar.

If anyone leaves with that woman tonight, it'll be me, or they'll be leaving in a fucking hearse because she's something I want.

And I'll be collecting all her pleasure tonight.

Sarah's been nursing that third glass of wine for the last half an hour. I've watched her politely speak to everyone who approaches her and turn down every man who's asked her to dance.

But my favorite part is how she always finds my eyes in the room after she does, seeking my approval, and each time, I give it with a wink. I like this little game we're playing. This silent understanding we're establishing.

Nothing unless I say so.

Dominic walks up with his wife, Drew, and slaps me on the back. "We're taking off, brother. My girl's tired."

Nodding, I lean down and kiss Drew's cheek. "Sweet

dreams, beautiful. Make your boy take care of the kiddos tonight."

She smiles back at me, squeezing my arm, and looks over her shoulder to Sarah. "D... Stop staring at her and go talk to her already. I thought you had game."

A laugh rumbles in my chest, and Dom grabs for her as she squeals, covering her giggling mouth. He circles her waist, lifting her off the ground.

I shake my head, still smiling, "Get out...go home, trouble."

He sets her down, giving me a jerk of his head as Drew wraps her arms around his waist while they walk out to their waiting car.

Bringing the scotch to my mouth, I let the cool liquor slip past my lips, my eyes searching the room again. No Sarah.

She's gone.

My head swings around more obviously, searching as I see a glimpse of her silver dress walk around the corner toward the restrooms, her eyes finding mine as she pauses to make sure I see her.

The idea of pulling her into a dark corner with everyone only a stone's throw away makes my feet carry me with purpose toward where I've been beckoned.

I don't think twice as I round the corner into the dark, empty hallway, my hand gripping the corner of the wall, but my feet slow as I'm enveloped by the darkness.

The only light illuminating the space is coming from a bathroom door because it's open...cracked just enough so that I can see her standing in the entry area of the women's bathroom.

I move in farther, watching with interest, leaning my shoulder against the wall.

She's in front of a velvet, round pink ottoman that's in the middle of the room. Her highheeled foot is on it, dress split, exposing her thigh, with hands on her leg as she adjusts the goddamn garters she has on.

She's a goddamn vision.

My cock starts to push against the fabric inside my slacks, so I reach down, adjusting myself, relishing the feel of pressure against my dick.

Sarah brushes her shiny, straight hair over her shoulder, bringing her chin to it and locks eyes with me. Her gaze drifts down to my hand that's still on my cock, and the sexiest smile graces her lips.

Everything stops.

All my thoughts.

All the sounds.

All my breaths.

It all stops.

The only thing I see, hear, and feel is Sarah.

I see her hands reach for her ankle. Hear the sound of her fingertips running up her leg against the sheer fabric covering her supple skin. And feel her need, her desire, her fucking challenge.

Sarah's hands stop on her thigh, and my eyes drift back to her face, appreciative of the show. Bringing her leg down, she slowly turns to face me then walks toward where I'm watching.

The minute her hand lands on the door, she licks her bottom lip, dragging it between her teeth. "Let me know when you get tired of just watching."

My mouth opens, but before I can answer, the door closes right in my grinning face.

Fuck. I'm going to break this girl in so damn hard tonight.

I turn and groan, looking down at my half-hard cock, and shake my head as I walk back out to say my goodbyes.

Time for me and Sarah to become more intimately acquainted.

CHAPTER TWO

SARAH

I pat some cold water on the back of my neck to try and cool myself down. Holy hell. That man is a gorgeous piece of meat, and I desperately want to take a bite.

The water runs over my fingertips, falling in between them as I smile at myself in the mirror. I can't believe I just teased him like that. It's as if all good decision has flown out of the window.

But fuck it. Weddings are for one-night stands. And it's been a while. *A really long while.* I deserve to let go. *Finally.*

The first time I laid eyes on him, I couldn't help but add him to my fantasy reel.

I've only met Dante in passing a few times and always when it's business related. Thank god his business is his sex club, Church, or I would've never gotten a glimpse of him shirtless. Talk about perks of the job.

He's insanely hot.

Dante's a six-foot-two god, with his delicious olive skin and shaved inky-black hair on display in a muscular frame covered in tattoos.

Tattoos that run from his neck over his shoulder and all the way down his arm to the hand that I hope wraps around my throat as he fucks me into sheer bliss.

A half-laugh escapes my lips over my dirty thoughts, and I step back from the mirror, giving myself one last look.

Here we go.

I grab the door handle, pausing for a moment and wondering if he'll be on the other side. But the moment I open it, I know he's gone, even before I look down the hallway.

Dante has a presence. You can feel him in the room. Everyone can. He's a dangerous, powerful man, and that's catnip for this pussy.

I walk back into the party, heading straight for the bar. I'm going to need some more liquid courage, but a waiter approaches with a glass of red wine, extending it out to me.

"This is from Mr. Sovrano. He said to tell you to say your goodbyes; the two of you will be leaving soon."

A half laugh escapes my mouth, and I'm certain I look stupefied as I accept the wine. I did tell Dante to let me know when he was tired of just watching. What did I expect?

"Thank you," I answer, searching over and around people for my dirty benefactor, but I don't see him.

Warm breath sends goose bumps up my neck, and I grin. Sneaky.

"You look stunning tonight."

I stop mid-sip, realizing it's not Dante behind me. Pivoting and taking a step back, I'm met with a familiar face. A client of Church, a very prominent CEO of a telecommunications company and the pig that's been sniffing around me for months.

No matter how many times I say I'm not interested, this guy's stayed persistent. I could tell Dom and Luca; they would kick him out...or maybe worse. But I won't, because I can handle him myself.

I'm not the kind of girl who needs rescuing. Never have been.

"It's nice to see you, Bill, but I don't remember you being on the guest list," I reply snidely, rolling my eyes and turning to the side, effectively dismissing him.

"I wasn't," he answers with an amused laugh at my dig. "I was passing by, coincidentally, and thought I'd pop in and say congratulations."

"Well then, I'll let you get to it," I answer, turning my head toward him, but when I turn away, I'm met with a scowling Dante glaring at me. *Uh-oh, Bill.*

I can see exactly what Dante's thinking, and a small, mean part of me thinks I should just wait. Let it all play out and watch Bill dig his own grave.

Men like Dante don't show favor to thieves. And for tonight, he's made it clear to everyone in the room that I'm his for the taking.

I haven't missed the signs. You'd have to be blind for them to go unseen.

It's been the most barbaric, power-driven foreplay I've ever experienced. Each time I turned someone down, he gave me his approval. I watched his intentions blister his face every time someone leaned in too close or brushed my shoulder.

And every time a man mentioned my name to him, I could tell, because they would always look at me one last time before pretending I didn't exist.

They weren't allowed to consider me anymore. Not after Dante said so. I've loved every minute of it. Because for tonight, I want to be owned.

My unwelcome guest puts his hand on my waist, causing

my head to swing down to where he's touching me. I look at his smug face with irritation and smirk.

"I wouldn't do that if I were you, Bill."

"Why? Do you bite? Because you know I like that..." he whispers, tugging me in toward him.

Dick.

"No. But he does." I point, watching Bill's face drop as a very pissed-off Dante stalks toward us.

Bill's hand falls from my waist, and I reach down to smooth out the fabric.

"I'd get going before he gets here," I offer, taking another sip of my wine.

He nods, stepping backward before turning to head to the door as I smile against my wineglass.

Dante slows as he approaches me, glowering over at where Bill is leaving the bar.

"Someone I need to kill?"

"No, tough guy." I laugh into his amused face.

His eyes crinkle in the corners as he grins down at me, taking the wineglass from my hand.

"Tell me something, beautiful. How come you turned down everyone who asked you to dance tonight?"

His tongue darts out, running along his bottom lip as he traces his fingers softly down my arms and over the top of my hand, intertwining our fingers.

I stay planted in my spot as he takes a step backward.

"How come, Sarah?" he growls, pulling me forward, forcing me to take a step closer.

"As if you don't already know," I tease.

"Humor me."

"Because I don't follow any man's lead," I answer bravely as we almost seal against each other.

Dante brings my hand to his lips, pressing a soft kiss on the top before he turns it sideways and bites, making me jump, a small gasp escaping my lips.

"We'll see."

His free hand brushes over the curve of my hip, settling against my flesh exposed by my backless dress, as his other releases my hand and snakes around my neck to grip me at the nape.

My fingers curl around the lapels of his tux, lost in our bubble, as my chest begins to rise and fall with the delicious bite of sexual tension.

We stand in silence as he holds me in place.

"We're dancing," he grits out.

I shake my head and grin, opening my mouth to protest, but Dante gives my body a little jerk, cementing me against him and making me wet.

"I wasn't asking." *Holy fuck.*

Our bodies begin to sway, pressing against each other in just the right way. He's fucking me in front of a room full of people, and nobody's the wiser.

Dante leans his face down close to my ear, his tongue running over the sensitive lobe before he whispers in a low, gravelly voice.

"See, following is easy. You just needed the right man to lead."

Dante's hand is burning a permanent mark into my back as we walk through the lobby of his building. We barely made it through the song before he had me whisked away into the car.

The entire ride, we drove in silence, his hand on my thigh, indecently high, where he kneaded and stroked his fingertips deliciously close to my center.

I felt feral—I could've mounted him right there and rubbed up against him until I came.

Jesus, he's making me crazy.

He leads me into the elevator, giving a nod to the attendant. A couple tries to enter but is stopped, and they gawk in confusion toward us as the doors close them out.

Dante stands silently with that sexy damn smirk and leans forward to enter a code on the pad. The metal box begins to move as he pulls his phone from his pocket and types out a quick message, glancing up to the corner of the elevator as he finishes.

My gaze follows his just in time to see the tiny red blinking light go dim then black.

Did he just have the cameras turned off?

His hand leaves my back as he shoves both hands in his pockets, reclining back against the wall and turning his head to look at me.

"Take off the dress."

My eyebrows shoot up as I look back at him. "I'm sorry, what?"

Dante's jaw tenses. "Don't make me repeat myself. Take off your goddamn dress. Leave on the garters. I want you naked in my home."

He jerks his chin for me to start, and as much I want to say *"fuck off"* ...I want to say *"fuck me"* more. Dante's filth is right up my alley.

My hand reaches for the strap of my dress, pushing it off my shoulder as I grin. "The cameras?" I question just to be sure.

"Off," he answers, running a finger delicately over my collarbone. "I'm gonna fucking destroy you tonight, Sarah."

"Promise?" I breathe out haughtily, letting the other strap fall, taking the dress down my frame.

He rises to his full height, pushing off the elevator wall, and lets his eyes roam my body, now only covered in lace panties and garters.

"Perfection."

My nipples pebble against the cold that sweeps over my bare chest as Dante lifts a hand, his finger finding my mouth and pushing inside.

I suck, pulling in my cheeks as the elevator dings. The doors slide open to reveal the entrance to his penthouse. He takes a step out, blocking the door with his foot, and pulls his finger from my mouth.

He traces the wetness down over my neck and chest as my head falls back, all the way to my nipple, circling the hard bud.

I hear him laugh appreciatively when I shiver.

"Walk inside to the living room and sit...ass on your feet. Tonight, you're mine to do with as I please, without question. This is the only time I'll give you a choice. The minute you set foot in this house, that's my permission until you say your word. You understand?"

My eyes connect with his, and I take a confident step forward, gripping his chin and pulling it down to look at me.

"I understand completely...until I say stop. You'll dominate, and I'll submit. But you understand that you get tonight and only tonight?" I purr as I release him, and he nods slowly.

"Make it count," I dare as I saunter the fuck out of the elevator and straight into hell.

Chapter Three

Sarah, One Week Later

My phone buzzes for the five hundredth time, causing my shoulders to tense as I hit ignore. I need to change my number. But I know that's just another Band-Aid until I'm found again and old wounds are torn open.

It's been three years this time: three years of bliss.

And now it's over. It's crazy how my life changed for the better and the worse in one night.

The vibration starts again just as fast as it ended. "Go the fuck away," I breathe harshly, turning off my cell and throwing it into the bottom of my desk drawer.

Closing it with more force than necessary, I take a deep breath and try to calm my nerves before reaching for one of the many portfolios I have strewn across my desk.

Work. I need to focus on work.

The stacks of unvetted potential members in front of me seem never ending, but it's only because I'm trying to get as much done as I can before I disappear.

For the first time in a long time, I allowed myself to care about something, and I don't want it to go to hell when I leave.

When, not *if*, I leave.

The thought makes the tightness grow in my chest again.

My time is ticking here, and I hate it. I don't want to leave Chicago. My apartment. My people. The life I was beginning to live.

Jesus, I'd just finally started to let myself breathe again and desire something.

Goddammit.

The calls started the night I left Dante's apartment. I was on a high put there by a man I was determined to keep as a one-night stand, but even as I left him sleeping in his bed, I knew that would be a fight I might not win.

And I was okay with that.

But then all possibilities leapt off the side of his building, crashing to a bloody death as soon as my phone rang.

When I answered, the familiar voice on the other end said, "One step closer," before the line disconnected.

All good things come to an end. That's the saying.

And when my family finds me here, they'll make sure to bring all the bad with them and end my peace.

Family is the wrong word to describe them.

They're the worst of the worst—desperate for power and corrupted by greed. I grew up with petty criminals, con artists, and thieves. Men with no loyalties and no interest outside of their own.

It was "eat or be eaten" in our house, especially after my mom died, and I got really tired of being chewed up and spit out, so I escaped.

I ran.

Ran as far away as I could from that Boston ghetto, landing

first in California, then Louisiana, Florida, Utah, Oregon, and now Chicago, Illinois.

It's been eight years of changing locations every time they get wise to me. It always starts with calls and then they find my location.

But I'm a ghost each time.

New name, new look, but the same me. At least I hope she's still in there...deep down, hidden under all the necessary survival. My eyes stare off into my office as my thoughts settle in—I haven't stopped in eight long years.

A huge part of me hoped they'd forgotten or lost interest this time. Sooner or later, they have to give up. Whether it's because they tire of this game or they're behind bars, I just have to keep running long enough to outlast them.

The hard part to swallow is that I'd started to believe I'd really escaped this time. Found the one place they'd never find me. I thought I'd won. Despite my past, I'd let myself build a small life, making friends with people instead of living anonymously.

My biggest mistake was letting the one man I knew better than to touch, put his hands all over me.

Girls with secrets like mine don't get a happily ever after.

I fucking know better. The cruelest thing I've ever done to myself was have a taste of a man that's left me with cravings.

The landline on my desk rings, making me jump and a small surprised breath suck in between my lips. My hand instinctively reaches for the handle, but I draw back, chewing the inside of my cheek and staring at the phone.

There are only three people who have this number.

The three people who own this business.

One of which I've been thinking about all week.

I wait, staring at the phone as it rings and rings, then finally stops. Tapping my nails against the desk, I narrow my eyes, hating that I'm actually entertaining thoughts about Dante.

I feel like such a chick. And I hate it.

I don't like feeling regret or hope or any of the bullshit that people who grow up in fancy houses with loving families feel. Each time I do, it just morphs into anger, which fuels my hate for everything I don't have.

And right now, what I don't have is time, but I'm greedy. The moment he finished with me, I wanted him to start again and never stop.

Thinking about it makes heat crawl up my skin, my arms erupting into goose bumps. I reach up to rub the back of my neck, tilting my head to the side.

"Fuck," I breathe out, rolling my shoulders.

I'm a girl with secrets that need to stay buried and skeletons that have to stay hidden, and Dante—he's the guy I can't seem to keep a straight head around.

Not that he's tried to pursue me.

I was just pussy to him. I made sure of that.

I can't be mad. But I am...at myself. And maybe him, but I won't admit that because that makes me way too weak.

I'll never be that for any man.

Then again, the last time I said that, I ended up trussed up and spanked.

My tongue darts out over my lip remembering how he held me still and kissed my lips softly, whispering, "Good girl," into my mouth.

"Look at you," he croons "You were made for this."

Dante runs his tongue over my neck, sinking his teeth into the curve of my neck where my shoulder meets, marking me again.

My ass stings from where Dante's palm left me red and begging for him to fuck me.

The pain is sensuous and erotic, and my eyes droop heavily from the sensations that've made my clit swollen and desperate.

Dante reaches down between my legs, rubbing his large hand on the inside of my thigh, close to where all my need has pooled.

A moan rips from my throat, my hands pulling against where I'm strung up. Thick black leather cuffs have my wrists bound together and locked in above my head.

I'm helpless and at his mercy.

Who am I kidding? I was at his mercy the moment he laid eyes on me.

"I promised you a reward," he murmurs, as his mouth travels down my body, "but I'm selfish, so this is as much for you as it is for me."

Dante reaches above my head and unlatches my wrists, my arms falling heavily to my sides as my chest still heaves from the teasing he's been inflicting over the last hour.

His strong hands grip my waist, hurling me into the air and over his shoulder like a rag doll. I squeal and laugh loudly as he walks his naked frame over to the bed in his room.

My tongue traces the symbols inked on his back before being jerked back over his shoulder into his strong arms. He's holding me like a man holds his bride, except this man is looking at me like I'm his dinner.

"Don't. Fucking. Move." He growls, curling me like a barbell, with his muscled arms, bringing my pussy directly to his face and diving in.

A breath leaves my body as the memory dissipates from my mind like a slow, delicious burn. *Damn.* The memory of him leaves me almost as flustered as the man himself.

"Jesus," I say to myself. "Get it together, Sarah." I squeeze my thighs together.

I pick up the phone receiver and punch in the voicemail number to check to see if a message was left.

Nothing.

It was probably just a wrong number.

I look at the clock. Seeing it's 1:00 a.m., I give my head a little shake, trying to refocus on the file in front of me, but it feels impossible. Between not sleeping and overworking, I'm exhausted.

Closing the portfolio I was trying to read, I sink back into my chair and close my eyes for a moment to let them rest.

I can feel myself drifting, my eyelids impossibly heavy. There's no way I could open them now if I tried. My breathing begins to slow, so I take a deep breath in and let out the tiredness that's settled into my bones.

The small hum that comes from the minifridge next to my desk acts like a sound machine, coaxing me into sleep.

I'm not sure how long I've been dozing, so when my eyes shoot open, my mind takes a minute to catch up. *Somebody slammed a door.*

I sit in the silence second-guessing myself, stock-still and waiting for another sound.

Another loud bang echoes through the room, and my spine straightens, the tiny hairs on my neck standing on end as I hold my breath.

What the fuck? Someone's here.

My mouth opens to call out, but I close it just as quickly, hearing shuffling and a deep thud vibrate through the walls.

Get up, Sarah, my mind urges.

Thoughts begin filling the gaps left by fear, willing my feet to move as I scramble from my chair and make my way to the slightly ajar office door.

Who the hell could be here? Nobody that's supposed to be.

My eyes shoot to the clock, seeing it says 2:00 a.m. Shit. I need to stay calm. *Stay fucking calm.* But I have every right to be afraid.

Nothing good happens in the middle of the night. Nothing.

I slowly push the door closed, twisting the handle so that the lock doesn't make a clicking sound, and flick the already dim light off in my office. With my back pressed against the wall, I think of all the scenarios that could happen.

None of them end with me making a new friend.

Whoever just busted in the door isn't here with any kind of good intention.

I start to slowly walk in the darkness of my office, familiar with the layout, as my eyes adjust to the blackness. The clanging of metal on metal has me holding my breath again, freezing in place.

They're in the prep kitchen. It's an empty space about twenty feet from my office used as a setup for caterers when we have parties.

And where we have knives.

I need a weapon.

Damn, my gun's in the bottom drawer with my phone. Fuck.

My mind starts to reason with me, rationalizing the threat. *Maybe it's a homeless guy looking for food?*

Chicago winters tend to make people on the streets pretty damn desperate, and now that we're at the beginning of December, it seems reasonable...maybe.

I can handle this. I can scare him off. That's all this is.

I begin to walk again, feeling for the desk and guiding my way around it. Jesus, my pulse is thrumming so fast I'm almost scared it can be heard. Rounding the desk, I squat down, running my hands over the drawer handles until I find the one I need.

The drawer opens smoothly without a sound, something

I'm grateful for, and I reach inside and pull the loaded Glock from where it's hidden along with my cell.

Pushing the button on my phone, I wait for the screen to light up. I'll call for help and hole up in here until it arrives. It's going to be okay, and if I have to, I'll take care of myself.

I've done it before. I can do it again.

Voices begin to carry, and I squeeze my eyes shut, putting my forehead on my knees, trying to make out what they're saying.

"You thought we wouldn't find you? That you could fucking run?" Holy shit.

I can't make out who it is, the voices are too faded. But the anger in the voice, the unsaid promise of death—that's something all too familiar.

My head shakes from where my face is buried into my knees.

"You'll never get away. I'm always two steps behind," the deep voice rumbles.

My head pops up, eyes growing wide. *Two steps behind...* My father always says he's two steps behind.

Footsteps sound closer, making their way toward my door. Is he here? Is he taunting me from the hall?

No. It's not him. It can't be. I need to focus. I can't panic.

But my breath starts to feel shallow and erratic. Cold sweat beads along my forehead, and I grit my teeth together, willing the feelings away.

"No, no, no," I whisper to myself as my memories come flooding back.

"You stupid bitch. You can run. You think we won't find you? A fine piece like you. We own you until I say otherwise. Or until you're dead. Get used to it."

My eyes spring open, ready for the fight. It may not be

them, but I'm not taking any chances. They'll kill me this time or ruin me until I wish I were dead.

I won't go back. Not again. Not ever.

I release a breath in a whoosh as my free hand reaches to the top of the desk, helping to pull me to standing, with my finger ready on the trigger of my Glock.

I look down at my phone to see it's still coming to life.

"Come on. Come on," I urge the phone silently.

The screen finally comes to life, but before I can punch in 9-1-1, the door swings open and bounces off the wall.

The phone falls from my hand as I jump in surprise and swing the gun out in front of me into the darkness.

I don't hesitate. I know better. I won't go back.

So, I fire.

CHAPTER FOUR
DANTE

Motherfucker. I've been shot.

A scorching pain sears my shoulder, and my hand hits the wall, unintentionally turning on the light as I duck down.

Everything happens in slow motion. Vincenzo yells from down the hall, and I feel myself answer, but I can't hear it.

I don't even know what the fuck I'm saying because my arm feels like it's on fire.

I shake my head as my mind tries to speed back up, but it's like I have a lag. My left hand reaches across my chest to my shoulder, but all I feel is wetness.

"Fuck," I grit out, seeing the streaks of crimson seeping through the arm of my white tuxedo shirt.

A noise in front of me calls my attention.

"You. You're a fucking dead man," I shout as my head jerks, my vision blurred by the quick movement.

I feel someone pulling at my body, tugging me to stand up. I'm gonna kill whoever the fuck did this. I launch my hand out and grab at the soft flesh in front of me, squeezing so hard a rageful grunt pulls from my throat.

I'm going to kill this motherfucker. Squeeze the life right out of him.

My eyes become clearer, fixing on the asshole I have a hold of by the throat.

But all I see is Sarah.

Her crystal-blue eyes are wide, filled with shock and shiny from her tears. Her pupils dilate as she's denied breath as my wrathful grip increases.

What the fuck? Someone shot me... Why is Sarah here?

Rage courses through my body as she slaps at my grip, sputtering coming from her lips, when suddenly understanding smacks me in the face.

Sarah shot me.

My eyes narrow on her angrily, my words becoming a growl. "Put the fucking gun down."

I loosen my hold enough for her to wheeze in a grateful breath.

"Dante. Fuck." She coughs, still holding the gun in her hand, waving it at her side.

I tighten my grip again, glaring at her, and she nods against my hand, dropping the gun to the floor.

I release her instantly, and as she takes a heavy step backward, I kick the gun toward the door.

"Jesus." She breathes heavily, taking in more of the air I was denying her. "What the hell are you doing here? Why the fuck wouldn't you announce yourself? I could've fucking killed you! You're such an asshole," she yells, her voice coarse and raspy as she rubs her neck.

I'm an asshole? "Why the fuck do you have a gun?" I roar.

She isn't the kind of girl who carries a gun let alone knows how to use it.

"What the fuck is going on?" I yell again.

Her hand stays on her neck as she shakes her head at me. "Obviously I didn't know it was you, Dante. Jesus, what are you doing here?"

My eyes dart to the handprint on her throat already blooming red and purple on her alabaster skin.

I could've killed her. I was killing her.

I instinctively reach out, but she flinches away from me.

"I'm not going to hurt you," I promise, but the skepticism on her face is ironic. "You don't look at me like that. You fucking shot me."

I jerk my head, motioning for her to step closer to me, and take her chin between my fingers as she does. I tilt her head to look at her neck closer, letting out an irritated breath.

Sarah's eyebrows shoot up in surprise. "How are you mad? Did you hear me? I could've killed you, Dante."

I twist her head the other way to look at the marks, scowling as I do.

"You aren't that good of a shot." I painfully smirk, inspecting my shoulder and letting her chin go. "You grazed me. It'll hurt like hell, but I'll be fine."

Footsteps come closer from the hall, and I know it's Vincenzo. Sarah looks toward the noise and backs away, putting her eyes back on mine.

"Vincenzo, sto bene. Rilassati. L'ho gestito." *Vincenzo, I'm fine. Relax. I've got it handled*, I call out as he fills the doorway.

Depositing his gun in the back of his pants, he looks at me confused.

I motion with my head to the gun at his feet, and he looks down, bending to pick it up, then looks back to me. "What the fuck?" he asks, shaking his head. I push the door slightly more ajar, allowing Sarah to come into full view.

"Come ho detto." *Like I said*, Vincenzo states, surprised to see her.

His eyes take in the scene and appraise what's happening and then land on my bloodstained shirt. "She shot you?"

"She did," I answer, still staring at her, my curiosity beginning to fester.

"*She's* right here," Sarah replies sarcastically.

Her arms cross over her chest as we stand in the silence, and I let my eyes search hers.

The longer I stare at her, the more her face gives nothing away.

Sarah's defensive. Interesting. My question niggles at me in the back of my mind. *Why the fuck is this girl carrying a gun inside a club that nobody would ever touch?* Something's not right.

I turn to Vin, reminded of the other thing not right. The business we brought to Church tonight.

"Where's the guy we brought in?"

"Chained to the cabinet...and quiet," he answers, but I'm staring at Sarah again. And she doesn't react. At all.

I nod, pulling at the top button on my tuxedo shirt as I study her, struggling against the pain in my arm to pull it free.

Sarah steps toward me and slaps my hands away. "Stop it. Let me," she breathes, taking over undressing me.

She pulls the buttons closer to her, and I breathe heavily as my arm burns like hell.

"Careful," Vincenzo directs sternly.

But I lift my hand to quiet him. "Lasciala lavorare." *Let her work.*

"Jealous? You want to undress him?" She winks at Vincenzo, and he grumbles and looks away, taking a step just outside the door—enough room to give us privacy but also to remain on guard.

I grin down at her, whispering, "Like old times..."

I don't miss her small grin as her fingers pull at each button to reveal more and more of my bare tattooed chest. Just like she did that night.

Despite the pain, I can't help the filth that's taking over my thoughts as I watch her eyes travel over my muscles like she wants to eat me up.

"Stop looking at me like that. You told me I only got one night," I tease, seeing her bite her lip. *My kind of girl— thinking dirty thoughts in the middle of bedlam.* "Now, answer my question, beautiful."

A sharp pain shoots through my arm, and I wince as she tugs the sleeve on my good arm to pull the shirt from my body. She gives me an apologetic look and much more gently removes it from around my back.

"Good girl," I mouth, giving her a wink.

She stills, her eyes faltering, and I swear I can smell her excitement. Fuck I like that—her response to my approval.

Sarah gives her head a little shake. "Hold this."

She puts my free hand on my shoulder, holding the shirt in place, so she can uncuff the side where she shot me. "It's your own fault. You do realize that?" she accuses angrily, averting her eyes.

If she was looking at me, she'd see the amusement on my face. Balls of steel, this one.

People don't speak to me this way.

Ever.

Not just because they respect me—it's mostly because they fear me.

And that's justified.

But this badass doesn't seem to have the sense to feel fear. It's what drew me in the most when we met. I liked listening to her mouth off then just as much as I'm enjoying it now.

Actually, more now, because I know she likes the punishments I'm itching to give her.

"You're a brave little thing. I can't tell if you're fearless or careless," I growl as the material brushes over the wound when she pulls it off me.

"Neither." She smirks, and we lock eyes for a moment.

Folding my shirt long ways, she drags it under my arm, her hands brushing my skin, and wraps it around the wound, tying it hard to stop any bleeding.

"Easy," I complain as she tightens it more.

Sarah's eyes dart to mine. "Don't be a baby."

Fuck, there's something about her eyes. I noticed it the night I danced with her at Luca's wedding. There's a whole lifetime that's been lived behind those damn blues.

The corners of my mouth lift minutely against the dark expression that's taken up residence on my face, and I lean my face closer to hers, watching her features freeze. "The circumstances are shit, but it's nice to see you again."

Sarah peeks through a forest of lashes and licks her lips. Damn, I want more of her.

"You didn't have to get yourself shot to see me. It's a little extreme, Dante," she teases, fucking flirtatiously.

That mouth is going to get her in trouble.

My hand runs slowly up the middle of her chest, stopping only to feel her heart beating, and slides upward again until I find my favorite place—wrapped gently around her neck. Tilting her head back, I bring my lips close to hers.

She lets out a small warm raspy breath, peering up at me with hooded eyes.

My lips skim hers as I speak. "Baby, I would fuck you. Here and now, bleeding all over you, letting it mix with our sweat and cum."

Damn, the way she's staring at me, like she wants it too, has my chest rising and falling faster.

"And I'd love every minute of it," she whispers, so quietly I almost miss it.

"Fuckkk," I roar, tipping my head back.

I need to control myself, but this girl brings out the absolute worst in me. No fuck that, she requires it.

Sarah wants me to do my worst to her. But now isn't the time. I drop my face back to hers.

"You gonna answer my fucking question now?"

Her eyes dart to mine, and she pulls from my grasp as I smirk. "You didn't think I forgot, did you? It'll take more than a little flirting to distract me, Billy."

"Billy?" she questions, her eyes filled with confusion.

"Yeah, like Billy the Kid."

She rolls her eyes, letting out a growl. Oh, this little kitten's mean.

"No. I'm not going to answer," she states bravely.

"I gotta hear this. Why?" I ask, amused with her indignation.

Sarah cranes her neck to look at Vincenzo then back to me. "Because one question leads to more. And If I wanted you to know, I'd tell you."

I laugh out, and she scowls. Fuck. She makes my dick hard.

Vincenzo takes a step in, ready to make her answer. Because, like me, he knows something's off here, but a small shake of my head is all that's needed to cause him to retreat.

"The fact that you won't answer means I need to know the story. I'm going to find out, so cut the shit."

That's the reality. She can protest, but I'll get my way. She knows that. And I can tell she knows by the way she starts fidgeting and chewing on the inside of her cheek.

She looks at Vin again, like she's contemplating her next move, before turning back to me. "Are you going to make your goon do the dirty work? Or is this friendly?" she questions warily.

Something about the way she says "friendly" pisses me off, as if I would hurt her, but if she wants a monster, that's what she'll get.

My voice drops low with my anger. "We aren't friends. We fucked and you snuck out.

Friends don't do that, and they're honest when asked a question. But if you keep pushing back, I'll let him watch as I get my answers."

Sarah's finger pushes into the center of my chest. "Do you think that scares me? You better do worse than that because I've known some real monsters in my life, Dante Sovrano."

She might look furious, but I see the disappointment in her eyes. And that makes me angrier. If she'd just fucking come clean, I could stop pushing, and she could stop making me into an enemy she doesn't need.

"Tell me what the gun's for."

Sarah throws her arms in the air, turning around and walking back to her desk. I reach for her waist to stop her, but my arm is slow moving. Placing her palms on the top of the dark wood, she hangs her head down between her shoulders.

"Tell me," I growl out to her back, but she doesn't turn around. "Tell me what I want to fucking know, Sarah?"

"I can't," she yells, slapping the desk.

My mind keeps trying to connect dots between what I know about her and why she would be here, now, in this position.

"What's got you too scared to tell me? Is it a *who*, not a *what*? Someone I know...someone from Church?" I press, running my hand up her back and feeling her tense.

"Leave it, tough guy."

Oh shit. Memories from the night we were together flood my thoughts. Sarah turns around, shaking her head, reaching out to place her hand on my bare chest.

"It's not what you think..." she whispers, but I cut her off, rage blurring my vision.

"The guy from the party... It's the asshole who was hitting on you? Did he threaten you?" I growl with deadly fucking intent.

If this asshole has Sarah carrying a gun, afraid for her safety... *Motherfucker.* My head tips back, anger straining my features. "I'll bury him, Sarah. But first I'll make sure he knows what fear really is."

"Fuck," she breathes. "Stop. Dante. This has nothing to do with that guy."

A crease forms between my brows as she answers. "Then who?" She blinks, but her mouth presses closed.

We're back at the beginning. That's fucking it. My patience has run out.

I grab the middle of her shirt, bunching it in my hands and making her body arch toward me, when ringing comes from the floor. My head swings around to look for the intrusion.

She pushes against me to circle the desk, but my hand cages around her arm as I point at it. "Vincenzo."

Where's the fire? Not so fast.

"No. I got it. Don't, I'm good..." she spits, as she hurriedly tries to pull away from me, but I hold her bicep tight in my good hand, planting her in place.

"Let go," she snaps, jerking her arm.

"Not a fucking chance. Settle down or I'll chain you to the cabinets with the guy in the kitchen." I warn, and she stills.

"Please give me my phone, Dante."

Her eyes are pleading. But I don't care.

This is the closest I've seen to fear from her. No fucking way am I giving her that phone.

"Not until you tell me everything I want to know. Or maybe the person on the phone can?"

Vin picks it up from where it's ringing and looks at me, and I nod. "Answer it."

He hits the Answer button and puts it on speaker, then sets the phone on the desk. I look pointedly at Sarah for her to answer.

But she doesn't, shaking her head, her angry glare locked to mine. Damn. I can't believe I didn't see it before because those eyes really do say it all.

There's a bite as vicious as a viper in there behind the sexy smiles and flirtatious laughs.

This girl has hellfire running through her veins, and whoever she doesn't want me talking to is most certainly the person who put it there.

My hand tightens around her arm as I bend down, bringing my lips close to her ear. My voice is quietly strained, trying to contain my anger. "Start talking." She shakes her head again, unwilling to listen, holding her ground.

I didn't expect any other response.

I reach out for the phone to say something when a man's voice fills the space.

"Sarah." His Boston accent is thick on his tongue. "I know you're in Chicago. Now you know I am too. See ya soon, girl."

The line goes dead, and all the heat I felt in her body before drains in an instant. All that fight gone.

She's ice-cold and trembling. The incarnate of fear. I believe that she knows real monsters because this woman is fucking terrified.

Her back presses against my shirtless chest, and I realize I've pulled her into me protectively. I'm nobody's hero. I barely even know this girl. But there's a code among criminals: no women, no children.

And whoever that was, broke the code...and broke it hard on Sarah.

Chapter Five

Sarah

I can't breathe. Fuck. They're here. My family's here in Chicago, ready to drag me back kicking and screaming.

Time's up.

Dante's warmth washes over me from behind, making my eyes squeeze closed. He's holding me close—too close. I'm suffocated by all his maleness.

My body pushes against the strength of his unmoving arm, needing to escape his comfort.

I can't think straight when Dante's touching me. And I need my mind crystal fucking clear right about now.

"Is that who you thought I was when you shot?" he asks quietly from behind me.

Struggling harder against his hold, I release a breath in a rush as Dante's arm leaves my body, setting me free.

My body springs forward, feeling even less centered than before. I wrap my arms around myself, not answering and staring at the bar in the far corner.

Dante spins me around and locks eyes with me, anchoring

me by my waist as his eyes search mine. His voice fills with the seriousness of his words.

"Whoever that was won't touch you, Billy. Not now, not ever. Do you understand that? I can protect you."

My head shakes as I stare at him, feeling an angry heat crawl up my neck.

Dante's words should be music to my ears. I should cry and fall into his arms, thanking him for being my salvation, my savior. My very own criminal dark knight.

But all I feel is angry. Really fucking angry.

Because I'm not that girl—the one who needs *his* kind of help. I don't need another villain disguised as a hero.

I've got me. I'm good.

"I told you to leave it. To *fucking* leave it," I spit, swallowing down the tremble in my voice. "Now you want to protect me?" I huff, pushing his hands off of me. "At what price?"

"What the fuck does that mean?" he barks as I turn and walk toward the desk, swiping my phone off the surface and making my way to the drawers.

"Exactly what I said," I answer over my shoulder. Reaching down, I open the drawer harshly. Vincenzo takes a step back, and I narrow my eyes at him as I pull my bag into my arms.

"You're an asshole, too."

He opens his mouth to speak, but Dante beats him to it.

"Concedici un momento. Chiama l'uomo e portalo qui per suturarmi. Di a Matteo di scoprire chi sta cercando di trovare la nostra ragazza. Lei non ci dirà niente. Ma voglio delle risposte, come ieri."

Give us a moment. Go call the guy, get him here to stitch me up. Tell Matteo to find out who's looking for our girl. She won't tell us anything. But I want answers, like yesterday.

My head swings between them, and I suddenly wish I spoke Italian because I know that was about me.

Vincenzo nods and walks past me, bringing a hand to my shoulder and rubbing it gently, before lifting his phone to his ear and rattling off more Italian.

What the hell?

Dante's head follows Vincenzo out and only turns back toward me when the door closes, leaving us alone.

"Now. Explain yourself."

Dante's voice is eerily calm and steady as he leans his hip against the desk and crosses his arms over his chest. He's not asking anymore, not in any form of the word. Whether I like it or not, I have to come clean.

If he was anyone else, I'd lie, weasel my way out of this with a bullshit explanation and disappear, but too much was said in the call. Dante understands the implications. He can read between the lines because he speaks the same language.

I take a deep breath to steady myself, preparing to say the words aloud that've been a secret for eight years.

"My father and brother are coming to collect me. Take me back home. But I don't plan to be here by the time they arrive," I confess.

The words feel like acid on my tongue, making me wish I could stop speaking and run. I pull my purse farther onto my shoulder, shifting my weight, feeling uncomfortable in my own skin.

His eyes narrow as he studies my face.

"Why'd you leave them?"

Because I hate them. Because they sold me as a low-level buy-in to sell heroin. Because they tried to ruin every bit of goodness inside of me.

"Nope," I answer flatly, watching his expression darken.

Dante motions his head for me to come to him, but I don't

move. I refuse because the way he's considering me looks a lot like pity.

"Don't do that," I bite out.

"Do what?" he answers, standing and making his way around the desk to where I am.

"Treat me like something fragile. I'm not that woman, at all."

The strength in my voice isn't surprising as I face him. It's expected. I'm a survivor, and I won't have anyone take that from me or sweep that under the rug with their fucking pity.

"Got it. But that's not how I'm treating you," he counters, taking my purse from my shoulder and dropping it to the floor next to him. "I'm treating you like someone about to run. Like an animal that's been cornered. I'm being cautious, Billy, because I don't want you to bite. I can help if you'll let me."

I don't answer. I won't. So, I just shake my head. He has no idea the levels my family would sink to get what they want or the despicable intentions of the people they're involved with.

I'm sure Dante could handle them, but it wouldn't be without some kind of damage to the things and the people he loves.

The people I love.

Dominic, Luca, Gretchen, Drew, their children...everything is fair play in this kind of war, and I can't live with that. They don't deserve this destruction.

But he's right. I'm going to run. I haven't pretended anything differently. And if he tries to stop me, I really will sink my teeth into anything that gets in the way.

Dante brushes a lock of hair from my face, tucking it behind my ear.

"Why do they want you back, Billy?"

The action is tender and soft, and my eyes close, to rob me of one sense so that I can relish another. His tatted hand cradles my jaw as he waits for my answer, and it reminds me of our first night—our first words spoken once I crossed the threshold.

"You're so beautiful sitting at my feet, Sarah. Thank you," he whispers, running his hand over my head and letting his fingers weave through my hair. I lean in to his touch appreciatively as he speaks.

"Tell me how you knew I was what you needed."

"I felt it. Your power. Your possession. And I wanted to be collected." His finger dips down under my chin, raising my eyes to his as I continue. "We're depraved, Dante. I recognized your darkness because it's mine as well."

Dante's voice pulls me from my bubble. "Answer me," he whispers. "Why are they coming for you?"

I lock eyes with his as I give the answer. "Because I fucked up a deal for them, and they want me to make amends."

The muscles in Dante's jaw work overtime as he lowers his face closer to mine.

"How do you make amends? With money?"

His voice is a low whisper; it's deadly and restrained.

"With my body...with my life. Whatever works." I answer honestly.

His thumb runs under my eye, but I know it's dry. I don't cry anymore. I wouldn't even know how.

His eyes bore into mine, like he wants to say more, but he doesn't. Shaking his head, Dante drops his hand and takes a step back.

"Motherfucker."

He smacks his hands together roughly. I can feel his anger; it's vibrating off him. Dante looks back to me as he keeps putting distance between us like he's trying to protect me from the rage that's evident all over his face.

"Ask me for help," he growls, fisting his hands at his sides.

He knows I won't ask.

"No. I'd be making a deal with the devil, and you'd want my soul in return."

I was sold once. That shit won't ever happen again.

Grabbing my purse from the floor, I look over my shoulder at the door and back to Dante. He takes a predatory step forward, but my feet instinctively carry me backward a few steps, and I reach out for the wall to steady me as I get tripped up around the desk chair.

"Ask me, Billy," he grinds out louder, rubbing his stubbled jaw angrily and stalking directly into my space, pushing the chair into its spot with a loud thud.

My hand shoots out to his chest, stopping him in his place.

"Men like you...you don't do things out of the goodness of your heart. There's always a price. And no matter how small it seems, it's always too steep." His eyes falter as he pushes my hand off his chest, but I continue. "My decisions are mine, Dante. My consequences are fucking mine. I won't make transactions with my life."

A sneer grows on his face, a deep guttural rumble pulling from his throat. He grabs a glass from the bar next to us and hurls it across the room as his voice booms in the space.

"So, I'm just some monster that would rob you of your life? That's who the fuck I am to you?"

The crystal smashes against the wall, and I flinch, refusing to look at the tiny shards ricocheting through the room.

"No, you're the nightmare that controls all the monsters. You're the thing I wouldn't be able to escape."

Dante runs a hand over his shaved head and takes two steps backward, letting out a laugh.

"Who said you're able to escape now? Donna testarda." *Stubborn woman.*

I draw my brows together, worried by his words, as the

sound of footsteps grabs my attention and pulls my head in the direction of the door.

Two fast knocks sound against the outside, and Dante walks past where I'm frozen, saying, "Entra," and pulling his cell phone from his pants pocket. The door opens wide, and Vincenzo steps aside just as Dante reaches the doorway.

"Where are you going?" I shoot out, confused by what's happening.

Dante turns and looks at me, a smirk growing on his face. "I gave you a choice. You could've just asked, but you had to do this the hard way. Try and remember what happens next is for your own good."

Turning his head, Dante brings the cell to his ear and speaks into it quickly in Italian. I can't understand anything he says except for when he says, "Done." But given his demeanor, I don't think it was good.

Dante covers the phone, turning to look at Vincenzo, as he keeps his back to me.

"Porta a casa Sarah, e tienila lì e non farla uscire."

My stomach flips at the finality in his voice, mixed with the uncertainty of his words.

And for the first time, I'm actually scared.

"Why the fuck are you speaking in code?" I yell to Dante's back. "What's going on?" It's as if I haven't spoken. I'm invisible. Neither man turns to look at me.

My eyes blink rapidly as I look around, needing an escape. I need to get the fuck out of here. The door closes with a loud bang, and I jump, my head swinging around to see Vincenzo standing alone.

"All right, sweetheart, we can do this the easy way or the hard way. Sarah, don't choose the hard way because I like you, and I don't want to have to—"

Cutting him off, I toss my bag on the ground, letting it

land with a thud, and walk to my desk, eyeing exactly what I need. I grip the silver metal scissors in my hand and turn, narrowing my eyes.

Vincenzo takes off his jacket and folds it, banking it over the armchair. He tilts his head and gives me a hard look before rolling up his shirtsleeve.

"Fuck. That's what I thought."

CHAPTER SIX

DANTE

'm the monster she can't escape? Her pride is her monster. Whatever happened to Sarah is far worse than she's letting on. That's for damn sure.

Fuck. The disgusting possibilities of what she didn't tell me run through my head, making me see red. I have to get out of this fucking room. We're getting nowhere, and I'm only going to do something I'll regret.

My gaze drifts down seeing the light reflected off a tiny piece of glass from the tumbler I tossed against the wall, and I close my eyes. *What am I doing?*

I open them and look to Vincenzo, standing next to me in the doorway, waiting for direction.

But I have none. I'm undecided. Conflicted.

On one hand, her shit isn't my problem, and if this girl wanted my help, she'd ask. She's been given a hundred opportunities tonight. I need to walk away and let her handle her own fucking life because helping her is inviting trouble...and I choose for more than just myself.

I have to look at the bigger picture.

But men are animals, our triggers are hairpin, and Sarah is a big fucking trigger for me.

I can't help but feel protective. She's unknowingly hit a nerve. One I never expose because it's so raw that it clouds my judgment.

I hit the number staring back up at me, hoping for a push in the right direction.

Whichever that may be.

The line rings twice before Dominic answers abruptly.

"What's up?"

"Abbiamo un problema." *We have a problem.*

"It's 4:00 a.m., Dante. The sun's up...we can't hide the body just yet. I just got to the office," he laughs, and I hear papers shuffle in the background.

"La tua falsa sorella è nei guai. Sono al club." *Your fake sister's in trouble. I'm at the club,* I say, clipped.

"What the fuck? Hold on. I'll patch in Luca."

I'm met with silence, then more silence, before the line echoes, and I know I've been put on a conference call. Luca's voice takes over.

"Explain."

"Non ora. Ascoltami, so che lei è importante per te, ma non so quanto cupo e caotico possa essere il suo problema, quindi prima di decidere ho una domanda da farti. Cosa vorresti che facessi?" *Not now. Listen to me, I know she means something to you, but I don't know how dark or deep she's in with her mess. So, I'm asking before I decide. What do you wish me to do?*

"Protect her," Dominic barks without hesitation with Luca doing the same on the heels of his words. "How the fuck is that even a question, dick?"

I let out a frustrated breath. "La donna testarda ha rifiutato l'aiuto che ho offerto. Non sono un cazzo di eroe, fratello.

Ricorda con chi stai parlando..." *The stubborn woman refused the help I offered. I'm not a goddamn hero, brother. Remember who you're speaking to...*

"You aren't a monster either. Remember who the you fuck *we* are," Luca pushes angrily.

"Since when has pushback stopped you from doing anything needed?" Dom questions.

I let out a long breath before answering them. "Questa merda è molto più complicata per me. Voi due lo sapete. Di tutte le persone...voi dovreste saperlo." *This shit is so much more complicated for me. You two know that. Of all people...you know.*

Dominic interjects, a seriousness woven into his words. "We do, but Luca's right, Dante. We choose not to be like our father or our uncle. You don't have to make their decisions all over again."

I hear him, but I won't risk my family for Sarah. She's nothing to me. Ultimately, she's just a girl I fucked. But even as I think it, I don't like the way it sounds.

I may not love her, but that night...what we did, I feel connected to her in a way I can't shake.

"Ho bisogno di un motivo migliore. Io prendo decisioni che riguardano tutti noi. Dimmi perché le ho dato valore se lei ha rifiutato il mio aiuto? Dimmi, perché continuo ad insistere?" *I need a better reason. I make decisions that affect all of us. Tell me why I put value on her when she's turned down my help? Tell me why I force my hand?*

"We choose to protect our family, not let greed and self-interest rule our lives. She's family, Dante. She's important to us. To me and Dom," Luca adds.

There's only one answer I can give. Luca knows that. He's given me my reason.....my excuse.

"Quindi lei è importante per me." *Then she's important to*

me, I answer, nodding my head, making peace with what I'm about to do.

"Hey. Do we need to be concerned about what's coming?" he asks solemnly.

I look back over my shoulder at the woman standing wide-eyed and wild in the center of the room and wonder if I could've actually let her go it alone.

Hating that I might have.

Relieved I won't have to know.

"Non lo so. Ma lei sarà protetta. Consideralo...done." *I don't know. But she'll be protected. Consider it...done.*

Pulling the cell from my ear, I cover it and tell Vincenzo to take her to my house and lock her down.

She starts yelling at me for an explanation, but right now, I need to get stitched up, grab a drink, and get my goddamn head straight.

Like I said, she's bringing trouble, and I just opened my doors wide to greet it.

I bring the phone back to my ear as I walk down the hall. "Since it's technically Saturday morning, let's plan Sunday dinner. Come to me because I'm going to have a pissed-off little houseguest."

"You're sending her to your place?" Dom laughs loudly. "You sure you needed us to push you in the right direction? Sounds like you've already turned down the bed."

I walk through the entry of the kitchen, stepping over the fucker we have chained to the cabinets, giving him a kick as I do.

"Scumbag. I'm not going to fuck her. At least that's not why I'm taking her to my house." I laugh.

"Again," Luca counters with too much amusement in his voice.

"I'm gonna make you swallow your tongue for that. And who says I fucked her? You just saw us leave together."

The doc motions for me to stand next to a silver metal prep table, and I do.

"Mind your business, assholes. And name a safer spot for her to be?" I challenge, wincing as the man pulls the shirt from the nasty wound.

"No. You're right. There's no place safer than your dick... nobody ever goes there." Luca chuckles, Dom following.

"Fuck you." I laugh, half groaning as I hang up, the needle inserted into the tender flesh wound numbing my arm instantly.

Antonio walks in from the back of the room, catching my attention.

"We good?" I question, looking down at the body and back to him.

"Yeah. I don't think he'll steal from us again. But try and rat on us, that's a different story."

My eyes drift to my arm as I'm sewn back together with the black wire.

"We need to send a message" I say absentmindedly, watching the needle slide into my skin and curl out again, bringing the skin taut. "Hey, Doc, you got more of that stuff?" I question, motioning with my chin to my arm.

He nods as he works, not taking his eyes off what he's doing.

Antonio clears his throat, and I look up to a jerk of his head. My face turns sideways, meeting the fiery blue eyes that are glaring at me. Sarah's standing in the doorway with fury etched on her face, Vincenzo behind her.

Her eyes drift to my arm being stitched up, and her face drops, but only for a fraction of a second. It's enough that I saw it.

"I see you managed to get her to cooperate. I'm impressed, Vin." I smirk.

Vincenzo shrugs. "Your girl and I have come to an agreement. No more trying to stab me, and I won't put her in the trunk."

"His girl?" she throws out and rolls her eyes.

I almost laugh, but instead, just smile because, to them, she is. I threatened everyone at the party who came near her. So, it makes sense.

Sarah narrows her eyes as she begins to walk toward me. Vin moves to stop her, but I give a head shake. Her eyes shift, taking in the guy chained to the cabinets as she walks around him, completely unfazed.

Stopping in front of me, she shakes her head. "Vincenzo told me what's happening. I'm not being held hostage at your house, Dante. Think again."

Her eyes are locked with mine in a standoff, but she's already lost.

"How'd you convince her to be reasonable, Vin? Because I seem to be coming up empty." I laugh, breaking our eye contact to look at him.

He holds up his gun and waves it. "We played a little game called Glock, paper, scissors. Glock beats scissors."

Antonio lets out a laugh, quickly coughing to cover it up. But I let mine shake my chest.

"Hold still, please," the doc directs.

"I hope it hurts," she hisses, making my smile grow.

I crook my finger for Sarah to come closer. "Make coffee when you get home—I'm gonna need some. And tell Vin everything he needs to know. And I mean everything."

Fuck. If looks could kill, I'd be a dead man. I grin down to her enraged face. "I told you this is in your best interest. Make peace with it, Billy."

"If you think you're going to lock me up, you're high. Fuck that. You said, 'ask me for help,' and I said 'no.' How hard is that to understand?" she snaps viciously.

"Stop assuming I care about what you want. I don't. I'm the great big bad, remember? You'll do as you're fucking told."

Sarah laughs loudly, narrowing her eyes at me. "I don't follow any man's lead. Including yours, Dante Sovrano."

I'm amused at her choice of words. "I remember the first time you said that to me. And do you remember what happened?" Her eyes falter, then double down with anger. "That's right, beautiful. I wasn't asking then, and I'm not asking now. Go home."

I turn my head, effectively dismissing her, but when she doesn't move, Vincenzo comes and grips her arm to pull her out, causing me to watch. Something about seeing his hand on her arm makes the words jump from my lips.

"Attento. Se lasci un segno, ti rompo il collo." *Careful. If you leave a mark, I'll break your neck.*

He must loosen his grip because Sarah looks at him and then back to me, confusion all over her face as he escorts her out.

"You're finished," the old doc says, giving me a sly grin while he stitches my arm.

I give a half laugh, knowing he isn't talking about my arm. I look back to the hall where they've disappeared, a frown taking over my face.

"Yeah. She's growing on me."

A grunt comes from the ground, and I look to see our rat friend waking up.

"Finish up, Doc, and leave me some of that wire, will ya?"

Antonio walks to the counter and snags a small carving knife, looking it over before turning to me.

The doc places a bandage over my arm, then digs inside his bag, gathering the things I requested before he faces Antonio.

"My car?"

"Waiting outside for you," Antonio answers, slapping a wad of cash on the counter. The doctor swipes the money as he walks out and doesn't look back.

Muffled cries rise from behind the duct tape on our shackled friend as he takes in his surroundings. Squatting down, I look him in the eyes.

"Hey, Frank."

I grip the tape at the side of his mouth and rip it off, slapping my hand over his mouth roughly as he screams.

"Shhh..."

Antonio walks over and hands me the carving knife. I flip it back and forth between my fingers before I look at Frank again.

"I've had a helluva day, so I need you to try and be still when I cut out your tongue."

He starts to kick his legs, flailing his body as he screams into my palm, but I stare into his eyes as Antonio holds down his ankles.

"Go ahead. That's it. Get it all out..." I whisper, leaning in closer. "Your squeals sound a lot like the way fucking rats sound before they die."

His head begins to shake as tears fall from his eyes, but I press my hand harder into his face, crushing the back of his head into the cabinet.

He's sobbing with deep guttural regret. I don't blame him. He knows he's going to die.

"Frank. Shh, shhh...stop. It's okay, because after I do it, I'm gonna stitch you up real nice, so everyone knows they have to keep their mouths shut or I'll do it for them."

I roll the sleeve on the new dress shirt Antonio brought for me, as I sit in the back of my black SUV, noticing a speck of blood crusted over the bone on my wrist. I wipe it on my pants a few times to get rid of it and sit back, letting out an exhausted breath.

The windows in the car are heavily tinted, keeping the sun out, something I'm grateful for, seeing as I've been up for twenty-four hours now.

What a fucking night...or day actually.

I pull my phone from my pocket when I feel it vibrate.

"Speak."

"Cleaning crew is at Church. We should be good to open on schedule. I'll keep an eye on things here tonight. Then it's closed for two days, so we should be all good," Antonio clips out quickly.

"Perfect. Let me know if anything goes down. And let me know when you get rid of the rat we found in the kitchen. Nasty fucking animals," I answer, knowing he knows what I mean.

I want to know when he dumps the body where it needs to go to ensure my message is received loud and clear.

"Will do."

The line disconnects, and I sit staring at my phone. I want to call her. No, it's worse—I want to check on her. A smile tugs at the corner of my lips as the picture plays out in my head when I remember how mad she was in that kitchen.

She didn't even give a second thought to the asshole chained up. I laugh, relaxing back into my chair. I don't know whether to call her a psychiatrist or propose because this girl is definitely one of a kind.

What amount of crazy am I walking into, Billy? I say to myself before shooting off a text to Vincenzo.

Me: How is she?

Vincenzo: Asleep. An hour after we arrived but not before she took a swing at me. But you should be all clear. Good luck.

I can't help but laugh because this girl is no joke. I'm gonna need all the luck I can get.

CHAPTER SEVEN

SARAH

My eyes flutter open, the sun beaming in on me from the floor-to-ceiling windows in the bedroom I'm sleeping in.

I roll over, turning my back to the light, feeling heavy from my exhaustion and hot from the clothes I slept in. I hadn't planned on falling asleep so quickly, but everything hit me all at once. So now I'm in full winter attire and feeling like I'm on fire.

I tried to convince Vincenzo to stop by my house or a store, just so I could grab some clothes, but he deemed me untrustworthy.

One little left hook, and I'm a monster. Fucking baby.

Sitting up, I unzip my black leather boots and pull them off, dropping them to the carpet next to where I'm lying in my cream-colored decorated jail.

I can't believe I slept like this all night. *What time is it?*

I look around the large space for a clock, but I don't see one. The whole room is fairly bare. Clearly a guest room, housing just a bedroom set and a light wood entry table.

I would check my phone, but seeing as how the assholes confiscated it last night, I can't.

"Vincenzo... Are you standing outside my door?" I yell as I roll my neck and cross my arms to pull off my sweater, pausing only to wait for the answer.

"No, it's Matteo," the familiar voice answers.

I grin because despite my circumstances, I like Matteo. He works with me at Church sometimes and always manages to make me laugh. We're around the same age, so we've always gotten along well.

"I'm changing, so no opening the door," I call out with less snark than I would've given Vincenzo, but still full of the fire I feel.

I look at the door again, waiting for a response. It's strange to have to just trust him, but I don't have a choice. There aren't any locks on the doors. At least not on this room or the en suite bathroom.

"Got it," he answers.

My skin tingles with instant relief as I remove my sweater and let out a breath. The cooler air envelops my body, making me shiver from being so overheated. Lying back, I unbutton my jeans, my hips doing a shimmy as I begin to pull them down.

A light tap at the door echoes through the room just as it opens, catching me with my damn pants down around my hips.

"Dammit! Matteo, I said no coming in," I snap, pulling them back on.

A deep laugh accompanies the freshly shaved face that's walking toward me. The door closes behind him. And I see red.

"You," I spit, immediately angry, jumping to my feet my pants still undone.

"I see someone's still angry." He smirks, setting the drink container and bag down on an entry table by the door.

"Oh, I'm more than fucking angry." My body lunges forward, ready to lose it on Dante.

"Who the fuck do you think you are? You've put me in a prison. Where's my phone...my purse?" I yell, launching myself at him, but he lifts his arms up and skirts my advances.

My body bounces off the table, causing it to shake, and misses him.

"Watch the coffee, wildcat." He laughs, sending me into more of a fury.

I let out a small guttural scream and swing at him, for any part of him. But I'm caged in by his much stronger arms.

My head swings around for something to use, something that will hurt him, and I kick my legs out trying to twist out of his hold.

"Relax," he growls, pinning me in place.

"Are you fucking kidding? You brought me here against my will. And you want me to relax?" I pant, already exhausted from the fight. He's just too strong.

"Yes. I want you to fucking relax and hear me out. I'm not trying to ruin your life—I'd like to help you save it. And frankly, Billy, what's the alternative. How the fuck are you getting out? Because you aren't going through me, sweetheart."

My eyes scan the empty space in front of me as I let his words sink in. He's right. I'm not. And I'm wasting my time and my energy fighting when I should be more strategic.

Nodding, I stand still as Dante slowly lets me go. I pull away quickly and turn to face him.

"I'll get your phone and belongings for you, so long as you promise not to use them as a weapon." He lectures as he steps over to the table where he placed the items he had.

"Fine," I answer, narrowing my eyes.

Dante's amused expression still evident, he motions his head for me to follow him as he picks up the bag and drinks. "Now, where were we? You were taking off your pants, right?"

He has to be joking.

"In your dreams, buddy," I snap.

"Almost nightly." He winks, making my nipples push against the lace fabric of my bra.

I roll my eyes and cross my arms over my almost naked chest. "That's all you're ever getting."

"We'll see."

He sets what I assume is breakfast on the nightstand and sits back casually on the bed, patting it for me to join him and grinning at me like the devil.

I hate how sexy he looks. And how much it makes me want to... *Damn traitorous body!*

"Am I getting a choice?"

"No." He answers as I walk to the bed and take the spot next to him, leaving space between us.

"All right. I'm listening." I huff, patting my forehead. I'm on fire and not in a good way.

"You've got to be hot." He grins with a devilish gleam.

"I am, but you aren't taking me out of these pants, you asshole."

"You sure you don't want me to? Because if memory serves..." he croons, leaning down on his elbow closer to me.

I hate him.

"That's all we are...a damn memory," I snap, pushing him back as his arm wraps around my waist, and he rolls me over, so he's on top of me.

My breath stops short as he stares at me because god help me if all this anger doesn't make me want to fuck him more.

Dante's leg presses in between mine, and my traitorous body wants to rub up and down until I scream.

"Let's do this, then talk. I haven't stopped thinking about you..." he says low with that heavenly gravel.

Dante's hands run up my body, and my eyes close, sucked into the sensation as he whispers in my ear.

"Those slinky little black stockings weren't nearly as tight as these jeans...and I managed those just fine. The trick is to start at the ankle."

His lips brush my neck, and a quiet mewl pulls from me.

Dante sits up quickly, grabbing my jeans around my ankles. A gasp escapes my mouth as he tugs hard on the jeans, pulling them down over my hips.

My head immediately shakes as I lift my bottom, trying to pull my skintight jeans back up as I realize what the hell I'm falling for.

"Hell no. Get your hands off me. No help required. I can take off my own damn pants," I snap, pulling my ankle from his hand, but he grabs it again harder.

"So you agree. You should take them off." *Fuck*.

His hands travel quickly down my legs to my thighs, and with a swift pull, he jerks my body closer to him as I let out a surprised squeal. My ass is flush to his thighs, my ankles at his chest, and my eyes are set on his.

Dante parts my legs slowly, letting them fall to either side of him, and hovers over the top of me. His hands find a place on either side of my head, making the bed dip.

"Billy, I want to take them off."

I hate how sexy his voice is, and I hate that my body is already begging. But I'm not giving in.

I press my heels into the mattress and lift my pelvis, so we're pressed together. I can feel his length hardening against my throbbing clit and the roughness of his jeans hard against the top of my silk panties. Dante raises his brows as I begin to teasingly wiggle against his cock.

I bite my lip, feeling the stab of need that fills my core as I rub myself against him. A small moan vibrates up my throat, overtaken by the sensation.

His eyes close, a groan coming from him. "Fuck, Billy."

My breath comes out in pants as I press against him harder, and he shoves a hand under my shoulder to grind against me harder.

"Hold on...I'm almost there," I say in a raspy breath, and his eyes shoot open to watch me.

They're filled with a primal intensity of want, need, and dominance. But mine are narrowed as a mischievous smile spreads over my face.

"All done." I announce dropping my ass back to the bed, pulling the zipper up quickly and fastening the button.

Dante starts to laugh, shaking his head. "Sneaky. I should've known." Walking his hands back as he rolls off me and sits up. "I can't say I've ever gotten hard over someone putting *on* their pants before."

Sitting up and scooting against the headboard, I shrug. "I told you I wasn't here to play some concubine role. Keep your dick to yourself."

I reach for my sweater, but Dante shakes his head.

"That's gonna be too hot. Take this."

He tosses the paper bag to me. It lands in my lap and brings with it the smell of blueberry muffin, which makes my stomach grumble.

Dante grips the back of his T-shirt over his shoulder and drags it over his head. "Here. Wear this."

I nod my head, averting my eyes as I take it from his hand to slip over my head. Fuck he's hot.

His smell clouds my senses. It's the faintest scent of cigar mixed with soap.

Dante stands and retrieves the drinks, and I'm not sure I

could cool down if I wanted to now. Between the grinding and his shirtless body, I may actually explode.

Especially when I sneak a glance at the way his jeans hang from his hips. That damn vee on his insanely sculpted abs points to everything I want and refuse to touch.

I realize I'm staring and look back to his face now adorned with his sexy grin. The one that announces his amusement over making me squirm. I smooth down the oversized shirt and roll my eyes, trying to dismiss him.

"Coffee?" he offers, holding out a to-go cup.

"Thank you," I say as impolitely as possible, still not ready to be nice to my warden. "What time is it?"

I bring the drink to my lips and take an appreciative swig, almost spitting it out as I do. Dante turns to look at me as he lowers himself down on the bed next to me and stretches out his long legs. "Two o'clock. You okay?"

I scrunch my nose and hand him the cup. "Dante. That's not coffee."

He takes the cup from me, exchanging it with his. "You got mine."

I bring the coffee to my lips, sighing into the steam. "What kind of psychopath drinks orange juice?"

He runs his hand over his exposed stomach and lifts his chin to the bag in my lap before diving his hand inside.

"It's refreshing and healthy. All that caffeine makes me aggressive." He smirks, rummaging around for something to eat.

I've got something. Jesus, I'm such a whore.

"Very cute," I chastise, pushing his hand out of the bag and grabbing the muffin. "Here." I place the bag on his chest.

He pulls out another muffin and takes a bite, chewing for a minute before adding, "You taste better."

I let out an irritated growl and stand up, abandoning my muffin.

"What's going on? My head is spinning, Dante. You bully me into your home and then say you want to help...how? By bringing me breakfast? And don't make me even have to mention the flirting." My arm waves in the air as the other holds my coffee.

He puts down his cup on the nightstand and folds his arms behind his head. God damn him. He's the picture of arrogance. So fucking calm in the middle of my storm.

His voice is smooth and calculated. "I didn't bully. I passionately coerced. You weren't exactly open to compromise, Sarah."

"I don't remember being given any alternatives to imprisonment," I quip.

He turns his body toward me, propping his head up with his hand. "Then let's make a deal."

I'm shocked at his nerve, and my mouth drops open, my arms crossing over my chest. "A deal? You don't know the meaning."

Dante rolls onto his back, heaving his solid frame up, and plants his feet on the floor. His head hangs for a moment as he sits with his back to me, his muscles deliciously on display. He cracks his neck before standing and turning to face me.

"You need to hear me out, Billy," he says more seriously. "And I'm not really open to hearing no."

This dick!

I take a step backward, narrowing my eyes. "This is bullshit." I turn and walk for the door, hearing Dante's footsteps sweep over the plush carpeting.

I swing the door open, barreling through toward where I remember the living room was.

It takes a minute, but I realize that we're alone, causing me to stop abruptly. I'm instantly engulfed by Dante's body. His arms wrap around me, stopping me from falling forward, and pull me into his body.

"Where is everyone?" I ask quietly as he rights me, my back against his chest.

There's something about this, the way he's holding me, the place we're standing. It's reminiscent of that night. I can tell he's remembering too by his silence.

His voice drifts over my ear, goose bumps spreading over my neck. "They're only here when I can't be."

His hands slide over my stomach and turn me around to face him. We're so close. If he moved just an inch, his lips would be on mine.

And I'm not sure I'd push him away.

I lift my chin, and his eyes fix on my lips. He feels it too. The familiar pull between us.

Screw it. Kiss me. Fuck me. Let me take a hit.

Dante's lips skim mine as my eyes flutter shut.

"Careful what you wish for, Billy. You can only tempt me so much before I'll want it...and trust me, I'll get my way."

Shit. What am I doing? I blink a few times and shake my head, the moment between us broken.

"Oh, this is gonna be fun." He revels in gauging my reaction. "You ready to listen to me now, Billy?"

CHAPTER EIGHT

DANTE

Sarah starts walking again, letting out a frustrated breath. She doesn't even have a destination, but she's clearly so pissed that she just needs to move.

I wonder if she's more pissed that she almost kissed me or that I didn't let her.

"Sarah," I call out from where I stand.

"No, I'm not ready," she says over her shoulder. "Because you're going to try and decide for me, and I only like that in the bedroom, Dante."

Fuck, I like that, too.

I take quick steps to where she's traveled to and grab her by the waist, hauling her backward midstride. She lets out a surprised yelp, and I twist her around, bending as I throw her over my wide shoulder.

"I remember. Quit fucking walking around already," I growl as I stalk over to the couch.

She smacks at my back yelling, "Put me down."

I deposit her on the oversized gray sofa, watching as she melts into the down cushions.

She's a wild mess, her hair swinging around her flushed face.

My eyebrows raise as a warning, because I won't chase her again.

"You keep fucking acting up, and I'll tie you to the goddamn bed. We clear? Now, are you ready to listen?"

"Fine. Speak. It's not like I have a choice but to listen," she barks, pushing her hair from her cheeks.

I can see from the look in her eyes that she expects me to be a smartass, to yell or growl at her. But that's not getting me anywhere with Sarah. The harder I push, the harder she pushes back.

It's why I can't stop thinking filthy damn thoughts.

I lower down in front of her, bringing us face-to-face, caging her in with my arms planted on either side of her legs. Her breath catches as I bring my middle finger to her forehead, gently sweeping a strand of her hair out of her eyes.

We're close, intimately close, and I can see the war in her expression. She hates that it calms her.

My voice is tender as I speak, which takes concerted effort on my part.

"Let's try this another way. Stop fighting me. Let me try and help. Give me a week, maybe two. You don't even know where they are, Billy. I can get eyes on them, and worst case, I buy you some time so that you can get lost, but with a nice head start."

She starts chewing on the inside of her cheek, considering what I'm saying. Sarah takes a deep breath and nods.

"You're right. I don't know where they are. And they won't know I'm here. But I need terms of my own for this deal, something that gives me control of this crazy fucking situation."

"Name them, Billy."

I can't help but grin because every tiny step with this girl feels like a goddamn world victory.

Her small hands push against my chest, trying to move me back. She needs the space, but she's not getting it. She tries again, but my eyes dart to her hands then back to her face with a shake of my head.

Sarah glares at me for a moment then answers.

"First, tell me what you want in return? And don't bullshit me."

"Nothing," I answer honestly, "I'm serious, Billy. Just let me help. Trust me, this is more about me than you."

The curiosity in her eyes has me pulling back. Now I need the space.

"Why do you keep saying that? Why do you care so much, Dante? We had a fun night, it was great, but this seems like an insane gesture just to secure a second date," she jokes, but the tension doesn't ease in my shoulders.

I push up to half stand, angling my body to join her on the couch. Taking a deep breath in, I squint my eyes at her before my face relaxes. The answer she wants to hear isn't the one I have to give.

She wants to hear that I'm a good person, altruistic. But I'm not. I'm just a guy who can't forget his past and likes to see people get what's coming to them.

So, I tell her a half-truth.

"Because you mean a lot to my brothers. What's important to them becomes important to me. Simple as that."

Her eyes crease in the corner from her fond look at the mention of Dominic and Luca.

She looks beautiful when she does that.

"Or, maybe I'm doing this for good karma," I add, smirking.

She grins wider. "Your smile gives away your lie."

"You don't believe in karma?"

"No, and neither do you, or you'd never take matters into your own hands. And I don't believe that you actually think any decision you make is wrong," she accuses humorously, pushing at my shoulder.

I reach up and grab her wrist as she does it, locking eyes. Hers search mine, and I swear I can see a debate brewing in her mind. She wants to tell me something, but the minute she looks away, I'm certain she's thought better of it.

My eyes drift down to the hand I'm still holding, and I gently flip it over, leaving her palm up. I begin to trace the uneven lines and crevices etched into her flawless skin as I speak.

"True. But what does the reason matter so long as you get a hand with these assholes?"

"You say that as if I asked for your help," she says quietly, watching my fingers skim against her skin.

I can't help but want to touch her. Whatever's going on between us, like this, is as electric as the anger she has for me.

"No, but you'll take it...eventually. Because you are far from stupid, and you know when to submit." She scowls at my choice of words, but I grin. "That look is my favorite."

"You're exhausting," she breathes out.

"Only because you're fighting it," I counter.

"Fighting what, exactly? Your assistance or your advances?" she challenges, leveling a glare at me.

"You hate me now, but that shit's like throwing gasoline on the fire. You might not want my help, but that won't stop you from wanting me, Billy...and after last week, I'm not so sure which one you actually want me to ask permission for. Because forcing my kindness takes away you feeling weak for asking. And forcing your body...well, that just gives you what you crave."

"Shut up," she whispers, biting her lip.

Just like I thought.

"Tell me I'm wrong, Billy. I dare you."

I start to let go of her hand, so I can lean in to kiss her, and her eyes dart down.

"That's the love line," she blurts out, obviously hoping for a subject change or a reprieve.

I run my finger over the small crease that she pointed out nestled inside her palm, grinning because I've made her nervous.

"It's supposed to tell you how many times you'll marry and how long you'll stay in love.

If you believe in that stuff." She shrugs, suddenly seeming shy.

Since when does Sarah get shy?

"Why is yours so short?" I tease, with a smirk, but it drops as a small frown tugs at her lips.

She gently twists her wrist from my hand and pushes to stand, keeping her eyes from mine. She traces the line on her palm, and her eyes grow sadder before she speaks.

"Because all the space in my heart is taken up by my hate."

I don't like any part of what she just said because it speaks to me. It mimics me. Like two broken mirrors aimed at each other, aligned with the same cracks. I stand, locking eyes with her and taking her chin between my fingers.

"We'll see, Billy. Don't tap out yet. You still have time."

Her hands find my chest, and she closes her beautiful blue eyes. As much as I want this moment, I don't, because I can't be the good guy. There's no redemption, no absolution for a man like me.

As if she can hear my thoughts, she pushes back, but I don't budge, forcing her to take a step backward. My hands sweep over my face, rubbing my stubbled jaw roughly.

"I'll give you two weeks, but we aren't doing this..." Sarah says, motioning between us. "No more flirting. No more touching. No more you," she adds, waving her hands up and down my bare chest. "We're not playing house, and by that, I mean fucking, because I'm going to need a clear head, and all of *this* doesn't help in that department."

I shake my head, irritated that she's trying to take the inevitable off the table. Sure, the timing is complicated. But I want this girl. She wants me. If she thinks I'll allow her to fucking deny me after last week, she's crazy... I'll push her until she comes crawling.

"You wanted terms. Are those it? No fucking?" My voice is gruff as I ask, unwilling to hide my irritation.

"Yes," she states, tipping her chin defiantly.

If I thought for one fucking moment this was about anything other than trying to stick it to me because I made her come here, I'd rethink my next move. But it's not.

Dragging my bottom lip between my teeth, I cross my arms over my chest.

"Looks like we're in for negotiations then, Billy. You thought I was a bully before? You don't have a fucking clue what I'll do to get back inside that tight little pussy. We're happening."

"Wanna bet?" she grits out, angry at my challenge. "I'm not as weak as you think."

I laugh and bring my hands together, rubbing them back and forth.

"Billy, I like when you fight back...remember?"

I see her fingers dig into her hips, and her breath hitches. Dirty fucking girl. The elevator dings, and I know Matteo's arrived with her bag, so I stroll past her pissed-off face as I make my way toward the entry.

Matteo has a small black leather duffle in one hand and a matching one in the other as he greets me.

"Hey. She's got so much stuff, so I just grabbed pajamas and sweats. And a bunch of girly shit that smelled good from her bathroom counter."

I laugh, catching her following me out of my peripheral as I walk.

"Perfecto. She'll live if it isn't right. She's not going anywhere."

"She's right here. Can you not talk about me as if I'm not in the room," she snaps, walking toward Matteo to grab one of the bags.

"Hey, Sarah," he greets, handing over the duffle.

She leans in and kisses his cheek, cutting her eyes at me after she does, resulting in my smile.

"Hi, Matteo."

"So you're nice to him..." I laugh, knowing what she's doing.

She walks into her bedroom without answering, and Matteo laughs and opens his arms.

"Everyone likes me. I'm charming."

"Attento." *Careful.*

Matteo holds up his hands in mock surrender. "Understood."

Her door closes, and we walk back into the living room with the remaining bag. Matteo places it on the couch as he half sits down on the armrest, crossing his arms over his leather jacketed chest.

"Did you find out names? Vincenzo swears he saw his life flash before him when he questioned her." He laughs.

I shake my head as I walk to the bar by the kitchen, glancing out of the window that spans the wall, and grab a glass, pouring myself a scotch.

"I'd call him a pussy, but I came pretty close to her right hook this morning."

He starts to laugh, but it fades just as quickly.

"Is that mine too?" Sarah questions from behind me, and I look over my shoulder at Matteo, who shakes his head to let me know she didn't hear us.

"Yes," I answer, turning around and ignoring her to speak to Matteo again. "Keep her out of trouble."

"You're leaving me here?" she says surprised, as I walk toward her.

"Yeah. I've got shit to run and people to find." I stop in front of her and look down. "Matteo will get your stuff. Play on your phone. Girls like that, right? They do that shit all the time."

The look on her face could actually end my life. Before she can spit fire, I walk off toward my bedroom door, calling over my shoulder, "I gotta change. No coming in."

"Don't worry. I won't. I have a bet to win."

Chapter Nine

Sarah

"Sarah." Matteo pushes against the doorframe. "Dante's going to be so pissed when he finds out you tied me up and searched the house."

I laugh loudly and look at him.

"You're such a pussy. One, if he cared about security, the asshole would have locks on his doors or at the very least on his desk. And two, he already knows. And three...if that's your story, that I tied you up, you're as good as dead."

"Very nice. Good to know you'll mourn me. Great friend you are." He laughs as I open up another drawer from the desk in Dante's office.

The size of his office is enviable; it's probably the size of my bedroom in my apartment. A muted black bookshelf, filled with books, runs from floor to ceiling on one side, and on the other is his large stone-gray desk.

The room is masculine and strong with a faint smell of cigars. It's definitely Dante, but I don't believe that he uses it often because other than an errant pen, everything is neat and organized, each item having its place. It's unnatural.

Yep, he's a psycho, or this is a front.

My head pops up when Matteo lets out a breath, reminding me to answer.

"I'm a hostage, and you're an accomplice in that. Our friendship is void. And believe me, Dante is well aware that I'm searching his house...which is why I'm coming up empty. He isn't stupid, and he also knows you're a little afraid of me."

"You're lucky you're a girl," he shoots back, laughing.

"No, you are." I exact, closing the last drawer when I come up empty.

Matteo walks inside the office, past me, and turns to come up from behind. He presses his hands on my back, pushing me out with enough force that my feet are made to take the steps.

I start to laugh and try to dig my feet into the ground, but he pushes harder.

Of all the guys, Matteo is the least intimidating. He's so easygoing and charming, living like he doesn't have a care in the world. The downside is he comes with annoyingly crude humor, and I'm fairly certain he fucks anything that walks.

"Come on. There's nothing here that's interesting," he complains, "Other than his overly sorted pen container. But you didn't think you'd be smarter than the FBI and find the smoking gun, did you?"

I reach my hands out to grab the doorjamb, stopping us just inside the room.

"No. I'm not an idiot. But I'm trying to figure him out, and you should help me."

Matteo lets out a groan. "Later. I'm starving, Sarah. Snoop later, cook for us now."

"I can't cook, you sexist dick," I snap loudly.

Matteo spins me around to look at him, confusion on his face. "Seriously?"

"No, I can." I smirk. "Come on. But you're so entitled." I laugh, letting the door go and exiting the room.

We walk down the hallway from Dante's office to the stairs. "How many women do you have cooking for you on a weekly basis?"

"As many as I can eat," he answers, bouncing down the stairs in front of me.

"Jesus. You're disgusting." I laugh.

When we hit the bottom of the stairs, we head toward the kitchen, and I smile at him.

"Would you give it all up for you know who?" I question, wagging my brows.

"Sarah," he answers, my name a warning.

But I know his dirty little secret. I've seen him sneak into the downstairs' rooms at Church to have his way with the one woman who has him hooked.

"I don't want to talk about it. It's complicated. Too complicated."

I shrug and start opening cabinets, unfamiliar with the kitchen, searching around for something to cook.

Matteo takes a seat at the island by the sound of the stool dragging against the floor. "But I'll tell you my complicated story if you tell me yours."

I grab a box of pasta and turn around.

"No way. There's nothing to tell." I lob the box at him, and he catches it midair.

"Bullshit. What's the deal with you two? And what's this for?"

My hands smack against the counter, and I look at him humorously.

"You are going to learn to cook for yourself. And why do you care...you want to take a shot?"

He laughs but stands and comes around the counter as I go in search of a pot.

"And *get* shot? No fucking way...you belong to Dante." His answer makes me swirl around.

Matteo is standing there grinning at me while holding a shiny silver pot.

"I belong to me," I state firmly, jumping up to sit on the counter.

I wave a finger at him and wonder how he seems to know his way around a kitchen.

"I never said I couldn't cook, just that I don't have to. Now, come on and spill it."

All that charm and wit wasted on a manwhore.

"Is this what it's like to have girlfriends? I'm glad I passed." I laugh, watching him turn on the faucet over the stove to fill the pot.

He laughs loudly as he sprinkles salt and olive oil into the water. "Let's make a deal. I'll tell you one thing, and you tell me one thing."

Against my better judgment, I nod because Matteo is hard to resist. That damn charm and those puppy dog eyes win out every time. But he's the definition of a wolf in sheep's clothing. I feel bad for the women who fall for his shit. But for better or worse, he's a friend.

"I like her...you know who I'm talking about," he starts, giving me a knowing look, and I nod. "But I fucked her sister. It meant nothing to us, but it will to her, because you know how she is with her. So now, it's really damn complicated."

"You fucked—" I gasp before he cuts me off.

"Eh, eh, eh. I will not confirm or deny a name," he answers, tutting at me.

I shake my head at him but secretly love the soap opera of it.

"Your turn, beautiful." He grins and leans against the counter.

I take a deep breath and pick at a piece of fuzz on my sweats. "I like him. Too much."

"That's it?" he deadpans, before checking the water.

I roll my eyes and rest back onto my hand.

"Yeah. I don't say that lightly. I don't ever stay in one place very long. My family always finds me, but this time, I went unseen for so long, and that fucked with my head. I did shit I shouldn't have."

"Dante...you did Dante," he teases like the asshole he is.

But I ignore him and continue.

"And now he's going to stay with me, curled up inside me, like a reminder of possibilities I don't get. It's like this shitty lump in my throat that I can't get rid of and can't swallow down."

Matteo grins, and I see the dirty thought about to come out, so I toss an orange at him from the bowl next to me. "Don't."

He catches it midair and tosses it back. "I wasn't going to. I was going to say, so you really like him. And if I had to guess, you keep telling yourself that you can't miss what you don't have...right?"

Nail meet head.

"Something like that," I answer.

"Well, sweetheart, life doesn't work that way. You've already taken a bite, so you can't forget the taste. Might as well have some fun while he sorts out your crazy-ass situation."

Does he make sense, or am I looking for an excuse? My eyebrows draw together as I look down at my thighs on the countertop, contemplating what he's said.

Nope. Not going to figure that one out today. I shake my head and look up, snapping my fingers at Matteo.

"Shut up and cook. I'm hungry, bitch."

"Soo fucking lucky you're a girl."

Before I can answer, his cell buzzes, and he looks down at the number, hitting the Answer button quickly. "What's up, boss?"

"You beckoned," I drawl sweetly, standing in front of Dante in the middle of the dimly lit little Italian restaurant called Mama's in my sweats, flip-flops, and an old T-shirt that says Al's Autobody.

I've never been here, but I've heard the guys talk about it plenty, and considering when we got here all that's been spoken around me is Italian, I figure this place is pretty authentic.

"Sit." He juts his chin to the space across from him and takes a bite of his entrée. "Do you want some wine?"

I can't help the irritated look that plays across my face before I blurt out, "Why am I here, Dante? This is embarrassing."

He looks up, maybe surprised by my candor, and picks up his napkin to wipe his mouth.

"Oh, don't be a gentleman on my account. I know the real you; might as well treat the plate like a trough." I grin, sitting down and scooting into place.

He laughs and lifts the red wine toward me. I grab the stem of my wineglass and hold it up for him to pour.

"I thought we'd have dinner together. Is that so terrible? And you look beautiful, Billy."

I lick my lips, almost feeling bad as he straightens the wine bottle and places it back on the table.

"I had a lovely dinner being prepared for me back at lockdown." I bring the delicious and much-needed glass of wine to my lips and take a sip.

Dante drops his utensils down by his plate, leaning back into the soft cushioned red banquette. "How is it you hate me for helping you? Explain that. You'd think you'd be nicer."

I hate the way he looks at me, because I know the only reason I'm pushing back so hard is that I can't risk him finding out everything I'm tangled up in. He's too stubborn and pushy, and my little fight would go from street match to a world war.

But that look. Like I'm ungrateful...no, like I'm disappointing him. It's gutting me.

"Don't look at me that way."

My voice is quiet as I take another sip of wine.

"What way? Like I'm surprised that a smart girl like you wouldn't know how to show your appreciation? Or that I'm disappointed that you haven't offered yet?"

What. The. Fuck.

That's the last answer I expected from his lips.

I huff out a laugh and swallow back my wine, bringing the glass down harder than necessary. "Nice to see your true colors, Dante. First, I'm appreciative of favors when I ask for them, and even though we made a deal today, that doesn't mean I'm suddenly the damsel you want me to be. And I'm not at all sorry that I haven't offered to blow you yet as a show of just how grateful I'm *not*."

Dante silently stares at me for a moment, possibly contemplating my death, but fuck him. He tips his head back, and a deep rumble fills the space as he laughs.

He picks his knife and fork back up then cuts into some peppers. "I don't want your body as gratitude. No, that I want you to offer freely. It's more fun that way. I just meant you could figure out how to fucking be nice, Billy. But I see I was asking too much."

He keeps laughing to himself as he takes another bite, and I hate how much of an asshole I feel like. I grab the bottle and pour myself another glass.

"I'm sorry. I'm the asshole. You're right. We made a deal, but you said we still had negotiations, so that thought is still lurking... I need to be careful with men like you...you can't blame me too much."

His brow furrows as I speak, and he reaches for his own wineglass.

"Men like me? Men like your family? Tell me about them."

The waiter approaches with a plate and sets it in front of me, and I blink at Dante.

Of course he ordered for me. That's a fight for another day.

I place my napkin in my lap and close my eyes, taking in the delicious smell of the dish in front of me. "I already told Matteo their names. Their rap sheets will say it all."

"I know you did, but I want to hear it from your lips."

I take a bite of my salad and hum in appreciation around my fork before sliding it out from between my lips.

"I'm jealous of a fork." He teases, and I laugh.

Dammit. He got a real laugh out of me.

"If everything here is this delicious, my mouth will be making sweet love to this fork all night long." I grin and take another bite.

"I like you," he states low and deep, dripped in the gravel his voice takes on when he's turned on as he leans in.

"I'm likeable," I agree, enjoying the way he's surveying me way too much.

"How do I get you to give in?" he croons, grabbing the fork as it pops from my lips and putting it in his mouth.

Goddamn him for being so sexy.

"Let's make a deal." I half smile. "If you find my family in the next forty-eight hours, I'll drop to my goddamn knees and let you do your worst."

He pulls the fork from his lips and offers it back to my smiling face. "Gorgeous and devious. You're trying to make me fall in love with you, aren't you?"

Dante relaxes back and shakes his head. His expression makes my face drop. A cold shiver runs up my neck as my stomach flips because he isn't amused. He's validated.

The look on his face tells me that whatever I just said told him more than I wanted him to know.

His voice drops low as his smile fades more, giving way to the face of a man who knows he's been misled.

"So sneaky. See, you're cheating because I need their real names to find them. Don't I, Sarah?" I start to counter, to tell him I gave their real names, but he holds up a hand to stop me.

"Do you think I believe that you're operating under your real name? I had you checked out, and you're too clean. Not even as much as a traffic ticket. I don't trust anyone who's never done anything left of right."

I don't even open my mouth because it's the only way to clamp down another lie that will fall out in an attempt to cover my ass.

"Are you going to tell me what I want to hear, or am I going to have to drag it out of you, gorgeous? And before you say no, just know that your silence makes me want to dig even more...because you're hiding for a reason."

My eyes drop to the table, needing a minute before I look up and say what I should've said from the beginning.

It's hard when you come from my life to ever really trust, but it's easy to know when to fold and not dig yourself in deeper. I lift my head and ready myself for his reaction to what I'm about to say.

"You're right. I've been playing you. Withholding their names. But Dante, you having me here, in your house, acting like some kind of dark knight...that's for you, not for me. I'm just biding my time. In two weeks, once you've played this out, I'll slip away, nobody the wiser," I admit without a hint of apology even though I feel guilty.

His hazel eyes take in my features, and I watch him as he does. Fuck. He's so unreadable.

I can't tell if he's pissed or impressed.

"Do you play chess?" he questions nonchalantly as the waiter clears our plates and sets down bowls of pasta in front of us.

"No," I answer, peering down at my food and wondering where he's going with this.

"The job of every piece on the board is to protect the queen because she's so powerful." His first two fingers run along the top of the wineglass. "Only people who are brazen, calculated, and willing to lose something important in order to win use her as a pawn to suck the other player's pieces in, so that they can eventually take down the other player's king."

My chest starts to rise quickly, seeing exactly where he's going. He wouldn't. No way.

"You would use me as bait...to lure them in?"

I wish I didn't hear the fear that I feel in my voice, but I do and so does Dante by the look of victory on his face. God damn myself, because now he knows what cards to play.

Dante leans in and tilts his head. "Only if you make me. Are you going to do that, Billy?" Making it my choice is so sadistic. He knows I won't say yes. I can't.

The idea of being out there, knowing something could go wrong, and I could end up back with that family, sends a chill down my spine. I won't go back to Boston. My name surely carries a bounty too big to hide from, because the only thing as scary as the Sovrano family is the Irish equivalent, the O'Bannion crew.

But those ties that bind—the ones I shot dead on my wedding night—will be buried with me. Not even my father and brother would tell for fear they'd be killed because they knew too much.

That's my only solace.

They won't rat me out to the head of the Irish mob or to Dante if he finds them for fear they'd have to come clean about their back-door deal with the weakest link in that crew.

"I need an answer."

Dante's intimidatingly calm as he asks.

"O'Malley. Patrick and Christopher O'Malley."

He sighs. "That wasn't so hard, was it?"

I grab my wineglass and throw it back, holding it out for him to pour me another.

He picks up the bottle, extending it and letting the liquid roll in.

"I gotta tell you, this devious side...I like it. It suits you. Fire behind the ice."

"Jesus Christ, you're twisted," I breathe out, and he laughs.

Tonight, I'm going to get drunk. Really drunk. Because there's no reason not to. I'm in over my head with him. And if I'm going down, then I'll do it with a lot of fucking wine.

As if he hears my thoughts, Dante looks at me and grins.

"Billy, tonight we have some fun. Tomorrow we can fight."

CHAPTER TEN
DANTE

S oft snores come from her throat from where she's lying next to me, tangled in my sheets. I've been watching her sleep most of Sunday morning, knowing the minute she wakes up, she'll be ready to have my head.

And I won't blame her. I was all too happy to keep her glass full last night. The more she drank, the more she liked me. It doesn't take a rocket scientist to see which side I'd be on.

I smirk remembering how much we laughed and how much she flirted. If I wondered whether or not the attraction was shared, I wouldn't have to guess anymore.

I'll need to remember that red wine brings out the monster in this girl. I like it.

Her eyes begin to open, and her head tips back as she yawns. An arm pokes out from beneath the covers, stretching above her head and making the covers pull down, exposing a beautiful pink nipple.

My head leans forward, but I stop. Fuck, I want to take it between my teeth and roll my tongue over the sensitive flesh until she's desperate for me. But that would most definitely ensure my death, so I take her lips instead.

I press a soft kiss down onto her mouth, hesitating to see her reaction, feeling her breath tickling my lips and making the parts I just warmed, cold.

A breathy moan comes from her lips, and her body rocks forward as her hand weaves up my neck, pulling me in closer. Our lips tuck between each other's, and my hand slides around to her back to pull her naked body flush against mine.

Our tongues caress and glide over each other like it's a dance we've been doing our whole lives. Sarah reaches down between us and wraps her hand around my engorged cock, pulling a groan from my throat, vibrating our mouths.

I softly knead her breast, pinching her nipple, rolling the hardened bud between my fingers.

Her hand stills, and my eyes pop open. Her own icy blues are wide as she pulls back slowly and swallows, evident that she's pondering something violent.

"Good morning, Billy," I say calmly. "You might want to let go of my cock before you make any rash decisions."

She flicks it hard toward my stomach with a little growl, making me gulp in a breath. She sits up quickly in bed, leaving the rest of her exposed, glaring down at me as I rub myself from her mishandling of my dick.

"I'm going to kill you. You know that, don't you? How could you?"

Sarah grabs a pillow and hits me with it before bunching up the comforter and pulling it around her, her grunts and breaths filled with exasperation.

Who is she trying to kid...she was awake.

"Violence isn't the answer," I tease, holding up my arm. "And I didn't do anything to warrant that verdict. It was just a kiss. I thought you were awake."

"Bullshit," she spits, pushing off the bed and taking the blanket and sheet with her, turning to look at me. "Jesus Christ. Cover yourself up."

I grin, lying back completely nude.

"I can't. You took the blanket and the sheet. You were adamant that we sleep in the nude last night. Who am I to say no to a beautiful woman?"

Beautiful is an understatement. She's fucking gorgeous like this. Hair wild, flushed and ready to do some damage. She's fucking perfect.

Sarah marches to the middle of the room where she threw off most of her clothes last night and bends down to pick them up.

"Real classy. I was smashed. And I remember almost everything...the only thing I'm foggy on is why I'm naked in *your* room. You could've put me in my room."

"You just kept saying 'I'm not allowed to wear clothes in the house' and 'my place is next to you.' It was actually pretty entertaining and accurate. I prefer you in the nude and in my bed."

"Where the fuck are my sweatpants?" she yells, sorting through her clothes as I shrug.

My name is called out from inside the house, and I know the guys are here, so I push out of bed. "No clue, but I have business. So you keep your pretty little ass in here until I'm done."

Throwing on some gray sweatpants hanging over a chair, I grab a T-shirt and head to the door.

"Dante. I'm not staying in here and waiting until you get done with your lackeys. I'm going out in a damn blanket if need be and going to my room."

The thought of her walking out, even in a blanket, pisses me off. There's no fucking way anyone sees how fucking sexy she looks right now. No, that's for me alone.

Turning, I look at her, no humor on my face. "You'll sit your ass down and wait. I want you like this when I get back. Today, we negotiate, Billy."

I walk through the door as Sarah glares at me from where she's standing next to the bed and let the door close behind me with a loud bang.

It's been twenty minutes, and we've managed to go through most of what we needed to talk about. But I'm antsy. Not because of this meeting but for the one waiting for me behind the door I can't stop staring at.

Turning my back to my bedroom door, I try and listen to what Antonio is saying, but all I hear in my mind are the breathy little moans that accompanied our kiss this morning.

Fuck that girl is hot.

I try to refocus, silently cursing my dick, but when I look up all I see are frowns and "oh shit" looks before I hear, "Good morning, fellas."

My head swings around, and silence fills every soul in the room, except for mine. All I feel is rage crashing inside my veins, making a ringing sound in my ear.

I'll fucking kill her.

Sarah's standing in the entry, wearing a smile and next to nothing—just a lace bra and a hot-pink G-string. Every part of her showing to the four assholes sitting on stools at my kitchen island.

"What the fuck do you think you're doing?" I bark, smacking the counter, watching her saunter to the fridge as everyone looks in different directions.

They better fucking look away.

"I'm getting some juice. What are you doing?" she answers, her head swinging to me lazily as she reaches inside for a carton of orange juice.

Matteo lets out a very nervous laugh, and my hand reaches to the small of my back instinctively for my gun, but it's not there.

Fuck. I'm ready to shoot people. This girl has me all fucked up.

Antonio smacks Matteo's shoulder, giving him a head shake, having seen my reaction, as Sarah bends to look inside the refrigerator. Her bare ass comes into view, sending me straight over the edge.

"Unless you want me to keep you there and make that ass bright red, I'd stand the fuck up."

She looks over her shoulder and winks. *Motherfucker.* I grab her shoulder and stand her up, turning her ass around and out of sight.

Sarah looks up at me and grins. "What's wrong, Dante? You seem angry. Should I have put a blanket around me?"

Before I know what I'm doing, my hand slams the fridge door shut as I loom over her, but Sarah just blows a kiss, uncapping the lid and drinking right from the carton.

"Oh, you're having fun, huh? All right. All right, I see what you're doing," I growl, trying to restrain my temper.

Dropping the container down, she looks at it musing. "You know, orange juice is starting to grow on me." Her eyes drift to her chest as she grins. "Whoops, I spilled some."

Her finger darts across her chest, wiping up a bead of orange juice and bringing it to her mouth. My fist instantly connects rapidly with the steel refrigerator, one time, two times, three times, but she doesn't even flinch.

That goddamn smile grows though.

And I snap.

I grab her waist and start pushing her backward toward my bedroom. "Put your fucking clothes on...or so help me god, Sarah, I'll..."

"What?" she cuts in, trying to throw my hands off her, but not succeeding as I keep pushing her backward. "You'll do what?" she challenges as I turn her back to me and shove her through the door.

"You're about to find out," I growl.

The sound of chairs scraping the floor echo through the room as the guys all begin to file out, leaving us to battle this shit alone.

"Sit. I'll be out in ten minutes," I bark, and the noises immediately stop.

Sarah starts off toward the bathroom with a string of curses, but my hand shoots out and grips her shoulder, keeping her in place.

"Let go," she snaps, full of anger.

I come right beside her and bend to her ear, my intention laced in my words.

"Are you trying to get these men killed? Is that what you want? Because all of this," I grit out, covering her breast with my hand roughly and hearing her gasp, "is for me."

She's already breathing heavy, and everywhere I touch feels like an electric current buzzing between us.

"You don't get to order me around, Dante."

Her voice is filled with defiance, but she doesn't make a move to push me away. She fucking wants this, even more so now. Everything we've been feeling. All the push and pull. It's become a ticking time bomb, and we're about to blow.

My hand massages her, and her eyes flutter closed. "Anger is the most powerful aphrodisiac there is, and right now, Billy, I'm gonna take out all my fury on your body."

I move my hand down her chest, letting her shoulder sink

into me, our breathing in sync as I move farther. Letting my fingers skirt over her stomach, I glide down toward her thigh, and trace the top of her panties. My finger dips just inside and runs back and forth over her skin.

"You don't ever teach me a lesson using what's mine."

I take her earlobe between my teeth and pull, tilting her head and sucking.

Her voice is so breathy that she sounds like she's coming. "I'm not yours."

A fighter until the end. Breaking her is going to be the highlight of my day.

"Try saying it more convincingly next time, Billy."

My hand dives down, pressing against her clit, and her knees almost buckle. I wrap my hand around her waist and start to rub her without mercy. No warm-up needed. She's all desire and pent-up animalistic need. Slow isn't what she requires. Sarah needs to come hard and fast.

Her hand reaches up, grasping my shoulder, as her body bends forward from the overwhelming sensation.

"Fuck. Oh my god," she whimpers, pushing her hips into my fingers and digging her nails into my shoulder.

My hand pulls to a stop as her ragged breath drags from her lips and her eyes find mine.

"What are you doing? Why are you stopping?" she questions, shaking her head, confused. She grabs at my wrist, but I don't move.

My fingers begin a slow skim over her tender clit, and she shivers, as a smile plays on my lips. I lean down close to her, whispering my seductive threat.

"Not a fucking word. If you make a sound, I stop." My fingers begin to move slowly again, and her body jumps. "They don't get to hear you. I told you all of this is mine, including your pleasure...all the little sounds and fucking moans. If you share it, I'll starve your fucking pussy to death." I push past her clit and thrust two fingers inside her, and she slaps a hand over her mouth. "Good girl. You want me to forgive that little stunt? Then prove your fucking worth, Billy."

This time I don't stop. She's held in place with my arm around her as I finger fuck her harder and harder, alternating between her clit and inside her pussy. Her hand presses over her mouth tighter and tighter as her body begins to jerk.

She's completely at my *mercy*. Unless she says it.

"You wish this was my cock, don't you? Fucking you raw. Making you breathless, while everyone waits outside, only a few feet away."

Sarah's nails dig so hard into my shoulder that I'm certain she's marked me.

"You like that, don't you? The idea of being caught, seen... or maybe it's the idea of being mine. To do with as I please." My fingers pump faster and faster. "Fucking you while everyone watches you get owned."

Sarah muffles her moans over my words as I finger her. Our eyes stay locked, trained on each other, intimately connected, and I know she's almost there. I push another finger inside her to bring her over the edge. "Open your fucking legs and give me *my* pussy," I demand, needing more room to fuck her.

As she does, I feel her stomach contract, and her eyes close. Her warm walls constrict my fingers, holding me inside of her as she rides out her orgasm. She lays her head against my chest as she convulses violently.

Slowly her body calms, and I slip my fingers out, her body giving a tiny undulation as I do. Sarah's body slumps against me, but I let her go, forcing her to hold herself up.

"Now, sit your ass down on the bed and wait for me, because when I come back in here, I'm going to eat your pussy and then fuck you until you can't breathe. Am I understood?"

Her eyes meet mine, and I bend down, giving her lips a soft kiss, then whisper, "Because to the victor goes the spoils."

I told her we were happening. She should learn to listen.

A faint "Shit" is all I hear as I turn my back and walk outside to finish my meeting.

Chapter Eleven

Sarah

Holy hell, what just happened? One minute I was Petty Betty, half-naked and on my high horse, and the next I was turned to Jell-O and left here to wait for my...punishment? Reward? I can't decide which.

He said it as if it would be a punishment. But after what Dante just did to me, I'm okay with being fucked until I can't breathe.

Dammit. This is why I didn't want to do this with him. Then again, maybe Matteo was right.

I snicker to myself at the thought, falling back onto the bed. I was supposed to win this battle. He wasn't getting the best of me.

Famous last words.

Jesus, he was so intense and angry. So possessive with all the "this is mine" growling.

There isn't any reality in which I wasn't surrendering. He's a goddamn beast with all his dirty talk and skillful fingers, and this is ultimately what I wanted. Deep down.

I wanted to fuck him the minute I saw him again. That's probably why I wouldn't stop pushing. He needed to break. Take what he wanted. Because I was never going to offer myself up.

Still, that makes *me* "the loser" in our little game. I caved first. Although, technically, I didn't actually say yes, just insinuated it with all my heavy breathing and compliance.

"Shit." I sigh to myself, letting the loss sink in.

The only thing worse than losing is losing to a smug bastard who knew he was going to win.

My hands run down my body, cupping my center as I sit up. This is definitely going to be sore later. Taking a deep breath, I push off the bed and stand up to walk to his bathroom.

I make my way toward the massive glass-encased shower and turn on the water, letting my fingers weave through the water to test the temperature, and watch the steam rise and billow as it begins to cloud the glass.

Shutting the shower door, I reach behind me and remove my bra, then my panties, letting myself back inside to the rain of warmth from the water.

I stand, quiet and still, letting my shitty decisions and insane life wash off me. I think the best in the shower, and right now, after what just went down, I need to think.

My thoughts are all over the place as I wash my hair with the shampoo he has in his shower. It smells fresh, like something that would be named cool breeze.

Leaning my head back, I snigger at the idea of Dante owning something called cool breeze, rinse the soap out of my hair, and open my eyes, finishing with the conditioner.

Grabbing the soap, I lather the sponge in my other hand and begin to make tiny swirls over my body as more questions pop into my mind.

I wonder if he knows I was awake the whole time he was kissing me?

He has to. It was just too tempting. Like a forbidden bite of the apple. Damn, but my body feels like heaven and not hell. But just because it happened once doesn't mean it will happen again.

I run my hands down my legs, realizing I need to shave...for all the sex I won't be having from this point on. *Lies. All lies.*

Looking around, I come up empty. No razor. That's a problem.

Opening the shower door, I peek my head out and scan the counter, spotting a shiny silver handle. I tiptoe out, careful not to fall on the slick marble flooring caused by the excess water, and nab it to use.

Halfway back, a throat clears, calling my attention to the doorway, and my head snaps to Dante leaned against the door-jamb with a grin on his face and his arms behind his back.

"Whatcha doing, Billy?"

I hold up the razor, naked and wet, goose bumps covering my body, and shake it at him.

"I need to shave my legs."

"I use that on my face," he states, amused.

"Then it should be up for the challenge of my legs." I counter as I walk back inside the shower.

The door closes, and I get back to business, ignoring him as if I don't care as he walks inside the bathroom.

Dante's back is to me as he stands at the bathroom counter, only a smoky shadow for me to stare at. He stands for only a moment, before turning to leave without a word.

The moment he shuts the bathroom door, I rub a clear spot in the glass to see what he was doing, curiosity getting the better of me.

No way.

A grin graces my face as I look at a small stack of clothes, neatly folded and placed on the counter.

He brought me clothes. So, what? It's not a big deal, but if that's true, why am I smiling like a loon?

Oh man, I'm in so much trouble.

Hating him is going to be harder than I thought.

Showered and changed into new, clean sweats—fucking guys, this is what happens when they pick out clothes—I pad out of the bedroom barefoot and head back into the great room, but the house is empty, no guys, no noise.

There's no way he trusts me alone. Although, I already know the elevator only works with a key card. Tried and failed that on the first night.

I look around and notice my purse sitting on the coffee table in the living room, so I head over and open it, grabbing my cell out, but it's dead. Matteo was supposed to give this to me yesterday, but we got sidetracked by my impromptu dinner date.

I rustle around, searching to see if my keys are inside, but come up empty. *Of course he took them.* Noise comes from upstairs, and I hear Dante's voice reverberate against the space.

"Make sure. We need to be positive before we make a move."

Against who?

My head lifts toward the top of the stairs as I watch him walk down. He always walks ahead, like he's leading the charge. I'm pretty sure Dante sees himself as the person who protects the men behind him and not the other way around. That's probably why they're so loyal to him.

It's obvious by their demeanor. Anytime I've ever seen

them all together, it's clear that Dante is where he is because of respect not because of fear. His brothers treat him the same way.

Especially Luca.

It's what makes him so powerful. They would all die to protect him, and he would never even need to ask.

"You don't listen very well," he calls out, taking the last step, dragging me from my thoughts.

Vincenzo laughs but gives me an apologetic nod when I narrow my eyes at him. I'm still mad at him.

I shrug and lean back onto the couch. "We already know this about me."

"Hungry?" He says teasingly, letting his gaze drift over my body as he stands in the entry, never taking his eyes off me as the guys walk out.

"No, but I need to make a run to my apartment," I say, brushing my damp hair over my shoulder, "I need something other than sweats to wear."

"I'll arrange it," he answers, still admiring me.

Picking up my phone from next to me, I stand and head toward the stairs.

"Bye, guys," I call out, seeing them enter the elevator, with a string of goodbyes yelled back.

"I like you in sweats," Dante remarks nonchalantly as I walk past him and the house gets quieter.

I stop at the staircase and look over my shoulder. "I like me out of them. We all need to make sacrifices, Dante."

I crane my neck to make sure we're alone, and he nods, so I push the bulky pants down and kick them off, leaving me in my boy shorts. He bites his bottom lip as I hang them over the railing and grin.

If I'm trying to get him to attack me, it's working because

Dante looks as if he's planning to pounce, so I make my move and jog up the stairs quickly, holding back a laugh.

"Where are you going?" He grins as he watches me go up the stairs.

"To put my phone on the charger in your office," I answer honestly, stopping at the top and glancing down at him.

He crosses his arms over his chest and stares at me. "How do you know there's one in my office, Billy?"

I can't help but just smile and shrug before taking a step backward and turning around to walk down the hall to hook up my phone, hearing him yell, "Sneak."

The familiar scent of him sucks me in the minute I walk inside his office. I make my way to his desk and see the plug I need nestled on his desk, neatly wrapped and tucked away.

Hooking up my phone, I sit in the large tall-backed leather black chair and throw my smooth legs up on his desk, letting out a breath as I wait.

A piece of paper that has some meaningless scribble on it, clearly written in Italian, catches my eye, and I can't stop my fingers as they dart out to trace the lines of his slashes and hard indentations.

He writes the way he fucks. Hard and purposeful.

Shit. I like him.

Too damn much.

I close my eyes with a small laugh because stopping this crazy train wreck seems impossible. The saying goes, "where there's a will there's a way," but I don't have the fucking will. I've never been so attracted to a person before in my life. It's as if Dante knows all the right buttons to push.

And god help me if I don't want him to push all my damn buttons...maybe at the same time, while he uses his tongue. Fuck my life.

A tiny voice in my head plays devil's advocate. *It's not as if we're going to fall in love in the next two weeks. What's the harm?* Still tracing the swirls and squiggles, I smile to myself because I don't have a devil and an angel on my shoulders—I have two devils.

"You look good in my chair."

I grin at his deep timbre and let my head fall to see him enter the office. "I feel like a boss."

My brows give a little wiggle to accentuate my flirting.

"Mmm," he hums deeply as he walks toward the desk. "You wanna be the boss?"

The way he looks at me. Fuck. Like he's stripping me bare down to exactly where he wants me—it makes every part of my body light up.

"Yeah," I purr, rubbing my crossed ankle up my other leg slowly and then back down.

Dante sits against the desk, pressing a finger against the paper I'm tracing, and pulls it until it's too far for me to touch. He pulls it up, folding and putting it in his pocket.

"What would you order first? And remember, you have to be specific or shit gets lost in translation."

He might be letting me take the reins, but we both know that in this game, Dante always runs the show. Just the way I like it.

"Take off your shirt," I direct, tilting my head and biting my lip.

He reaches over his shoulder and drags the T-shirt off his body, smirking as he does, and tosses it onto the chair next to him.

Fuck, he really is gorgeous. My eyes take in all the colorful swirls and patterns on his hard chest and arms. His body alone is intimidating, but it's the accessory to his intention. That's what really makes him the man he is.

"You like what you see," he states, appreciating the compliment my eyes are giving him.

"I was just thinking that tattoos make good men look dangerous."

His head lifts as his thumb skims across his lip. "I am fucking dangerous. So, what do they make me?"

"Authentic?" I grin, as he nods, letting out a half laugh.

His eyes lock with mine, and it's as if everything fades away around us. All the pretense and sarcasm, all the bullshit. It's just me and him, both wanting the same damn thing from each other.

Dante licks his bottom lip, and I watch his tongue glide across, wishing I felt that on my body.

"You gonna look at me all day, Billy...or are we gonna fuck?" The roughness in his voice hits just the right button.

I uncross my legs, letting one slide away from the desk, and leave my legs spread apart. "Why don't you make good on your threat from earlier and stop wasting my time with all this foreplay."

I swear it's admiration I see in his eyes before he does exactly what he promised.

CHAPTER TWELVE
DANTE

I swear I can still taste her on my lips, like fucking honey. My tongue darts out past the seam of my lips when the thought passes through my mind as I relax into my seat in the back of the SUV. The car switches lanes through traffic as I pull my phone out and dial Sarah.

She's displeased that I left her behind today—at least that's what I gathered when she told me to "go take a stroll in heavy traffic." But bringing her with me wasn't an option.

The call goes to voicemail after a few rings, making me crack my neck, trying to relieve my irritation at being ignored.

I hit Matteo's information, since he's her designated babysitter, or at least the only one she doesn't try to stab or punch.

"Hey, boss," he answers on the first ring.

"Give her the phone."

The line is silent as I assume he's handing it over to her.

"Dante," she answers in her sexy little rasp, as if she expected my call.

I laugh silently, picturing her expression. "Why aren't you answering your phone?"

"Because it's off." She half laughs.

I can't help but join in. "You're fucking terrible, you know that?"

But she's crawled under my skin. She's stubborn and unreasonable. She's fucking infuriating and seems to find joy in making my blood boil.

And I like it.

"Go get it, Billy."

She cuts me off quickly before I finish. "Jesus Christ, Dante. Fine. Is that all? What do you want? Are you calling to tell me all about the outside world...just to rub it in?"

"You're safer in the house. The end," I grit out, unwilling to fucking talk about this.

"Bullshit," she spits. "You just don't want me to tell everyone what a tyrant you are."

I laugh loudly at her accusation. She's never seen my worst, and I hope she never has to because this girl is quickly becoming one of my favorite people.

"Sweetheart, they know. It's not a secret. But there's shit going down you can't be around for." I smooth my slacks, imagining her in a tiny lace string and how enjoyable it'll be to have a glass of whiskey while she rides my cock. "So settle down and put something on I'll like for later."

I hear Sarah take a deep breath before her voice fills the line, eerily calm. "You have completely forgotten who you're speaking to. You will fuck only yourself from this point on. And whatever the fuck is going down at family dinner that I can't be around for better never show her damn face while I'm here."

The line dies, and I place the phone down on the seat next

to me, picking it up to call back but putting it back down just as fast. A small laugh escapes my throat.

She thinks I'm seeing another woman. Sarah just got jealous, really fucking jealous. I don't think my dick has ever been this hard.

Fuck.

My car slows, a horn honking in the background, pulling me from my thoughts. We've stopped in front of a small florist shop in downtown Chicago. The minute I'm back in the present, my shoulders tense and all the humor from my conversation dies.

"We're here, boss."

I come every week to the bricked building on this busy street, usually on autopilot. It's a necessary chore—the duty of a doting son.

But I hate this fucking place because it reminds me where I have to go next.

I step out the moment my car door opens and scan the sidewalk, before closing my suit jacket and buttoning it to guard me from the chill in the air.

The clerk perks up as I step through the entrance and motions to the dark pink peonies on the counter.

"We've got them ready, Mr. Sovrano."

I nod, walking over and accepting the butcher-paper-wrapped bundle, tossing a twenty on the counter. "I won't be here next week. But the week after we'll resume."

"Absolutely, sir," he responds and jots down a note to himself on the pad in front of him.

I turn to the door, and my eyes are drawn to a case filled with roses, all varieties of colors, the petals slightly dewy from the water that's been sprayed on them.

"Would you like to add to your order, sir?" the clerk questions.

Would I?

I could send Sarah the whole fucking case and watch her roll her eyes at my outrageous behavior. Pretend she hates them, then watch the smile brighten on her face as I tell her that I'd do it every damn day if it meant she'd be that happy again.

I could, but since she's pretending to hate me...

My eyes linger on them for another moment before I shake my head, breaking my focus.

"No. Just what I have."

My driver pulls the door open, and I walk out, the tiny bell dinging again as I do.

"I got it," I say, grabbing the door handle and opening it.

Sliding in, I settle into the back of my SUV, placing the bouquet next to me in the empty seat. I look out of the window and catch my reflection, seeing the grin on my face. I've never wanted to buy a woman flowers. Ever.

And this pistol makes me want to buy the store.

My head shifts, and I let out a half laugh as I lean in toward the driver.

"Take me to my mother."

He nods as the car comes to life, and we slowly pull out into traffic. I undo the button of my suit jacket and reach into the inside pocket to retrieve my cell.

I hit the number and place it against my ear.

"Boss," Antonio greets.

"Did we verify?"

"We did. It's them. Her dad and brother. Dante, they're the lowest forms of fucking scumbags...the shit we've heard. È orribile. It's gonna make you lose it. But they're here, in Chicago, about a block from her place."

My fist strains against itself, making my knuckles white.

What kind of men hunt their own flesh and blood? Unless she betrayed them...turned on them.

The idea gives me pause. Sarah's definitely running because she's afraid, but until now, I never considered it's something she's due.

No. I throw the idea away the minute it enters my mind. Because I don't care if it is something she deserves—nobody touches her.

"Send Nico and some of the other guys to have a friendly chat."

By friendly, I mean for them to break bones and jaws, knock out teeth, and take their dignity.

"You want them gone?" Antonio questions seriously.

He's not asking me if I want them to be given plane tickets—he's asking if I want their lives. I hear the train run by him on his end, and I take that opportunity to answer, just in case it's not just *us* listening.

"Send them back to Boston. I don't think after a chat they'll be back. But if the boys feel it necessary to send them somewhere further, then I'm more than happy to front the ticket."

I hear him chuckle before he answers, "Perfetto."

"Hey," I add, "not a word to Sarah."

"Of course. One more thing. We did find the guy who they used to track her down. He was showing her picture around, asking if anyone knew her. What do you want us to do with him?"

"Bring him to the space. And tell Matteo to ask Sarah about her family...she trusts him, she might talk. We need to know more." Before I hang up, I add, "Antonio. When you grab our new friend...I need his jaw working in order for him to speak."

"I'll do my best." He laughs darkly.

I hang up just as we pull up to my destination. The car slows into the entrance, winding along the smoothly paved road flanked by oak trees. My mind wanders thinking of the last time I spoke with my mother.

The car turns, taking another road that leads down to a grassy area where a brook runs. We slow to a stop, and I exit, taking in a deep breath and exhaling, before reaching back in for the flowers.

It's the same each week. I hate coming. Despise remembering.

But then, I walk the thirty-seven steps past the stone-and-marble gravestones etched with the names of people lost and show my respects to the woman who gave me life but ended her own.

I run my hand over the white, cold stone, brushing away a few small leaves, and pull her flowers from last week out of the vase, replacing them with the new ones.

"Ciao, mamma. Ho portato i tuoi fiori preferiti. Non come la signora nella tomba accanto a te ... i suoi figli le hanno portato un mazzo di garofani. Roba da due soldi. Solo il meglio per te." *Hi, Mom. I brought you your favorites. Not like the lady a few down...her kids bring carnations. Cheap. Only the best for you.*

I laugh sadly as the words come out, thinking how pleased she'd be to have the fanciest gravestone with all the best flowers and how much I wished I could have saved her from the dirt that buries her body.

I inhale in quick succession on my forgotten cigar.

"You guys are like a bunch of chicks. I'm not telling you shit."

My brothers and I are seated outside on the patio, drinking the smoothest scotch and enjoying cigars. Family dinner is a ritual, and we abide by it every Sunday. It's a "have to" amongst us, but it's also a "want to."

It's one of the few times in my life when I can let down my guard and just be the man I am.

Luca tosses the same half-eaten roll at me, hitting my bad shoulder.

"Dick," I growl, rolling my shoulder. "I'm gonna choke you to death. With my bare hands."

Luca's eyes are filled with amusement as he leans forward. "Good luck with that, cripple. Listen, you don't want to tell us the good stuff? Fine. You're like a virgin in relationships. It's okay...we can ease you in. Warm you up, sweetheart. It only hurts a little."

I laugh at his crude humor, and Dom throws back the rest of his drink as his shoulders shake.

"If you aren't spilling the goods, at least tell us what you know about what she's involved in," Luca finishes, getting down to business.

I lean back, resting my arms out over the chairs next to me, deciding how to tell them.

But there's no point in sugarcoating it, so I give it to them straight.

"Not much past what I got out of her the other night. But Antonio says the guys are real lowlifes. Whatever the fuck she's tangled in smells foul. My gut says there's way more to the story, and I don't think I'm gonna like it."

My brothers stare back at me with hardened gazes. I know they feel the same way I do.

And I know they're thinking all the same dark thoughts I've entertained.

Luca lets out a long breath, running his hand through his hair. "Are we worried about her?"

I know what he's asking; I entertained the thought momentarily, too. We have to think this way—it's our nature.

"Would it matter? Really? Even if she did something to deserve what she's getting?"

His eyes hold mine, and I see his answer before he says it. "No, because whatever she did, that girl did it for the right reason. I don't care who she is to them; I know who she is to us."

"Agreed."

"Have the guys tracked them down yet...her father and brother?" Dom questions, pulling my attention.

A billow of smoke wafts through the air with my exhale. "Yeah. We found them—the assholes are a block down from her. Nico's gonna introduce himself tomorrow."

Luca leans in, worry darkening his features. "Does she know you know?"

"Nah, that's a fight for another day..." I answer, not elaborating.

Dom leans back into his chair. "Now, why would you keep that from her?"

I wave him off, crossing my arms. "I'm not keeping anything from her. I'm just ensuring the coast is really clear before she gets any ideas."

My brothers stare at me and then at each other. I hate that twin thing. It's always two against one with these dickheads.

My hand rubs my stubbled jaw as I grin, knowing they see right through my bullshit.

"Just fucking leave it, already..."

Dom smirks, slowly spinning a spoon around on the table, regarding Luca with amusement.

"You still on the fence about whether or not you want to help her?" Dom asks sarcastically.

Luca chuckles like the asshole he is. I level a look at my brother as he chimes in. "She's not going to miss this time when she shoots you for lying and keeping her here, so you can fuck her longer."

I smack the table, and he laughs harder.

"Fuck you. That's not why I'm keeping her here...I mean, it's not the only reason. And I never said we were fucking— stop trying to get information, you fucking perv."

I take a swig of my drink as they both sit there shaking their heads at me, unconvinced by my reasoning.

"I wish I was an only child again. It wasn't lonely. I take it all back." I laugh, reaching for the butter knife.

"Careful, you'll hurt yourself," Luca jokes, grabbing it before I can.

I growl, rubbing my face, irritated with my asshole brothers.

"Fine. I like her," I answer, bringing my eyes back to Luca's. "She's growing on me, and I don't think she'll have to run once I'm done with these jerkoffs. But she isn't the kind of girl who does any-fucking-thing unless it's her idea."

"Now that I believe." Dom states.

Luca puffs his cigar. "Aww, maybe you should make her matching bracelets, so she knows you really love her."

Dom laughs, throwing back his drink, and pats the table. "Or, wait. Wait. I got it. You could get her those little heart candies that say 'Be mine.'"

"I fucking hate you two so much."

My phone vibrates on the table, and I pick it up, shaking my head and pointing at Luca.

"You're the biggest prick of the two of you, you know that?"

He nods, smiling big. "Yeah. My cock is huge. You're right. Biggest one."

Dom howls as I stand and walk away to answer, my own laugh filling the line. "Speak."

"We have a problem. She wants to go to her apartment to get more shit. But now that we know what we know...how do you want me to handle this?"

Matteo's voice is hushed as if he's trying to stay quiet, so she doesn't hear. My arms cross as I hold the phone to my ear and turn my back to my brothers.

"I can't risk spooking her or giving her false hope. Have you made headway about her family?" I question, hoping that he has so then she may be more open to reason.

"No. The girl is a steel trap." *Fuck.*

If I demand, she'll react. If I request, she'll deny.

I shake my head, the irony causing an upturn in my lips when I realize that the only way I'm made happy is if she's happy.

"Dante," Dom yells, and I turn, waving him off.

"Take her. Call some guys to go with you. I'll meet you there. They're not trying to take her out. It seems as if she's more valuable alive."

"Done."

I end the call and shove my phone into my pant pocket, just as it vibrates. "Jesus. I'm the most popular guy tonight."

Luca laughs as I walk back to the table and take my seat. I open the message that's been sent from Antonio, and a frown forms on my face. Fuck.

> Antonio: We could use your expertise. When you can.

They aren't getting anywhere with the guy who's been

tracking her. If Antonio needs my help, I can't imagine the sack of bones I'm gonna walk in to see.

> Me: On my way.

I type back quickly, putting my phone away and focusing back on my brothers.

"I have to go. Business," I shoot out, downing the rest of my drink and standing.

I stub my cigar out but put it between my fingers. "Never waste a good Cuban."

Luca nods and lifts his drink. "Words to live by. Leave quickly before the girls come back down. They'll have your ass for leaving before dessert."

I laugh because it's true. Drew and Gretchen aren't going to let me hear the end of this.

Slapping Dom's shoulder, I lean in. "Do me a favor?"

"Name it," he answers, standing to walk out with me.

We stride through the door and back into the house. I grab my jacket from the couch and look at him. "Call Matteo and meet them at her place?"

He understands I don't want her there so close to the men trying to hurt her. "If I can't be there, then I need you with her. Have Matteo call me with any problems."

"She'll be safe. I got you. But you're going to owe Drew something big the next time you see her because now both of us are leaving early."

CHAPTER THIRTEEN
SARAH

"You don't think you're overdoing it? Maybe slightly?" I ask Matteo from the back seat of the SUV where I'm flanked by two serious-looking guys.

"Dante said to bring some guys with us. I brought some guys." He laughs. "Bitch to him when he meets us."

"I get it. It's fine. I'm just happy to get something other than sweats. You're the worst." I joke.

"You're welcome." He laughs again.

We ease into a silence as we make the drive to my apartment. I don't live too far from Dante, but I do live a few incomes from him, so the closer we get, the less shiny the buildings are, and the more necessary it becomes to have security.

It's funny, the first night I made it to Dante's, I thought of it as a prison, but all the windows here are the ones with bars.

"We're here," Matteo barks to the guys as the car slows and pulls to a stop in front of my building.

They exit first as I grab my bag from the floor and sort through it for my keys. My door opens as I hear them jingle. I twist my head to the open door and see a large, familiar hand extended to help me out.

"I'd know that watch anywhere. Hey, you." I greet, peering up at Dominic. "What are you doing here?"

Dom pulls me out of the car and into a squeeze, making me laugh.

"He couldn't make it. So, he sent a better model."

I push his shoulder as he lets me go, still laughing at his joke, but when I take in his face, I notice his smile doesn't meet his eyes.

I smooth out my shirt and point to the door. He nods, and we start to walk the concrete walkway to the steps of the brownstone that houses eight apartments.

"It's nice to see a friendly face." I can't help but notice the way he looks around as we walk. "Speaking of miserable people. Where is he?"

Dom gives a small shoulder shrug and winks.

"Business, gorgeous. You know, the kind you don't need to know about."

Grinning, he stops in front of the entry door and angles his body, so his back is to the wall. *Something's up.* I look over my shoulder, but all I see are Dante's burly soldiers staring back at me.

My eyes travel to Dom as I twirl my keys around my finger. "Something I need to know?"

"Not a thing." He answers and looks down at the door, motioning for me to open it.

I fiddle with the keys Matteo gave me back earlier and turn the lock, pushing the door open.

"How was dinner?" I ask nonchalantly, as we walk past a wall of gold-plated mail slots toward the stairs.

Dominic laughs and shakes his head, holding me back as the other guys take the stairs first.

"You mean the dinner where we set Dante up with the busty blonde who couldn't keep her hands off of him?"

My eyes shoot to his, and I swear I could kill him.

"Easy." He laughs. "I'd hate to be the one who got in your way. You can put your claws away. It was family only. But I couldn't help myself. You know, considering he told me and Luca all about your little false assumption."

I smack his shoulder and laugh.

"Oh, that's nice. Like a group of golden girls. The three of you are terrible people."

Dom nudges my shoulder with his much larger one. "Aww. We love you too, Sar."

I roll my eyes as we walk up the stairs, feigning irritation, mostly to hide the fact that I'm really very happy that I was wrong. I shouldn't care. But I do.

I don't want to share. It's as simple as that.

When I get to my apartment, I unlock the door and head inside with my entourage. The space feels so small and too dark, in a way it's never felt before. I flick on a light and toss my keys on the counter.

Everyone filters inside, the door shutting behind them, and I look at the guys, who are taking up all the room in my place. "I'm going to pack. There's only the one room, so you guys can hang here."

"Let them check it first." Dom directs.

I nod as Matteo and the others walk past me, keeping my eyes on Dom. "You sure there isn't something I should know?"

"You sure there isn't anything I should know?" he counters, and I scrunch my nose.

I love Dominic and Luca like they're my real brothers. I wish they were, which is why I won't say a word, but I also hate lying to them. Almost as much as I hate lying to Dante.

"Gorgeous, you know he'll find out the truth. Whatever that is. Right?" *Yep. I do.*

"Let's hope it's after I'm gone. Then we can all be spared the grief." I shrug, not bothering with pretense.

This is Dom—he and Luca have been my only sense of family since I started working at Church. I can lie by withholding, not by being false.

"Sarah. Don't push everyone away." I shake my head, opening my mouth to protest, but he stops me. "Like you always do. Let us help you. You have us. Me, Luca, and especially Dante."

I stare at his face, wishing that I could just cave and say "yes," but some things are for the best. I almost laugh when I think it, hearing Dante's words in my head: *"It's for your own good."*

Matteo walks back out and nods. "All good, Sarah."

I smile weakly at Dom and turn, walking inside my room, trying to suffocate the need to spill my guts, but it feels overwhelming. The longer I stay, the harder it will become. I know that. But there isn't anything I wouldn't do for these guys. Especially now.

I grab the last of the things on the list I have in my head and walk to my bed, sitting for a moment and taking a breath. My phone buzzes on my bed where I tossed it when I came in. I scoot myself back and lean over to reach it, lying down as I answer.

I hit Answer without bothering to look because I know it's Dante.

"Miss me?" I tease, smiling wide as I hold the phone to my ear.

"Oh, we miss you, Sarah."

Chills shoot down my spine, and I sit up straight as a board. My breath is still in my throat, my teeth grating so hard they may break.

"Christopher," I greet with every bit of the malice I feel for my brother. "Where are you?"

I don't think he'll actually tell me, but I always ask anyway.

I hear him laugh darkly as the sound of a car passing by with loud music mutes his voice.

But what gives me pause is the echo I hear from my side...

"Look outside, dearest sister."

My eyes blink rapidly as I stand, my head turning to the window as my feet refuse to move. *Go, Sarah.* I push forward, taking slow steps, then walk quickly toward my window.

My eyes dart to my bedroom door, worried someone may hear me or walk in. I stand by the corner of the wall and bring my fingertips to the soft cream curtains I put up myself.

Peeling it back, I peer out with half my face, scanning the sidewalk and across the street for my brother.

I hear a match strike, and Christopher inhale deeply, just as I see the bright red burn from his cigarette illuminate the dark space across the street.

Shit.

"Still smoking, I see. Here's hoping cancer strikes," I bite out, closing the curtain and leaning my back against the wall.

"Wouldn't that be your lucky day." He laughs with an exhale.

My eyes search my room as I try to decide what to do. I could tell Dom and Matteo right now. They could grab him and beat the shit out him...maybe worse. But then...

"What do you want, Christopher? You know I'm never voluntarily coming back. So why call, why torment me?"

His voice forces me to remember what he looks like when he sneers.

"You know exactly what we want. I suspect that's why you've made new friends, bitch."

He was watching me when I got here. If he's too scared of them, that means he knows or at least suspects who they are. Fuck. But maybe I can use it to my advantage.

I push off the wall and start back to my bed, running my hands through my hair.

"Yep. Good luck getting through them. You'll need an army. Might as well give up now."

"You forget we *have* an army."

I laugh at his empty threat and grab the handle of my bag. "Not unless you want to die too."

Christopher's voice is quiet, threatening, with a promise he plans to keep. "Times have changed, sister. And now that you have dangerous friends, we'll need a bigger gun. This isn't over. We'll see you around."

The line dies, and I feel like I do, too.

He has the O'Bannions on his side. He must have made a deal with them in exchange for me. Before I can think or process what he's just said, I grab my bag and rush out the door.

All heads shoot to my face, concern etched on theirs, not that I wait to dissect—my entire body is set to survival mode. I need to get out of here.

I wish I could burn this whole building down. Just the fact that he knows where I am, where I sleep—it's all tainted by their disgusting intentions.

I hate them.

"Sarah. What's going on?" Matteo calls out as I reach for the keys but throw them to the ground.

I won't ever need them again because I won't be back.

"We need to get out of here. Now," I yell behind me as I throw open my front door and practically run.

I hear footsteps behind me. They're all yelling for me to stop, but I don't. I just need to get out. I make it down a flight of stairs before strong arms wrap around me and pull me in.

"Sarah. Stop," Dom whispers into my ear, and I shake my head.

I struggle against his arms, needing to keep moving. "We have to go. Let go, Dom."

I feel it. The panic. The fear. It's all there. Hiding away, waiting to rear its ugly head.

"Whoa. Settle down. You're okay," Dom breathes into my hair, holding me as my body quiets.

The lump in my throat feels like a boulder. And that feels like the worst part. I'm holding on by a thread, and if I let go, I need to know I can pull myself back in.

But if I can't, Dante will.

"Call him. I need him. Call him please," I plead in a hushed voice, turning into Dom's chest and letting him hug me.

"Okay. It's okay, Sarah. I got you."

CHAPTER FOURTEEN
DANTE

I roll my head, trying to relax my shoulder muscles. We've been in the car too long for my liking. But I know it's necessary. The spot is a haul from the city but worth it when privacy is needed.

Helps to be in the middle of nowhere when people scream.

The gravel kicks up against the car as we pull into the old parking lot. There are three industrial warehouses on this plot. Two I lease out, and one stays empty for whatever we need it for. It's a perfect cover.

I look out the window, but I can't see anything past the tint on the glass until we pull past a dimly lit area that highlights the door. The car pulls into an overhang for the cars and stops.

My door is opened, letting in the cold night air, and I pull my black cashmere trench closed as I exit. The moment my loafers hit the ground, I see Antonio waiting at the door for me.

He looks worn-out, tired in the same way someone looks when they've been hitting a punching bag for hours.

Too bad for the guy inside it's him being hit and not an actual bag.

I walk toward the metal door and nod to Antonio as I slip inside.

The space is vast, empty, and dark, but the faintest smell of sawdust from some building materials stored inside fills my nose as we walk. My feet stomp against the cement floor, and it seems to echo off the steel walls.

However, not all the walls are steel. One is made with cement blocks.

And that comes in handy.

The guys have kept it discreet tonight, using only a few floor spotlights. They're aimed at the badly beaten guy strung up by chains and hooked to that handy-as-hell cement wall.

His face is bruised and swollen, a gash under his right eye congealed with crimson. The chains rattle against one another, a brutal melody of torture as his fatigue shows, and his body sways when his knees buckle.

Antonio falls in step as we walk toward where Vincenzo is leaned in talking to the guy, no doubt telling him that he'll make it all stop if he just gives us what we want.

"Did you make any progress?" I question, reaching into the inside pocket of my coat.

Antonio looks down at his red, swollen knuckles, flexing and straightening his hand.

"Not yet. He's sticking with the same story. He was hired over the phone, doesn't know who. Just supposed to send the info to an email."

"Bullshit," I counter pulling out a silver cigar case.

"Completely. But he's committed," he intones as we come to stand a few feet away.

I run the fire over the tip of my cigar and put it in my

mouth. Vincenzo comes to stand with us, his back to the guy, and I nod to him as I puff, relighting my Cuban.

Blowing out a puff of smoke, I look over Vin's shoulder and back to the guys.

"He works for someone big and bad. That's the only reason he doesn't buckle."

They both nod at me in agreement, and I know what I need to do.

"What's his name?" I ask, holding the cigar between my teeth, and shrug off my jacket.

Antonio takes it, folding it over a chair beside him. "Frank," he offers as I unbutton my suit jacket and hand that to him too.

"No fucking way. It's a bad week for Franks," I laugh to their amused faces.

Walking over, I uncuff my sleeves and begin to roll them up, exposing the veins on my tattooed forearms. I come to a stop in front of our half-conscious friend and take a drag of my cigar, then blow the smoke in his face.

He coughs, the chains rattling as he pulls away, mumbling a few incoherent words.

"Frank...hey," I bark, slapping his cheek. "Wake up, Frank."

More mumbles as his head bobs, hanging down between his upstretched arms. I look back at Antonio and Vincenzo in irritation. I told them to leave him conscious. *Assholes.*

"I missed cannoli for this. Wake him up."

Vin walks toward a safety spigot that has a hose attached like the ones on a fire truck and begins to pull it over.

"Ah fuck. I love cannoli...Mama's has the best in town. I'll kill anyone who says different." Antonio agrees, taking the hose from Vin.

I walk a few feet away, not wanting to be in the spray, and nod.

The freezing cold water turns on with a violent blast, shooting straight onto Frank's body.

He yells and bucks against the pain from the force of the water.

Vincenzo starts to cheer, clapping his hands. "There we go. Nice to see you again."

I hold up my hand, and Antonio stops the assault. I walk over and stand in front of his water-swept face, watching him cough and shake his head as he tries to get his bearings.

"Sorry. I'm sure you understand why that was necessary. I can't get answers if you're sleeping."

"Fuck you," he spits, the blood from his mouth landing on my shoe.

I look down, and my jaw tenses. "That was rude, Frank. How about you make it up to me. Tell me who you work for? Better yet, why'd the girl's family want you looking for her?"

He stares at me and shakes his head. I have to give it to this dick—he's loyal. A trait my first Frank could've used.

"Frank...I can call you Frank, right?" Vin comes up next to me, handing me a cloth for my shoe, but I pocket it. "See, the way I see it is you're too scared to rat on whoever sent you. And I admire that. I do. But that means my only option is to be scarier than whatever's back home."

"I'm not telling you nothing," he slurs in a deep accent. A familiar one.

"That's interesting. That's two now with that accent... fucking Boston. What's with you pricks?" I push, and he lunges for me in his chains.

I let out a deep laugh, stepping back quickly with my arms spread wide. "There's the spirit, Frank." My voice booms through the space as I begin to feed off his anger, clapping my hands together and coming face-to-face with him. "Tell me who you really work for. Cuz it ain't the dicks she's related to."

Frank sneers, his teeth showing the blood left in his mouth. *That's right. Give me a fucking reason to beat it out of you.*

"You can't protect that whore. He'll get his queen back. Even if he has to go through you. She'll go back to where she belongs, and when she does, she'll hurt real bad. But after six or seven of us, she'll get used to it or die trying."

My vision dims, my mind going blank as heat suffocates any and all reason. I act out of instinct. Primal fucking brutality. I'm not inside my mind even though I'm guiding my body.

I hear the screams, his wails, faint at first, then gaining in volume as my mind catches up, zooming me into focus. The smell of burning flesh engulfs my senses, and my knuckles burn from the strength of my grip on the back of his hair. It's so hard that I can feel tiny strands breaking free.

I'm holding Frank in place with my cigar pressed into his eye.

His pain swallows the silence as I press harder, but I can hear the small sizzle that fills the space. The cigar crumbles, breaking against my strength, and I mash it into his face.

When I step back, my chest is heaving. I'm unhinged. Pure evil. A fallen angel with a singular purpose.

"Nobody touches her. You hear that? Nobody!" I bellow, slapping his face.

I run my hand over my head, pleased as I watch him writhe in pain.

"You'll be the message. You're going to show them that anyone who steps foot in my fucking city leaves in a goddamn body bag if they try to come for what's mine."

Rage courses through my veins like a life source. It pumps through my body like a drug, giving me focus and power. I step in quickly, bringing down a swift hook to his jaw, hearing it crack under the pressure.

"She's *mine*. You wanna fucking steal from me, you piece

of shit?" I growl as I hit him again even harder, hearing another crack. "Who the fuck is gonna go through me? Nobody."

The sound is intoxicating, and I look at the ceiling, taking in gulps of air. I'll never let anyone hurt her.

I keep hitting him, again and again, his head swinging with every blow. Grunts and spit fly from my mouth as I unleash my rage on him, unstopping and unrelenting. His head hangs down, dangling after each assault, making me adjust my stance until his legs finally give. He's unconscious, maybe dead.

But I don't stop, swinging into the air and stumbling backward as his body swings away from me.

"Dante. It's done... Stop. It's done," Antonio whispers, putting his hands on my shoulders to steady me.

I lunge forward, but the guys hold me back, keeping me in place. I stand, breathing heavy and in a haze, staring at the body, knowing I've killed him.

Good fucking riddance.

"Come. Come...we'll take care of it," Vincenzo coaxes, pulling me backward.

Antonio's holding out my jacket for me to put on, but I reach into my slacks pocket, pull out the cloth I'd shoved in there earlier, and wipe my hands. Blood stains the rag as it removes the evidence of my indiscretion.

I fold it and lift a clean part to my face to wipe away some blood spatter that's hit my cheek and look at the guys. "Burn the body. But make sure he's found. I'm going to speak to our princess about who the fuck her family really is. Because the one thing I know is Sarah's been lying to me. To us."

I tug on my suit jacket, my breath still labored, and my head tips down. I see the spit still on my shoe. Grabbing my coat, I pull it on as I walk back to Frank's dead, hanging body.

Reaching out, my hand steadies his limp body as I wipe the shoe he spat on over his pant leg.

"Save me a spot, Frank, because it won't really be hell until I arrive." I turn and walk past the guys, and straight out of the building.

The moment the freezing air hits my lungs, I feel refocused, awake, pulled from my haze. Running my hands over my face, I stand and let my breathing steady, feeling calmer with each moment that passes.

My driver steps out and opens my door, letting me slide in and shutting it behind me as I pull my cell out and dial Matteo. I want answers, and I won't wait until I'm home.

He answers on the first ring.

"Boss."

"Put her on," I clip out.

There's silence, and then I hear her voice blast through. "Where have you been?"

"I want to know who the fuck your family is. And I want to know now."

CHAPTER FIFTEEN
SARAH

The hairs on my arms stand on end over the tone coating his words. His voice is gruff and angry. It doesn't sound like Dante. More like the men I'm used to. He sounds unhinged, rageful, and unpredictable. And I don't like it.

"Don't speak to me like that," I say calmly because he feels volatile, even over the phone.

Why is he angry? I was so relieved when he finally called, and now I'm totally thrown.

Dante lets out a growl as he answers, "I'll speak to you any way I like. If you know what's good for you, you'll answer my fucking question."

What the fuck? He's insanely angry.

I've been waiting hours for him to call. Hours. All I've wanted was to tell him everything, to let him help. To let him in. But right now, I don't trust that anything I would say to him could be seen with clear eyes.

"No. You aren't going to call me and start yelling for answers. Calm down and then we'll talk," I snap, irritated at his insistence. "I had a shit night. What the hell has gotten into you?"

"Right. Fucking. Now," he roars, banging sounding off in the background.

"What is wrong with you? You're acting like a lunatic," I yell back, throwing an arm in the air and turning my back to a watchful Matteo.

I can only imagine what the car will look like afterward.

"I'm a lunatic? Huh? You're right, sweetheart...I'm the asshole protecting a girl who's fighting me every step of the way and keeping more secrets than the truths she tells. Don't deny it...because that will just be adding to your lies."

My voice catches in my throat as I answer, "The only secrets I'm keeping don't need to be told."

"That's what I fucking thought. Nothing stays a secret forever. Remember that."

The contempt in his voice guts me. If I didn't know better, I would think he'd found my family.

"I won't talk to you like this," I breathe out quietly.

The line is bathed in silence, interrupted only by Dante letting out an audibly ragged breath.

"I found a guy. And that someone's left me with unanswered questions. Ones you will answer willingly. Or this time I'll make you."

The harsh control in his voice makes my eyes falter. My hand brushes up to my throat as I stand stoically, trying to keep my composure. Three hours ago, he was the only person I thought could bring me the peace I needed.

And now I realize how stupid I've been. I don't know what *means* he'll use, but this Dante isn't any version I've met before or one I care to.

"You can stow your fucking threats. Whatever you're

thinking in that head of yours, let me assure you that you're wrong. My life isn't as predictable as you may think."

His voice booms over the line. "How the fuck would I know anything about your life? You're one big goddamn secret. No matter how easy I make this for you, no matter how much help I offer, all you do is hide."

I start to pace as we speak. "That's all I know how to do, Dante." I wrap my arm around my center and say the words before I can stop them. "I can't believe that for a minute I actually thought you'd be what I needed."

My head tips back, and I stare at the ceiling, standing in place as we stay in silence.

Dante lets out a breath before speaking in a quieter tone.

"Even after all that's happened between us, you won't trust me. You refuse to believe that I know what's best. That I've got your back. Unbelievable. You aren't the girl I thought you were."

He's not seeking my answer. Dante's speaking aloud, like an affirmation, a validation for whatever he's planning to do next.

I could correct him. Tell him it's not true, but where he is, in this headspace, it's no good. Better for him to hate me because it's clear that Dante protecting me has become intricately woven into how much we like each other.

But me and him, we're for another lifetime.

And I can't trust him with the truth—tonight was evidence of that. So, I do what I do best and push back.

"*We* don't have anything to do with all this shit. And *we* don't even exist. We fucked. That's it," I spit angrily.

Dante's growl weaves around his words. "I'm gonna make you eat those words off a plate from where you crawl to lick me clean of the person who came before you."

There's hating me, and then there's *this*.

Rage burns my skin. He's a bastard.

I spin and look at Matteo, furious. I want to scream. Tear down the wall. But instead, I drop the phone from my ear and walk back the few steps to where Matteo stands. I can hear my name being yelled through the phone, but I hand it back, leveling him with a glare.

"Tell him that when he's ready to act like a sane person and be fucking polite, I might speak to him. But not a goddamn minute before." My voice raises even louder at the end as my temper spikes higher.

Matteo hands the phone back to me and shakes his head, but I know Dante heard me loud and clear.

"Sarah. You know who he is...stop stoking the fire and answer him."

"Fuck you! I won't ever be spoken to that way. And if he wants to kill me for it, then he can get the fuck in line."

Matteo puts the phone back to his ear and winces as he hears Dante yelling.

"Sorry, boss, but she won't speak to..." He nods his head. "Yeah. I think so." More nodding. "I can...I could try and make her..."

My eyebrows raise, but whatever Dante's saying cuts him off, and Matteo seems uncomfortable as he listens. His eyes dart to me, and I swear he looks apologetic. Matteo lowers the phone, his Adam's apple bobbing as he swallows and meets my eyes.

"Well?" I ask expectantly, waiting for an answer.

Matteo holds his hand over the phone and squares his shoulders.

"He says you have two choices. Take the phone back and answer, or take your spot on the living room floor, head bowed, hands on your thighs. Because either way, he'll get the answers he wants. It's your choice whether or not you enjoy the process."

My hand strikes out across Matteo's unsuspecting face, his cheek reddening immediately.

Leaning in close, I sneer, "That's for your boss, since we're passing messages."

Checking the time again, I crane my neck to the kitchen clock from where I'm sitting on the couch. Eleven o'clock.

I pour myself another glass of chardonnay, hoping he walks through the door this time.

It's been an entire day.

We collided, teeth bared and armor on, Sunday night, but he never walked through the elevator doors.

Matteo stayed with me most of the night, although he's not speaking to me after I slapped him, and then it was a steady stream of the guys ever since. But nobody will tell me anything. They're barely speaking to me.

If I thought my situation was bad before, now I know it can be worse.

Monday's about to come and go, and still no Dante.

I wish I felt nothing, that I didn't care, but I do. My nerves are raw and frayed. I've picked up the phone to call Dominic or Luca, but I haven't. Too many questions, too many explanations I won't give to do that.

My leg bounces with my unease as I stare at Antonio, who's sitting no more than ten feet from me. I know he knows what's going on, but he's the most standoffish.

I think he's still pissed about the scissors and Vincenzo. In my defense, I had no idea what was going to happen to me...it was survival of the fittest.

"Is he okay?" I breathe out, extinguishing the silence.

Antonio folds down the top of his paper and stares at me for a moment. "He's alive."

"That's not what I asked," I answer with a scowl.

He stares at me longer and nods. "He's Dante. You've fucked him over. He needs to get past that."

I draw my knees in, taking a sip of my wine. "How did I fuck him? He called me screaming like a psychopath. Demanding, being a bully. I needed him yesterday, not the other way around."

He laughs, folding his paper and setting it aside. "You underestimate your place with him. You've kept him in the dark. And for people like us, information is a means for survival. You've made him go at this blind. And because of his history, he's willing to do that for you. But I have a feeling he wants you to care about that even more than he needs you to agree with it."

My glass rests against my lips as I listen, trying to see the bigger picture.

My eyes lift to Antonio's, and suddenly, he doesn't seem so reserved, so removed anymore.

"I do care, Antonio. That's why I'm doing what I know I need to, but in another life, I think he could be a man who I..."

The elevator dings, and my head snaps to it as Antonio says, "He's here. Remember what you were about to say, beautiful." He stands and starts past me, giving me a hard look. "Especially in the next few minutes. Nobody said the job of queen would be easy, Sarah."

Before I can say anything, the elevator doors slide open, and Dante's hazel eyes meet mine.

Antonio blocks my view as Dante enters, so I take the moment to take another sip of my wine. I don't know what to expect, and Antonio's words aren't making me feel any better either.

I turn to look back again as a squeal accompanied by an overenthusiastic giggle bounces off the walls, and I stop breathing.

What the fuck.

The scene in front of me comes into focus as my mind scrambles to process what the fuck I'm seeing.

Dante's arm is wrapped around a leggy blonde who's come to stand by his side, his hand resting on her ass.

I'll break that hand.

Her boney fingers run over Dante's lapel, and I have the extreme urge to yell at her to get the fuck off.

Antonio walks inside the elevator, not bothering to look at me as Dante leads his Barbie doll inside.

I wonder if she's just as easily breakable as the real doll.

His face is buried in her neck as they walk, and I can feel my heart beating out of my chest.

I need to think straight. I blink my eyes a few times and look down, sweeping my eyes for the water I thought I had, but instead, grab my wine and down the rest of the glass.

"Sarah," Dante greets, coming to a stop, trailing his hand up and down her hip.

I can't look at him. My eyes are fixed on the movement of his fingers on her skeleton.

That's what she is. Skin and bones, no meat, no curves. Nothing. She couldn't be more opposite than me.

"What are you doing?" I blurt out, tearing my gaze from Dante's toy to his face.

"I'm going to bed. What are you doing?" he answers, coolly.

Motherfucker.

"You're serious right now?" I snap, tapping my nail against my wineglass.

"As a fucking heart attack," he sneers, tearing his arm in between them to point at me. "I can't even fucking see straight. I tore the car apart. You should've just answered me..." he barks, his gaze drifting to the open area in the living room. "Or been on your goddamn knees."

I huff, rolling my eyes. I can't say anything for fear that it'll give away how much he's hurting me. Because that I won't give him.

He grabs Barbie's face and tilts her head, sinking his mouth onto her neck and letting her go just as harshly. "So, she's here to do what you won't...to fucking listen."

I could kill him. His choice of words stabs me directly in the gut. I can feel the heat under my skin burning with my temper. He's brought this girl here to punish me.

And it's fucking working. Damn him because he's damned me.

"Okay," I say, taking a breath, hoping for some amount of calm. "Well. You have fun," I bite out, shaking my head "But let me point out that you didn't know—for two days—that I wasn't on my knees and you still brought this whore home?"

Dante narrows his eyes at me, disliking my point.

"You're the dick in this scenario, Dante. Not me for avoiding speaking to a lunatic."

"Um, excuse me," Barbie pipes up with a whine. "Don't let her call me a whore."

"Oh, come on, you know who you are, hooker," I snap as she scowls. "I don't have the desire to examine your poor life choices right now. Do what you're good at and be quiet. Or better yet, say something else and not even Dante will be able to help you," I offer with a smile.

The son of a bitch actually chuckles. "If I'm reading this

right—and I am—you care that I brought another woman back to my home?" He smirks arrogantly. "You're jealous."

I wipe my cheek, afraid of a tear that may fall. "You want me jealous. I'm not. I'm disappointed that you keep proving to me that you're like all the rest of the men in my life."

I see his hands fist and the anger spike like electric shocks through his body.

"No. That's bullshit. You fucking care. Admit that shit. Now," he growls.

We stand staring at each other, our eyes locked.

"I couldn't care less," I counter, lying through my damn teeth as his toy runs her hands over his shoulders. It's like she's in heat. Fucking bitch.

"Yeah?" he challenges, shrugging off Barbie's hand on his shoulder. "You don't care who I fuck, right? We don't exist, right?"

"Abso-fucking-lutely!" I bark, crossing my arms, still holding my wineglass.

Dante narrows his eyes at me as we stand locked in a fierce stare down. I refuse to look away until he admits he's being an asshole. Simple as that. I win. No other option.

"Unbuckle my pants," he directs in a low gravel.

I open my mouth to say "hell no" when I hear his buckle rattle.

That wasn't for me.

My heart stops, right in my chest. He's not talking to me. My head shakes as I watch her jump to action.

His hips jerk forward, and my eyes shoot to his waist as Barbie pulls the leather from the hook. I glance back to him, and he smirks as she unbuttons his slacks but leaves them zipped.

My chest begins to rise and fall faster as fight or flight begins to take over. Because that's a natural reaction when someone declares war. But my body is still trying to decide if I leave or kill everyone.

"Get down on your knees," he growls.

Her hand slides across his chest as she looks over her cheap-ass shoulder and steps out of her heels, slowly dropping to her knees.

My words get caught in my throat, eaten by the bile trying to come up. My arms drop to my side, and I stare at him, not even trying to hide the hurt behind my eyes anymore.

Dante's not my boyfriend, and I don't love him, but this still feels like a betrayal.

"You could stop this anytime, Billy. Just say what I want to hear," he says tenderly, and I want to scream.

His eyes don't leave mine, and I say exactly what he wants to hear, but it all stays in my head because he doesn't deserve to ever hear it.

I want you, just for me, more than I've wanted anything in my life. I haven't stopped wanting it since you first touched me, but I'm leaving and never coming back. And that's all for you. All my lies have all been for you, not against you.

My eyes blink away the thought and drop to the couch. I grab a pillow, tossing it in their direction. "Here, for your knees. Bruises are a hooker's dead giveaway. You wouldn't want everyone to know your trade secrets, sweetie."

Dante's jaw tenses, all the muscles rippling, but all I feel is empty. I'm done. I've reached the point where I can't care anymore.

"You didn't really expect me to fold that easily, did you?" I laugh, but it's hollow. Tipping my glass back, I remember it's empty. "Looks like I'm dry...I should put this in the sink."

From where I'm standing, I hurl the thin-stemmed wine-glass into the next room, only half aiming for the sink. Glass shatters everywhere as it hits the countertop, and I nod, enjoying the destruction as Barbie shrieks from the floor.

"All right, I'm going to bed."

I reach back behind myself and grab the wine bottle that's still a quarter full. Bringing it to my lips, I chug some back before walking from the living room. My eyes stay forward as I pass Dante and his new bitch.

His hand wraps around my arm, stopping me in place, but I jerk away, spitting fire.

"Have fun with your girl."

He turns his body toward me, his deep gravel saying more than his words can.

"*She's* not my girl."

"And now neither am I."

Chapter Sixteen

Dante

What the fuck was I doing?

That's the only question that's played on loop since I came home hellbent on making her regret what she said.

It was the look in her eyes that made me want to erase what I did. But it was her disappointment that stripped me bare.

I became another man who's hurt her, and that's the one thing I never wanted to be.

"Fuck," I growl, throwing the sheet back from where I lie.

Alone.

I rub my hand over my face, taking a deep breath and rolling my neck to ease the tension I feel. There's no going back from this. She'll never forgive that.

Won't matter that I didn't touch that girl.

I knew the fucking move was shit, but I was gonna shove those words down her damn throat. I was so focused on that she denied us. That she didn't care about what's sparking between us.

After all I did that day, the lengths I went for her and the *why's* that I did it—to know she's lying to me was too much.

I needed her to come clean, to want to have my fucking back. Fuck that. I needed her to want me. As much as I want her.

But that bridge was burned, blown up, and fucking decimated last night.

I groan as I roll out of bed and stand. Running my hand over my stomach, I head to the bathroom to shower and get ready for the guys this morning.

"Four days," I whisper to myself, thinking about how long it took me to fuck it all up.

I walk inside the bathroom, turn on the shower, and head over to relieve myself before undressing and sliding inside the hot shower to let the water drown me.

Standing still, I take stock, letting the hot water rain over my bowed head. Warm droplets fall over my cheeks and face as I keep my palms against the stone wall. My eyes close as I give in to the moment.

There has to be a move I can make. Something. This can't be how we end before we ever really got started.

I smack the wall, hating that I can't get her fucking face out of my head. The look she gave me...like I'd ruined her.

Why do I care? What does it matter?

I don't love this girl. I just fucked her.

Lies.

She doesn't even matter. She means nothing to me.

Lies.

We're gasoline set to a fire. We're a beautiful fucking disaster.

"Goddammit," I roar, pushing off the wall and running my hand over my head.

I wipe my face with one hand as I yank the shower door

open with the other and step out, not bothering to turn off the water.

Fuck it.

I grab the towel off the counter and wrap it around my waist as I stalk out of the bathroom, dripping wet and on a mission.

Pulling my bedroom door open, I growl out her name. "Sarah." My head swings around to take in the living room. When I don't see her, I yell again, "Sarah!"

Her bedroom door opens, and she stands inside the frame, staring at me with red-rimmed eyes and no fight left in her.

I broke her. I did that.

It brings me to a full stop. We just stand staring at each other until the elevator dings and voices carry through the space.

"Billy," I mouth, but she steps back inside her room and closes the door.

I can't move, but I have to.

"Hey, boss," Vincenzo greets, but I wave him off as I turn and head back to get dressed and turn off the goddamn shower.

We've been seated in my office for an hour and a half, and I haven't heard one word being said.

"Dante."

I turn my head to the guys all seated around my desk, not knowing who just called me.

"Over here," Antonio calls from the arm of the sofa that's in the seating area in front of my desk. "Where are you today?"

I lean my head back onto my chair and let out an exhale. "Jesus. Let's just say my mind is on a stubborn girl."

My face dips back to the crowd, and eyes drop, accompanied with sympathetic looks playing over their faces. Something about how everyone avoids looking at me tells me that's not for me.

"Is there something someone wants to say?" I offer, opening my arms to the passive-aggressive assholes.

Nico shakes his head, holding up a hand and going back to his phone. Vincenzo mouths, "No," but crosses his arms, choosing to look down at the couch.

"Matteo?" I question. He waves me off, clearly angry as he mumbles to himself.

But Antonio just stares at me, tapping the newspaper he always reads on his leg.

"Is there something you wanna say, Antonio?" I challenge, leaning in on my desk.

He tosses the paper onto the table in front of him and crosses his arms, narrowing his eyes like he's considering his words carefully.

Of all the men, he's been the least convinced about helping her. Antonio's more of a "none of my concern" kind of guy. But he would never go against me, so when he does, I listen.

He takes a deep breath, a crease forming between his brows. "That girl needed you. She asked for you, Dante. And we both know she doesn't do that. So that stunt...with that chick. It wasn't cool. She deserves better than that because she cares for you."

The muscles in my jaw work overtime as I try and restrain my temper over what he's just fucking said. He's acting as if everything I've done isn't in her best interest.

"You don't have a fucking clue what you're talking about. She's done nothing but tell me to go to hell," I bark, my head pulling back.

He stands and shakes his head, and I do the same. The tension in the room begins to brew as we look at each other.

"I know exactly what the fuck I'm talking about. But maybe you should listen instead of trying to bulldoze that girl."

I rub my jaw, wishing I could break his, and laugh. "No. Fuck that. Apart from the chick being kind of a dick move, I've done nothing wrong here."

My words are punctuated by my finger jabbing the desktop.

Matteo shoots up from the chair next to Antonio and throws his arms up. "Come on, D. The other day was different —she wouldn't even talk to Dom. Whatever spooked her was something she would only tell you. I've never seen her that vulnerable...she's such a badass. And you let her drown in that shit."

My face contorts into confusion. I look around to the other guys, wondering what the fuck Matteo is talking about, but they're all nodding in agreement.

"What the fuck are you talking about?" I bellow. "What the fuck am I missing?"

The room sits in silence, staring at me like I'm crazy. I smack the desk hard with my palm. "I said, what the fuck am I missing?"

"Dom's message, Dante," Matteo says as his face begins to drop.

How the fuck does he know my brother left me a message, and why does it matter?

"What about it?" I answer.

Antonio looks at Matteo and then back to me. "You didn't check it?"

It's like having to put a fucking puzzle together, and my patience snaps.

"No. Is there something you want to tell me? Spit it the fuck out...I'm not trying to solve a mystery, dick."

Antonio begins to speak when Matteo stops him. "No.

Listen to it. I would've shared the information that night, but I was too busy getting slapped for passing messages."

The look he's giving me takes a lot of balls. But I knew what I was doing when I did it. I reach for my phone, feeling much too dangerous for Matteo to keep pushing me.

"Matteo..." Vincenzo warns, shaking his head for him stop pushing his luck.

Matteo looks away and walks to the other end of the room. That's probably for the best.

I pull up the message before pressing the phone to my ear and listen.

"Dante, I don't know what the fuck happened. Sarah...I've never seen her like this. She just keeps asking for you. Go home. That's where I'm taking her—she needs you and only you, brother. Whatever you two are starting to mean to each other is all that's holding her together right now. Take care of our girl, because she's definitely yours now."

The message barely ends before I hurl my phone across the room. It shatters against the wall. I don't think; I act. I bust out of the room and down the hall toward the stairs. Everyone jumps to their feet, calling out my name and following behind me, but I'm not listening. She fucking needed me, and I answered her by bringing home pussy to make her jealous.

If I would've known.

"Dante, relax. She's been through enough," Matteo reasons behind me.

I spin around and walk back down the hall, grabbing him by his shirt and pulling him to me. Arms are thrown between us, trying to stop me from killing him, but I'm past the point of being stopped.

"I should break your fucking neck for not telling me. You were supposed to call me with any problems...not my fucking brother," I growl. "I should break your neck."

"Dante," Antonio says calmly, pushing me back. "Let him go. He thought you knew. We all did. D, come on. We thought you knew."

I let him go with a shove and look at them. "And you all let me act like a monster. You thought I knew...and you let me treat her like that?"

"Be reasonable." Vin shrugs.

I take a few steps backward, holding up my hands. I get it. There's only so much they can say; in the end, I'm the boss. What they did today was all they could do.

"I'm sorry," I concede to the group but glance to Matteo, who nods. "Leave us. I need to speak to her alone."

They each walk by me and give me a pat on the shoulder, but Matteo stops and looks at me. "It's not too late to make it right, D. No hard feelings. I would've done the same for my girl."

I nod as he walks down the stairs.

The house grows quiet again before I make my way to her bedroom. I don't knock or ask permission to walk in because I won't hear her say no. "Billy," I call as I open the door. "Billy, I'm..."

"Don't," she says almost at the same time.

She's sitting on her bed, dressed, with her duffle bags packed on the bed.

"What's this?" I ask, motioning to the bags, but I know.

She doesn't look at me as she speaks, keeping her eyes on her hands as her fingers weave in and out of each other.

"Our deal is done. I'm leaving. I appreciate everything, Dante, but I have to go now, and I'm asking you to step aside, to not push back." Her eyes lift to mine, shiny and honest. "Just be decent and let me go without a fight."

I run my hand over my head and walk to where she's sitting. "No. I'm not decent. I'm an asshole..." Squatting in front of her, I take her hands in mine. "I brought that girl here to make you mad. To force you to take back what you said, make you admit we mean something. But I sent her packing the minute you walked into your bedroom. I didn't touch her."

Sarah stands and slips past me, pulling her hands away and walking a few feet away. She keeps her back to me.

"It doesn't matter. I don't want this. It's too much."

"Stay."

It's not a demand. This time I ask.

"No," she answers resolutely, turning around to face me.

"Stay. Please."

She shakes her head but doesn't answer.

"Trust me, Billy. I know it's a lot to ask, but I'm asking anyway. I want you to say yes, but I'm not going to demand it... Stay and let me give you what you need."

I take a few steps, closing the distance between us, and bring my hands to her face. The moment my fingertips brush her cheek, an uneven breath leaves her body and she closes her eyes.

She's gotta hate herself for still needing the person she hates the most right now.

"How do I fix this, Billy?" I urge, my face turned downward to her, feeling like my chest is ripped open as she gives a small shrug, "You need a reason to trust me again? I can give you one... Ask me what I did Sunday night."

I shouldn't tell her, but I will if it makes the difference. I'll tell her everything if it makes her stay.

"It doesn't matter," she shoots out quickly, pushing my hand from her face. "I don't want to know. There's nothing you could say that wou—"

"I beat a man to death." Her eyes grow wide as I cut her off. "With my bare hands. I hit him so hard over and over that his bones crunched under my knuckles and all the breath left his body."

She shakes her head, wrapping her arms over her center. But I reach down and pull them from her one at a time. I don't want her closed off to me, in any way.

"Now ask me why," I growl, fighting the strength in her arms as she tries to put them back.

"It's none of my business," she whispers, eyes becoming shiny, as she pulls her wrists from my hold.

"For you," I say, hushed, cradling her face and locking our eyes "Because he told me that someone was coming to get you and that he'd make you hurt. The thought of someone trying to hurt you, someone trying to steal something I possess. Billy. It made me crazy. You're mine."

She tries to pull back, her hands gripping my wrist, but I bring my lips down to hers, pressing them gently down, and whisper again, "You're mine."

Her fight stills, and she stares at me as I pull back. "If you hurt, I hurt. And if I hurt, people die, so the same applies for you. I don't know why, I don't how, but you've dug your claws in me, and I don't want you to let go." Her hands travel up my forearms and back down, gently skimming my muscle. "I want you and I'm sorry I wasn't here. I should've been here when you needed me. It'll never happen again."

Her eyes search mine, and with everything in me, I silently implore her to forgive me. I need her to. All my cards are on the table.

She doesn't answer. She may never, but that's the crack in the door I need.

I pull her back to me. "Let me say sorry, Billy," I whisper into her lips. "Let me make it right."

My hands drop from her face to her hips, and I push my

fingertips underneath the sweater she's wearing. "I'm here, Billy."

Her eyes stay trained on mine, never giving anything away as a tear escapes and runs down her cheek. My lips kiss her cheek, soaking up the evidence as I slowly run my palms up the sides of her body and lift the cashmere off her skin.

"Let go. I'll be here to bring you back, Billy."

Her jagged breath releases in a whoosh, and I pick her up, pulling a leg around my waist as her arms wrap around my neck. The other leg follows, and I stand, holding her as close as I can get her as her face buries in the crook of my neck.

I feel her tears against my skin, and I tighten my arms around her. "I'm sorry. Let it all go. Let me take it all from you. I've got it." Her body shudders as she does what she's told. And for the first time, I've never been so grateful she's listening.

I kiss her hair as we stand, clutched to each other, like two pieces of metal being welded together. Intertwined and indestructible.

Her face pulls from my neck, and she looks at me. She's never been so beautiful. Our lips find each other, gentle at first, parting slowly until my tongue pushes into her mouth, deepening the kiss.

I pull away and rub my nose over hers as I turn us around, not ready to put her down, and walk to the bed to sit, keeping her straddling me.

Her hands pat my shoulders as she takes a deep breath.

"My brother called me. That's why I freaked. You have to understand, my family is an unimportant band of thieves, con artists, and petty criminals. They're the kind of people who are willing to make a secret deal to sell an eighteen-year-old girl to a low-level member of the Irish mob for the equivalent of a thousand dollars' worth of heroin to sell on the streets."

She can't even look at me, opting to look at her thumb that's brushing back and forth on my shoulder. It's as if she feels ashamed.

That one motion.

The way she looks down.

That's why they'll die. Nobody makes her feel small.

I reach my finger under her chin and tip it up to look at me and give a small shake of my head. "You don't ever look down unless it's at them. You don't have anything to be ashamed of, Sarah."

She closes her eyes, taking a breath, and shifts her gaze back to me with the fire I've become accustomed to from her. "But the joke was on them—I shoot to kill, remember? Something Declan, my unwanted groom, found out on our wedding night. If you can call attempted rape and torture a honeymoon night."

My hands find their way under her arms and tug her forward. I need her against me. Even an inch is too much space between us. I wrap around her back, letting her tuck back into the crook of my neck.

"Now you know everything," she mumbles into my skin.

"What family did the dead guy work for, Sarah?" I ask, knowing it's not what I want to hear.

She pulls back again to look at me. "The O'Bannions."

"As in the head of the Irish mob, O'Bannions?" I wish I was surprised, but my gut never lies. I knew that prick from Boston was working for someone bigger.

"One and the same. Christopher implied they would help him. I killed one of their own. They'll want my head once they know. Now you know why I haven't been forthcoming. I knew if you knew, it would complicate everything. Dante, I don't want to bring this mess to your house. I don't want this for any of you."

She's been trying to protect me. This whole time...her only job has been protecting me.

"I'll never let them near you. Do you hear me? They're dead men."

Her hands crawl around my shoulders, and I feel her squeeze me tight, and I swear my body relaxes. She needs our connection as much as I do.

"I forgive you." She takes a deep breath before continuing, "I don't just want you—I need you, in a way I don't understand. But I'm done fighting it and overthinking it. I want this...for however long we have. I mean, you beat a guy for me... I would've taken flowers though."

A small laugh pulls from my lips, and I grin, pushing a kiss into her cheek roughly.

"I'm gonna kiss you. Taste you. Eat you. Then fuck you...in that order, Billy."

CHAPTER SEVENTEEN
SARAH

Shivers run over my body, making me wiggle from where I'm lying on my stomach. I'm sated and thoroughly worked over. He did every single thing in the order he promised, and it was fucking divine and exhausting.

Finding my way back into Dante's bed is the best/worst decision I've ever made. Best because I can't deny I'm falling for him, and worst because of the same reason.

My lips quirk into a smile as Dante lets out a quiet laugh when I shiver again. His fingers glide slowly and seductively over my back, making swirls and designs across my skin, trading places with his lips every so often.

"Mmmm. That's feels so good," I breathe, my eyes closed as I enjoy the sensation.

"Look at you, with your claws back," he teases, brushing my hair off my shoulders, bringing his lips against my shoulder blades. "Are you purring, kitten?"

The warmth from his mouth spreads over my back as I feel the heaviness of his body.

Dante kisses his way up, teasing me with licks and wet lips until he's at my neck.

"Maybe." I moan, feeling his length against my rear as he settles on top of me.

"Spread your legs. I want this," he growls into my ear, pressing himself against my ass.

I do as I'm told, gripping the sheets as his teeth graze my ear. He grinds against me from behind, biting my neck just hard enough to make me suck in a breath.

Supporting his weight on one arm, he slides his hand over my ass cheeks and pushes past, thrusting two fingers inside my pussy.

"Fuck." I moan as he pushes soft strokes inside my wetness while whispering dirty words in my ear.

"You're so tight around my fingers, Sarah. Your pussy is needy, begging to be fucked over and over. It's greedy."

"Yes, it is."

My voice is breathy as I answer, barely able to concentrate as I'm held down by the weight of his body and finger fucked.

"You don't get to come before I get what I want, Sarah. Do you understand me?"

His voice is low and gravelly, but the authority in it is sending vibrations straight down to my clit.

"Tell me what you want, Dante. Name it and you'll have it." I grin, biting my lip as I push my ass into his hard cock and writhe against the sheets.

He lets out an amused laugh and sucks my neck hard, then mouths, "Good girl," against my skin.

Dante pulls his fingers from my pussy and draws the slickness over my tight, forbidden hole. And my breath stills. The motion is so exquisitely naughty and so fucking dirty.

Dante doesn't speak, just pulls from my pussy to coat my ass, over and over, in soft touches and quiet breaths. The silence only heightens the moment, the sounds my body is making creating a filthy ambience for his debauchery.

Thrusting inside me, he lets me ride his fingers until I'm panting and then traces the part up to where he wants to bury himself.

He's preparing me, caring for my comfort and lighting me up with pleasure. All my nerve endings are buzzing like live wires at his touch. It's overwhelming.

He draws up again, massaging and pressing his finger against the hole. My body tenses on instinct, pulling away from him into the bed.

"Hell no," Dante growls, gripping my ass cheek and holding me in place. "Don't you fucking pull back. Now you'll spread wider. I said I want this, and I'll take it."

Every word speaks a language to me that only I can understand. Because when he's dominant, I'm submissive...in bed.

"Yes, Dante," I breathe out, so hot that I might catch fire.

His hand slides under my stomach and pulls my ass back up slightly.

"Don't you move a goddamn muscle. Do you understand me? What's your word?"

"Mercy," I moan, biting my lip.

"Why is it mercy, Sarah?" he grits out, running his hand through my hair and gripping it, pulling my head up.

"Because I'm the only person you'll ever show it to," I pant.

He has me ready to come, and he's not even fucking me.

"That's right. You're the only person who gets that privilege. And I'm going to punish this ass tonight. It's a good thing you've done this before because I'm not holding back."

His words almost send me over the edge, and I have to use all my willpower not to grind into the bed, desperate for friction against my clit.

"Open up," he directs, bringing a pillow to my gaping jaw.

"Bite down." I bring my teeth over the fabric, muffling myself, ready for what's next.

"You're going to need that when I push my cock in your ass."

Dante spreads my ass cheeks and growls, "Not wet enough. No moving. And no fucking the bed trying to make that greedy little clit explode, or you'll go without for a week. Do you hear me, Billy?"

Goose bumps rack over my body as I nod.

Dante positions his strong legs on the inside of mine, keeping them spread wide.

"Goddamn your pussy is soaked." His fingers push inside, twisting and thrusting. "Listen to that. That's the sweetest sound." He pushes in again, and wet smacks fill the room.

My hands grip the sheets above my head as my teeth dig into the pillow that's been placed in my mouth.

He starts a sensual and excruciating exchange as his fingers are shoved inside of me with quick, hard thrusts, then dragged up over my ass. Thrusting and sweeping, pounding and massaging until I'm recoated in my own wetness again.

"Yes, god." I moan around the pillow as his finger pushes past the tight hole into my ass.

The act is so debasing, so barbaric, that I almost come on the spot.

A hard slap curses my ass, and my whole body vibrates from the delicious bite of pain, making me clench around his finger.

"What did you just say?" he growls. Dante leans into my ear, taking the lobe between his teeth, pulling and sucking. "Did you call me God?" he croons low and seductively.

I nod my head, smiling, because I know the rule. His name and only his.

"What's my name, Sarah?" he bites out as his finger pulls and presses inside my ass again.

I pull my mouth from the pillow, already breathless and ready to break. "Dante."

"Say it again." Two fingers push into my ass this time, harder and unrelenting.

"Dante," I groan against the fullness.

"So, you do know it," he accuses as I'm left empty and wanting to squirm.

I arch my back, jutting my ass up, begging for him to continue, but all I get is another hard slap. "Lie still."

My body drops, but his hand rubs and kneads my tender flesh.

"I don't want to ever hear you ever say any other man's name other than mine. Not even God himself. I'll be the only one who owns your pleasure. You got me?"

I nod, and he pulls my hips, so that I'm on all fours, head bowed.

"Let's make sure you remember. I wanna hear it. Each and every time."

I don't answer until his palm connects with my ass.

"Dante," I grunt as my body pushes forward with force.

Fuck.

"Can't hear you," he growls.

Another hard slap followed by kneading. My cheeks spread and close as he alternates between spanking me and comforting the bite of pain. He presses his cock against me, rocking me forward, and I moan, "Dante."

"There we go. Again."

His hand lands lower, hitting the tops of my thighs, faster and faster. Over and over, harder and harder until I'm screaming his name, arching my back, my pussy throbbing with need.

"Dante!" I scream, and he slaps my wet pussy.

I'm thrust forward roughly, my face buried in the bed, as he shoves his mouth down between my thighs, eating my pussy from behind.

My legs tremble as his tongue swirls and flicks around my clit. My nails dig into the sheets until I'm sure I'll rip through the fabric. He doesn't stop, doesn't relent. Dante grabs my thighs, forcing my back to arch to give him a better angle as he destroys my pussy, letting me drop to the bed as he growls.

He yanks me back, lining up to my ass. "What's my fucking name?"

"Dante" rips from my throat as he pushes inside my ass, using my juices as lube.

The sting around the rim stills my breath, but I love it. I want it to hurt.

"Ah, Sarah. Fuck. You're perfect. Come with me. Put your fingers on your pussy and come all over that fucking hand while I fill your ass."

My fingers scramble to my engorged clit, and I rub in frenzied, quick motions as his hips push into me, pounding my ass unforgivably.

We're animalistic, grunting and thrusting. Slapping sounds fill the room as Dante's hands claw at my shoulder and ribs until his hand finds purchase around my throat.

His palm covers my throat, fingers splayed along the side of my neck as I feel pressure. All the sensations begin to amplify. His hips grind into me as he slowly squeezes, owning my body, fucking me from behind and denying me air.

I can breathe, but he's in complete control of me, using my body to fuck himself.

"Come. Come all over your hand. I wanna hear those greedy little moans."

Whimpers and moans slip from my throat as he applies

more pressure, ramming unmercifully, until he hunches over me, gripping my breast with his free hand, fucking me like an animal.

"More," he growls. "More. Give it to me, Sarah. Give me all of you."

"Dante, Dante, Dante" is sung out in a ragged breath robbed chorus as my body tightens, my hips thrusting into the deep rub of my fingers, feeling my body filled from behind.

"It's never enough. I'll never have enough," he grunts as the wave of orgasm begins its crescendo.

Three hard strokes inside my ass, and I burst. My vision goes black as I suck in air, just as his hand gives, and Dante follows with his own release, warmth bursting through my body as he says my name into my shoulder.

We stay like that, bare and breathless, fucking spent, limbs heavy over the other's.

Completely intertwined. Completely lost in each other.

"I want you, like this, in my bed, forever," he mumbles, and my heart stills.

Because we still have an expiration, and I've never hated it more than in this very moment. I could live like this forever.

"Shower," I request as he lifts his body off of mine, pulling out. "Ahh. Give a girl some warning."

He pats my ass as he lifts off the bed. "Let's go, Billy. There's something I want to try with the showerhead."

Jesus. He's trying to kill me.

When I don't move, I'm dragged over the bed and pulled into his arms, my squeals and giggles surrounding us as I'm folded over his arm and carried into the bathroom.

CHAPTER EIGHTEEN
DANTE

"Tell me something." I grin, running my fingers through her wet hair.

Her body is relaxed back against my chest, as we lie submerged in my oversized tub. The water looks like milk from the scented bath shit she put in—she spouted something about it being relaxing. I didn't care. I was too busy staring at her ass as she added it to the tub.

"That sounds like a serious question brewing." She laughs, and her tits bounce lightly.

My hands knead and tweak her nipples, and she moans.

"How do you know I'm going to ask something serious? Maybe I'm going to ask what your favorite ice cream is."

"Ha. It's vanilla with chocolate chips and cherries. And I know that's not the question because you say 'tell me something' before you ask serious questions."

In any other circumstance, I wouldn't feel this pleased that someone knew me so well. But I love that she pays attention. My chest shakes her body as I laugh, and I reach out for the sponge and dip it into the water, letting it soak, before I bring it to her chest and make gentle swipes.

"You got me. Tell me this... What does your life look like if you hadn't been running the last eight years? What do you wish you could've done instead?"

Her hands meet mine and take the sponge from me. She dips it again as she sits silent and brings it to my knee.

She shrugs, but then she speaks. "When I lived in New Orleans, I always wished to do Mardi Gras. It's why I planned that Saints and Sinners party next weekend at Church. I thought the idea of all the masks and the ball seemed close enough."

"It's a great idea. I'm taking you...as mine."

Pulling her hair to the side, I run my fingers down her bare neck and place a kiss on her wet skin.

"Okay," she agrees, biting her lip.

"What else?" I coax.

She takes a deep breath and rolls sideways, so she's laying her face on my chest.

"I always wished I'd learned to surf in California. And in Florida, I really wanted to do the alligator tour thing, where you go out on the boat and see them."

I smile down at her wistful face. "That's all place-specific... Name something you've always wanted to do that you couldn't because you were running."

"Fall in love," she answers quietly.

Just give me time, Billy.

Fuck. Where'd that come from?

"What do you wish you could have done or had...you know, if your life was different?" she questions into my chest as I let my hands brush over her body.

"I have everything I want. There's nothing," I answer, slipping a hand between her legs.

"Lies." She accuses and snuggles into me.

"All right." My head tips back to the ceiling as I think, a sad smile forming on my mouth.

"Birthday cake."

I stopped celebrating when my mother died. Fuck, it's been a long time since I've eaten cake.

Her hand lays heavily on my chest as she kisses it softly. "Birthday cake? Why don't you have that?"

"No reason. Luckily for me, you're as sweet as cake. And I plan on eating you a lot."

I drag her up my body quickly to break her from the moment, and she squeals. "Tell me more. I want to know everything you've ever wanted to do." My fingers find her sides and dig in, tickling her.

She screams, squirming and laughing. "Oh my god, stop!"

I ease up and let her straddle me, brushing her hair from her face. Her giggles fade as she finishes answering.

"The opera. I've always wanted to go watch someone else's tragedy. Get super fancy and sit in one of those boxes."

"That sounds like that movie with the hooker?" I wink, dipping my head and pulling her nipple between my lips.

She laughs again and runs her hand over my head. "You mean *Pretty Woman*. But I'm not a hooker, so it doesn't relate."

I let her nipple go with a pop and look up, wagging my eyebrows. "You can be my hooker."

She leans in to kiss me, stopping just before she does, and pushes away. "You can't afford me."

My hands paw at her waist, trying to pull her back to me, but she giggles and pushes back to keep her distance.

"Nope. Too expensive for you. So sorry. No love for you."

I give up and eye her up and down. "You got like a sale happening or what?"

She throws her head back and laughs, and I attack, covering her neck with my mouth and pressing her breasts against me.

"Out" is all I make out before I feel her legs connect behind my back, and I lift us both from the tub, water splashing everywhere, coating the slick surfaces.

Our mouths are a tangle as we walk back to the bedroom, soaking wet, clutched to each other, reveling in the ways our bodies mold together seamlessly.

———

I feel the bed move, and my hand shoots out, but I come up empty.

"Come back," I growl, not bothering to open my eyes.

Her laugh makes me grin as I run my hand over the empty spot.

"You're trying to kill us. I need food and water. Tuesday's almost come and gone, and we've been in this bed all day. It's dark out, Dante."

One eye opens as I scowl. "Billy, if you don't get your ass back here, I'm going to chase you down and make you pay."

"Run slow...I need a sandwich first," she yells over her shoulder as she walks out.

My chest rumbles as I laugh and haul myself out of bed to standing. Cracks come from my neck as I roll it around and shake out my shoulders. I wasn't kidding—I'm gonna run her ass down.

I take a few quick steps, getting to the door just as she looks back to see me. Her scream accompanies her run as I bolt for her, catching her by the waist and lifting her sideways, hooking an arm under her leg.

Curling her up, I take a bite right on her ass and laugh.

"Ow!" she squeals. "You bit me!"

"You deserved it." I wink, before placing her to her feet and slapping her ass for good measure.

"Monster."

She grins as she walks in the nude to the refrigerator, her hand stretching around the handle to pull the steel door open and shakes her head. "Poor fridge. You need impulse control."

I follow her gaze to the barely noticeable dents, as I come in behind her and wrap my arms around her waist. Bending to rest my chin on her shoulder, I smirk. "It was better than tearing this fucking place apart or killing everyone for looking at your naked ass."

Her laugh vibrates against my throat. "Juice?" she questions.

"Mmm." I reach out and grab the carton from the cold shelf before running it over her nipple, making her jump.

I let her go and step back, uncapping the carton and drinking from it. She turns around, closing the door, and grins as she watches me. My Adam's apple bobs as I gulp down the liquid, not realizing how fucking thirsty I was.

"Thirsty?" I ask as I finish and hold out the carton to her.

"Very," she says seductively, letting her eyes travel down my body.

"Look who wants sex before food now..." I tease, setting the juice down on the counter
and stepping toward her.

"Stop. Nope...I may be turned on, but this girl is sore, so we're having a conversation first, and then eating, and then *eating*."

I laugh loudly, watching the mischievous grin spread over her luscious lips.

"Done. I'll have some food brought over from Mama's. Go put some clothes on and throw me some sweats because if we stay like this, you aren't lasting more than ten minutes."

An hour later, we're seated on the floor on blankets surrounded by pillows by the fire, trading pasta and drinking wine.

It's perfect.

"Question. Why were you in a tux the night I shot you?"

I laugh and take another drink of my wine. "Charity event with my brothers. I was called away...for the guy tied to the cabinet,"

"Ah...and the guy is...?"

"Not a problem anymore," I answer coolly, tossing an olive at her to dissuade any further questions.

"Sorry, curiosity gets me every time."

Her expression is teasing, lit with humor, as she sets the olive to the side in a container.

"That doesn't bother you?" I watch her closely for a reaction.

"Why would it? I know you don't make decisions lightly, and I'm positive that when they're the hardest to make, that you don't have any other alternative."

Well, Fuck me. She's too good to be true.

I lean back on my elbow, focused on her face and the way she glows in the light of the fire. I'm fucking awestruck. There's nobody like her. I'm falling hard for this girl.

"Okay, I have another one." She laughs, and I shake my head. "Why birthday cake? You said no reason, but that was crazy specific. Spill."

I push myself back up, waving her off. "Naw, ask something else. That's for another day, Billy."

Her eyes search mine, but I look away, uncomfortable where this is going.

"Dante," she says tenderly, moving the food out of the way, so she can crawl across our makeshift picnic and onto my lap.

My hands find her hips as she straddles me, bringing both her hands to hold my stubbled face.

"Talk to me," she whispers, locking her eyes to mine.

I can't lie to her. Not after everything.

"Kiss me first," I answer quietly, and she does.

I can count the times on one hand that I've said these words aloud. Once to my uncle and once to my brothers. But if there's anyone else I would tell, it would be her. Only her.

"When I was twelve, my mother made me dinner, kissed my head, and went to take a bath." I clear my throat, leaning my face into her hand and closing my eyes, searching for the resolve to say the rest.

Opening my eyes, I take a breath, letting the rest flow out. "It wasn't until the water started pouring out from under the bathroom door that I realized something was wrong."

Sarah's hands leave my face and drift to my shoulders, her fingers clinging to the cotton shirt covering my body, her face etched in concern.

"She was sad a lot. I didn't really understand because to me she was everything. So strong after my dad died and always so loving. Heart of gold, that woman. But she was a product of this life. Abused and wrecked at the hands of my uncle, forcing her to carry the kind of burden no woman should ever have to."

My brows crease as Sarah's eyes begin to shine. "I didn't understand. You know? I would've killed him then, not waited until later. Because she couldn't carry that anymore, the shame over the things he did to her, the fear that it would never stop. I didn't know..."

Sarah presses a hand to my heart and shakes her head.

There's so much understanding in her eyes that it makes me want to put my hand through a wall.

I clear my throat again, tensing my jaw before I continue. "She went into the bathroom, locked the door, and slit her wrists."

I can feel my body shake with the hate that still fills me, the regret that I carry inside of me over not being able to help her. If I could bring that motherfucker, Gio, back to life, I'd kill him over and over.

"I tried like hell to get that damn door open. But I was a kid, small, skinny. And no matter how many times I ran myself into it, no matter how many bones I broke, I didn't stop until my legs finally gave out and my shoulder was broken. Because I just wanted to save her. I needed to save her."

My voice breaks at the end, and a rush of breath pulls from my lips as Sarah's arms wrap around my body. But I'm numb as she squeezes me, kissing my face and my cheeks.

"Dante. I'm so sorry. That's why you need to help me," she whispers.

I nod my head, unable to speak past the emotion.

"And that's why you don't have locks on your doors. Isn't it?" she says quietly, kissing my lips over and over.

All I can do is nod as she kisses me back to life.

"I'll never stand in your way again. Kiss me. Be here, with me."

I focus on her lips and let my hands snake up her spine, one resting on the middle of her shoulder blades and the other on the back of her neck as I do as I'm told, kissing her as if it's the last moment I'll ever get.

Pulling back, I stare into her eyes. "How'd I get so lucky with you, Billy?"

"You keep earning me," she answers, leaning back in.

Chapter Nineteen

Sarah

"Good morning, sleepyhead." I smile as I move the eggs around with my spatula in the cast iron skillet. The food sizzles, and his muscles ripple as he rolls his shoulder.

"I smelled food." He grins sleepily, and I bite my lip, letting my eyes peruse his body. Of course, he's this sexy in the morning when he's not even trying.

Dante reaches down and rubs his cock that's already at half-mast under his black boxer briefs. "If you wanted this, you should've stayed in bed, gorgeous." He laughs, deep and full of a morning rasp.

My cheeks heat, knowing I've been caught thinking dirty thoughts as I go back to the work at hand. He walks in behind me and kisses the top of my head, swatting my ass and making me jump.

"Quit! I'm going to burn myself," I humorously scold. Pointing my spatula at a bag on the counter, I add, "You have a package."

Dante laughs and walks back around the center island to sit

at a stool and opens the bag that was dropped off, pulling out his replacement phone.

I lean to my left and grab the half-filled plate of bacon and sliced fruit to scoop eggs onto it. Steam rises off the white porcelain as I turn and place it in front of him.

"For you." I bat my lashes flirtatiously.

He grins and shakes his head, picking up a fork and turning it between his fingers. I lean my forearms against the counter and lean in, watching him take a few appreciative bites.

"Oh. I almost forgot."

Spinning around, I grab the already poured glass of orange juice from the fridge and put it in front of him.

"Voila."

Dante stares at me with the look he gets when he's sizing up a situation. But I don't pale under his scrutiny; instead, I blow him a kiss. He stabs a piece of cantaloupe and grins.

"All right. Spill. You've either poisoned me to escape, or you're trying to butter me up, and since I know you like my cock too much to kill me, I'm going with the latter."

I let out a dramatic breath and stick out my tongue.

"Fine. I'm caught. We need to negotiate. I need to go to Church. I'm not leaving it to your lackeys any longer. God only knows what's happening. I have the big party next weekend and too much to fuck around with not to be there."

"No," he answers, taking a barbaric bite of the toast.

My face immediately contorts into a scowl. I pull a fork from the drawer and lean over to stab a piece of fruit. "Try again. Nicer this time."

"No. But thanks for breakfast?" He chuckles, hitting his fork against mine as I steal more food.

"I should've poisoned you," I sneer.

He laughs and juts his chin, holding up a bite of eggs for me to eat. "I'll send someone to get your shit from the office."

I scowl as I wrap my lips around the fork, pulling the warm bite into my mouth and chewing as I grin. I swallow and shake my head. "No, send someone to deliver me *to* my shit in my office."

He drops the fork and crosses his arms. *As if that's scary.*

Rolling my eyes at him, I forge on. "No one is coming within twenty feet of me. And Dom will probably be there tonight. He always is...him and Drew."

"I don't want to know about Dom—I'm eating. Billy, you're killing me."

I wave him off and keep my eyes on his. "This would all be so much easier if you just agreed."

He leans over the counter, grabbing my wrist and pulling my hand up to kiss my palm.

"All right, you win. But you'll take Antonio and Matteo, and I'll meet you there."

I wink and give my shoulders a little shake before I pull his plate to me, eating the still hot eggs.

My night has flown by, but it's nice to be back in the saddle. Antonio and Matteo were only up my ass until we walked through the door, because I'm safe inside of here, and they know that. There's such a heavy system of vetting that to get through these doors is next to impossible.

But they're still watchful.

On the way here, I asked if they'd found anything new out about my family or tracked them down, and I was met with silence, answered only with headshakes.

Hopefully, no news means good news, but the worry is there in the back of my mind.

I stamp my approval on the last application we're taking for next year and stand from my desk, looking across at the wall that's been fixed from the bullet. It's crazy to think it's been almost a week since everything first happened. It feels as if months have passed, but in reality, it's only been five days.

I let out a sigh, relaxing my shoulders and heading to my office door to take a walk around the club. I try to every night; it's important to put eyes on the night's activities, gauge how the night is going.

I walk around the corner from the back hall and spy Antonio at the bar that lines the wall, with an ice water in front of him. He's so serious. If ever a person needed a drink and to get laid, it's him. I wave and he gives me a small head nod.

I continue on through the main room of Church, which is set up much like a hotel bar, with dark leather booths that line the red velvet-cushioned walls and tables flanked with highback club chairs scattered under twinkling custom-made chandeliers. The vibe is 1940s debauchery. I think it nails it.

The main floor serves as a gathering area for mingling and flirting; public displays are limited in here because it's meant as foreplay of sorts for all the other trouble you can find.

I walk through the room and hook to the right, which leads to a wide iron-railed staircase that leads to the communal room upstairs.

Clicks echo on the black concrete steps, accessorized with a rug colored with golds and reds that runs down the center. I quietly greet a couple coming down and pass them as the music begins to fade away from downstairs.

Unlike the main room, the energy up here is more fevered, more sexual, and doesn't need any help in setting the mood. Especially now, with the show beginning in the center of the room.

There are plenty of spectator events that run on any given

evening in this room. Some are requested by guests to perform and others are courtesy of Church, but tonight is special.

On certain nights, there's a baptismal of sorts— a bathing that happens in an egg-shaped tub that was custom-made and fully useable in the center of the room.

A woman is bathed, prepared, and brought to pleasure for the room to watch. It's incredibly sensual and erotic to watch someone cared for in such a way, and it makes me squirm every time I see it.

I stand toward the back as the crowd begins to gather and surround her. Some choose pews that are sectioned around the tub, and others opt to stand. The entire room is dimmed, creating shadows and dark spots for hands and moans to exist in privacy as a spotlight is shined from above down on the bathtub.

Desire is palpable. An elegant woman with honey-blonde hair sweeping her back is led through the room. She saunters behind her partner...her master, the crowd parting for her naked body as her sinewy body is led by the delicate gold chain that's connected to her bright gold collar.

My fingers trace my collarbone as I stare at the way she holds her head high, as if she wants everyone to see what's around her neck.

She does. She wants people to know she's owned. A familiar feeling pricks at me...am I jealous?

The man, who is in suit slacks and a white dress shirt, stops at the bath, reaching down to feel the water before taking her hand as she lifts one leg then the other to step inside. He nods, and she submerges herself into the water as he holds her hair up, letting it cascade outside the tub when she settles.

He removes his shirt and kneels down next to her, taking a sponge and drowning it in the water before he begins to clean her, long brushes over her skin, disappearing into the water, accompanied by sweet moans and mewls that pull from her lips as her head falls back.

The crowd watches the sensuality of what he's doing, and you could hear a pin drop. A thick blanket of need, urge, is covering the room, and people are beginning to transform into roaming hands and pressed bodies as they watch.

Breathing begins to pick up, with panting sounds coming from a scattered number of spaces, creating a symphony of sex. It's everywhere; you can smell it.

The sound of water splashing catches my attention as the woman stands on display for the room bathed in light that glistens off her wet body. Water slides down her breasts as his hands come to the front of her, kneading and caressing. His mouth finds her hard nipple, and his tongue traces it before he sucks.

She stands unmoving, her eyes fixed ahead of her, but you can see the pleasure she feels, that she's receiving from this act.

"You like what you see, beautiful?" a low voice comes from behind, and I almost come out of my skin.

I spin around and step back immediately.

"Jesus," I gasp, my eyes adjusting to the familiar face. "Bill." My eyes widen, trying to plant a fake look of polite surprise on my face. "Good to see you. You really shouldn't sneak up on a girl. Better men have been shot," I half joke, brushing my hair from my eyes.

He laughs and touches my shoulder, but I shirk away.

"Great to see you, Sarah. Having fun tonight?"

"As much as work is fun," I laugh. "It was great seeing you again. I really need to get back to it." I motion behind me as I take another few steps backward before pivoting around, almost running right into Dante's hard chest.

"Fuck! Is everyone trying to kill me tonight?"

"Move," he barks, glaring past me. "I'm about to scare the shit out of *him*."

A smile immediately graces my face, and I start to laugh, wrapping my arms around his waist. "Missed you."

I feel his body ease as his hands run over my back, gripping my shoulders and pulling me off him. His face leans down to mine. "I don't like that people don't know you're mine, Billy."

The scene behind me flashes through my mind, but I let it go just as quickly.

I push up onto my tiptoes and kiss his lips. "Dante. Everyone knows. You're a fucking lunatic."

He scowls but doesn't say anything back. Instead, he takes my hand and pulls me from the room as I laugh, trying to keep up with him. We head back downstairs, slower, and when we get to the bottom, he turns to me and grins. "Go to your office, change, and meet me back out here. I have a surprise."

My face lights up, and I smack his chest gently. "What? Change into what?"

He shakes his head, refusing to answer, and winks. "Go."

I walk past him and point my finger, wagging my brows. "Look at you, all romantic,"

I tease him as I walk back toward my office.

I push my door open excitedly and scope out a garment bag and shoe box laid across my desk. Closing the door behind me, I don't waste any time getting to the bag and unzipping it. Red peeks out from behind the zipper, and my smile grows even bigger.

"Oh...it's gorgeous," I say aloud as I fold the bag back to reveal a sublime strapless red evening gown. "What did you do, Dante?"

I pull it out and hold it up against me, it's *Pretty Woman*. I start laughing when I realize what he's done, and I'm in full-on swoon mode.

Undressing quickly, I shimmy on the dress and pull the zipper straight up my side. Fits like a glove. He couldn't have done better if he tried.

The bottom of the silk dress is pooled around my feet, and I have to walk on my tiptoes to grab the shoe box, opening it to reveal a pair of strappy crystal Jimmy Choos.

I gather my dress in one hand and place another on the chair in front of my desk to steady me as my door opens, pulling my attention.

"Thought you might need help," Dante suggests.

I let my eyes catalog him, realizing he's dressed in a sleek black suit with a matching tie.

He looks criminally debonair.

"I can't believe you did this." I grin, running my hands over my hips.

"Tonight, you get to hear other people's tragedies." He smirks. "And then we can play hooker."

I laugh and turn my back to him to grip the chair again for support to slip on my shoes. Hands envelop my waist. "Give," his deep gravel comes from behind, and I jump, looking over my shoulder.

"You shouldn't sneak up on a girl."

He tugs my waist and turns me around, taking the shoe from my hand.

"I can do whatever the fuck I'd like. Remember?"

I grin as he kneels down in front of me, my hands slip onto his wide shoulders.

Dante's hands slip under my dress, and I pull it up for him. He taps my calf for me to lift my foot. Dante's fingers trace my leg before he brings the shiny heel to my foot, sliding it on and gently wrapping the strap around my ankle.

"I'm like Cinderella," I tease softly.

Dante looks up at me slyly, his hand brushing up my leg,

disappearing under my dress as it falls back down. My head tips back, a small exhale escaping as his nimble fingers start their dirty work.

"No, Billy. You're more interesting than her."

My mouth parts as he rubs my clit, my breathing increasing with the naughty rhythm, but his fingers stop, disappearing from where I want them as he runs his hand down my other leg and looks up at me, motioning for the other shoe.

I narrow my eyes but reach over to the desk and grab it from the box to hand it to him.

Dante pats my foot before rising back to his feet and brushing off his knee. "Come on, Billy. We don't want to be late...I hear these people can be very particular."

I smile and nod my head, taking his hand as we walk out of my office, making our way out of Church, only stopping for Antonio to say something to Dante about an errand Nico is running tonight.

Dante leads me out of Church to our waiting car, and I smile as he opens my door.

"You are going all out tonight. You're going to get laid— secret's out, buddy."

He laughs deeply, throwing the bottom of my dress at me and shutting the door before getting in on the other side. The car starts the minute he does and pulls out onto the street.

My heart is in my throat. I can't remember the last time I felt this excited about anything. I feel free. I look over at him and rest my head on his shoulder as we drive, just basking in the moment.

The whole drive feels special. I feel special. And it's because of him.

My mind is doing flips with the number of thoughts that are circulating. I'm not sure how much time has passed; between the number of questions I've hurled at Dante about what's happening next, and the calls he keeps getting, it's kept me preoccupied.

We drive through downtown Chicago and change lanes, beginning to slow, and I lean closer to my window on the passenger side. The marquee lights from the Chicago Opera House shine through the window, covering my reflection in orange and red, as I try and memorize this very moment.

"If this is all it takes to get that look on your face...I'll rent the goddamn place out every damn day," he offers from next to me.

My head swings to him, confused. "Rent it out?"

Dante winks and takes my hand in his, giving it a kiss. "A little for you, a little for me. You'll see, Billy. Come on."

My door is opened, and the driver helps me out as Dante steps out behind me, placing his hand on the small of my back and leading me toward the doors.

An older, distinguished-looking man is standing at the front with a gold key. He smiles at me.

"You must be Miss London. The Opera House has never been more pleased to grant this request. You only get one chance to fulfill a lifelong wish, after all."

I beam back, my eyes jumping to Dante's, who's standing with a knowing grin on his face.

The man puts the key in the door and unlocks it, and I stare at Dante confused, but the door is opened, and I'm ushered through, still unsure about what's happening.

We walk through the massive, beautifully decorated, albeit empty space, and Dante just keeps that damn smirk on. My head swings around taking in all the details of the room as we walk. He leads me inside the dark theater, where all the seats are completely barren, and I look at him again.

"Dante, what's going on?"

He holds up a hand. "Patience."

Footsteps gather on the bright stage flanked by deep crimson curtains, pulling my attention. Person after person begins to file out, all dressed in jaw-dropping colorful costumes, with feathers, jewels, and makeup.

It's magnificent and absurd.

"Dante," I laugh, "what is happening?"

He leans down and kisses my forehead. "I thought you'd like to meet the performers."

My eyes grow wide as he pulls away. "Tonight's show is for you. And only you."

My hand jumps to my mouth. *How?*

I've been shocked into silence as we walk down to meet all the lovely people who will give me something I've always wished for. Scratch that—this blows my wish out of the water.

Dante leads me to a set of stairs that carry us up onto the stage as people begin to greet me by name, and my head spins. I politely thank them for making time for this extravagant gesture by a crazy man, pulling a laugh from Dante and the crew.

An eccentric man dressed in what looks like a jester costume motions to the seats behind me, speaking in a very thick accent. "Where are you sitting, goddess?"

I open my mouth to answer but look at Dante and shrug with a laugh. "I don't know."

Dante smiles and turns me to face out from the stage. The lights are dimmed, and the house lights are turned up, illuminating the room, and I gasp. Rows and rows of seats lead up to boxes that jut out from decadent walls of fabric. It's breathtaking.

Leaning down to my ear, he whispers, "Choose."

CHAPTER TWENTY

DANTE

"How was the show last night?" Antonio asks, seated at the booth in Mama's Ristorante.

Visions of Sarah mesmerized, leaning onto the ledge of the box seat she chose, jump into my mind.

Only to be quickly taken over by the sound she made when I pretended to tie my loafers and slipped under her dress, spread her legs, and ate her pussy while the music drowned out her own high notes.

"Good." I grin. "Tell me about last night."

"Like I said—" Antonio shrugs. "—there's nothing to tell. Other than they're long gone. Looks like they skipped out a few days ago, probably right after the brother called Sarah at her place. Our guy has eyes on them in Boston. Said it doesn't look they're trying to make a move. Everything's quiet."

"Maybe they got spooked, recognized some of us?" Vin throws out.

I don't like it. They've been after her for too long to just walk away. If they were afraid of us, we would have heard rumblings, talk spreading. But nothing? I don't like it.

"Keep an ear to the ground. I wanna know if they start talking with the O'Bannion crew."

"Got it," Antonio answers. "You gonna tell her the coast is clear?"

"I'm not sure it is," I say with a shake of my head.

His eyes narrow as if he isn't buying my bullshit, but I'm not having this conversation with him.

I rap my knuckles on the table and nod. "I gotta run and pick something up for Sarah. I'll handle taking her to Church tonight. I'm hoping to see that asshole who keeps hitting on her."

The guys laugh and look at each other.

I chuckle and Vin looks up. "Are we gonna need to hide a body or bail you out tonight?"

Smiling, I button my jacket and give a thoughtful look. "The future is unknown, boys."

"Shit." Antonio laughs, smacking the tableclothed surface, and Vin gives me a two-finger salute as I walk away.

I stop at the front to speak with the owners, Mario and Sophia, and listen to reasons why I need a wife, promising to start my wife search soon. Turning to make my way outside to the car, the chill hits me like a brick the moment the restaurant door opens. The driver stands waiting, as I rush inside, closing myself in.

Shit. Chicago winter is no joke.

"Where to, Mr. Sovrano?" I hear from the front as I shrug off my jacket, already warm in the car.

"The jewelers off of Sixth. I need to pick up a package."

The car pulls out slowly as my driver speaks over his shoulder, keeping his eyes on the road.

"I'm happy to run in and get it for you, sir. It's nasty today."

"No, no. This one's special. I'll get it myself." I stare out of the window, trying to envision how tonight will go.

I've never wanted to hear her say yes, so much in my life.

I step inside the walk-in closet and lean against the frame, watching Sarah slink the white dress down over her body, her hips giving a shimmy as she does.

The dress is completely backless, dipping down dangerously low. It hugs her curves all the way down to the ground.

I like her in white. I grabbed this dress the same day I bought the red one. But not even my imagination did her justice.

There's a slit that leads up to the top of her thigh, and it makes me think how easy it'll be to slip my hand inside the dress to her pussy. My fingers itch to try it out, but I have another mission, and it's weighing on me like an unkeepable secret.

I walk inside, setting the large black velvet jewelry box down on top of the cherrywood valet that takes up room in the middle of the closet.

"Let me help." I come up behind her and take the small straps that fasten around her neck.

My hands run down her bare arms when I finish, enjoying the feel of her, and I press a kiss to her shoulder.

"Thank you," she says, turning and smiling. "Is this a thing now? You buying me a dress every day?"

I grin, taking a step backward to grab the box. "No. The dress isn't the fun part."

"What's in the box?" She slyly tries to peek around me as I hold it behind my back.

"Something non-negotiable," I answer, furrowing my brow.

She crosses her arms over her chest and looks at me with a serious face.

"I can't agree to that until I see what's in the box. You're a fucking tyrant, and I'm not an idiot."

I laugh and nod my head. "I agree. But hear me out?"

"Okay," she agrees, suspicion all over her face.

"When we're at home or in the world, it can be your choice." I bring the box to the front.

"But when we're at Church, this stays on you. Without question and hopefully with pride."

I tap the box hesitantly before lifting the lid. Her eyes grow wide as her fingers dart out to touch the diamond-encrusted choker and matching wrist cuffs that shine in her eyes.

"They're gorgeous... Are they..." she whispers, stopping before she finishes, so I say it for her.

"They're real." I wink. "I thought it was elegant and beautiful, but not in a flashy way. It's unexpected. Like you."

She steps in close, poring over the pieces. Her hand runs over the sparkly extravagance but pulls away as her eyes shift back to mine, the realization setting in.

Sarah's hand travels to her throat as her eyes lock to mine. "It isn't just jewelry, though. Is it?"

"It can be, but not at Church. There, it would be your collar"—a spark in her eyes makes me hopeful as I continue—"and the wrist cuffs have been made with a reinforced metal, so I can hook them up to the chains downstairs."

Her tongue runs over her plump bottom lip as she drags it between her teeth. "You want to own me."

The way she says it, so matter-of-fact, without judgment or disregard—it makes my dick jump. Because hell yes I want to own her and fuck her...and love her.

I'd lock her down in my fucking house for life if I thought I could get away with it.

"Do you want me to own you?" I ask, tilting my head, watching the way her chest is rising up and down. "I know you like when we play, Billy. You like when I dominate. When I allow you the space to be vulnerable. I want that. Not all the time, not in our day-to-day life, but wearing this just means that others who play won't cross the line... Think of yourself as a walking lifesaver. Because there's nothing I hate more than someone trying to take what's mine."

Those gorgeous blue eyes lift to mine, and I see my answer. A smile grows across my lips, wanting to hear her say it.

"Answer me with your words, Sarah. Do you want to belong to me?"

"Yes," she breathes like it's the first breath she's ever taken.

I turn and set the box down, taking out the bracelets first. When I turn back, she's biting her bottom lip with her arms extended in front of her, wrists up.

"Good girl," I growl, wanting to fuck her on the spot.

I take my time placing the diamonds around her wrists, bringing each to my lips and pressing a kiss on her skin as I fasten them. When I finish, she gives them a little shake and smiles.

"They're beautiful. Thank you." She beams.

She's fucking perfection.

I reach out and grab her waist, pulling her flush to my body, and lean down to brush our lips together.

"Thank you," I whisper. "Good luck getting away now."

"Good luck getting rid of me." She smiles back.

"Turn around."

She does as she's told, and I pull the piece from its place on the velvet inside the box, lifting my arms around and placing the cold choker against her skin. She pulls in a breath, and I give a small laugh.

Sarah brushes her hair over her shoulder, and I fasten the piece, locking it in place. She can remove it herself, but it's designed to need assistance.

I feather kisses over her neck, hearing her moan as my hands roam her body.

"You look good as mine."

She turns around and levels a look at me. "Where's your choker?"

I laugh loudly, and she squeals as I pick her up by the waist, bringing her to eye level. "Billy, I think everyone knows who the fuck I belong to, and since women tend to be smarter than men...it won't be an issue. Nobody's trying to be on the other end of your temper."

She shrugs as I lower her down slowly, her hands wrapping around the back of my neck. I let her drift down my body, and she plants kisses on my face as I do. Setting her to her feet, I squeeze her ass and smirk.

"Let's get you to work and show you off."

The moment we walk into Church, eyes dart to her neck left and right. But Sarah doesn't fidget or seem concerned. She's undeniably comfortable with the meaning, the vow that's been said between us.

And I'm in awe of her. This girl was meant for this. Meant for me. I don't know what that says about how I feel, but I'm past the point of falling. I've fallen.

We walk into the main room from the entry, and I see Matteo sitting at the bar. Pulling her to a stop, I lean down and kiss her cheek. "Go work, I'll be at the bar with Matteo. I have to speak with him."

She gives me a nod and starts toward her office, looking back over her shoulder.

"Don't miss me too much." She winks.

I smile and make my way over to the large mahogany bar. The bartender notices me and begins to make his way over.

"Hey," I greet, taking a stool next to Matteo.

"Hey?" he questions. "That's what you're starting with?"

The shit-eating grin across his face is almost too much to look at as he swigs his drink.

He and I share this lifestyle in common. Not the one we're born into, rather the one we're sitting in. So I know he gets exactly what the shiny new additions on Sarah mean.

"Whiskey," I say to the bartender and face Matteo. "Hey is a typical greeting. I don't know what the fuck you're looking for...Merry Christmas?" I laugh, pulling my cigar case out from the inside of my suit jacket.

"No way. Come on. That's a lot of shine on your girl's neck. And it looks suspiciously like something some people use to claim a person they want to keep. Tell me I'm fucking wrong," he says, his face lighting up with a challenge. "You can't because I'm not fucking wrong."

Matteo takes too many allowances with me, but he gets away with it because I can't help but love the dipshit. And he's not wrong.

"I'm not telling you anything, prick. But yeah, she's mine. And yeah, I'm fucking keeping her for as long as she'll stay." I pick up my drink from where it's been placed in front of me.

"Well, goddamn," he replies, holding up his glass and clinking it against mine.

I open my cigar case and pull one out, running it past my

nose and inhaling the scent of tobacco. I place it between my lips. I fucking love the taste of these things.

There's a no-smoking rule here, but none of those apply to me. Matteo twists, angling his body toward mine.

"Are those the Cubans that Antonio got? They're too dry, they don't light well. You have to get them really wet," he complains, continuing his motion and turning his back to the bar.

His eyes have landed on the blonde who's owned his attention for the last few months.

She's gonna eat him for breakfast.

"You're out of your league with that one," I say with the cigar in my mouth.

He nods, focused on her. "I like a challenge."

I laugh as I pull the cigar from my lips and roll it between my fingers, but my amusement fades as the dirty thoughts grab me with both hands and shake.

"I'll be right back."

He answers with a nod as I walk back past the bar and toward Sarah's office, giving the door a rap before I push it open.

She smiles from behind the desk as I walk in, looking up from a stack of paperwork in front of her.

"Can't get enough of me, huh?"

I close the door behind me, turning to lock it. "Something like that."

Pivoting back, my lips tug upward at the ends as she leans back in her chair, waiting for my move. *Get ready, Billy.*

"Come here," I demand in a low gravelly voice, walking to her desk and sitting back against it to sit.

Sarah stands from behind me and walks around the desk with that sexy-ass hip sway and stops directly in front of me, standing in between my legs. "I'm here."

I place my cigar on the desk beside my leg and put my hands on her hips, taking a deep breath.

"Thoughts are strange sometimes. The way they connect. For instance, I was drinking a glass of whiskey, and as I did, I thought of how much I enjoy whiskey and how I swear I could taste a hint of honey."

She gives a half laugh, her fingers finding their way to the lapels on my jacket. "You came in here to tell me you tasted honey in the whiskey?"

"Yeah." I breathe out low, dragging my bottom lip between my teeth.

She taps a finger against my chest gently and laughs. "Are you drunk already?"

I take in how flushed her cheeks are and how her breasts push forward slightly as she speaks to me.

"No." I answer, dragging out the word. "But you know what else tastes like honey?"

"No." She shakes her head, but her mouth stays slightly agape. Sarah's sucked into our game.

"You."

"Oh."

Her eyes blink, and she presses her lips together, excited by what I just said.

"See. Then Matteo told me these cigars—" I reach down, picking up the forgotten smoke, and bring it between us. "—that these particular cigars are very dry...that they need to be wet to really give the best experience."

Sarah shifts her weight, and I know she's wanting to relieve the ache that's building inside her. I tilt my head and run the cigar past my nose again.

"So, I thought, since it needs to be wet, I might as well coat it in honey. And then I'll have all my favorite flavors with me," I explain, giving her a half smile.

"Oh."

This time she says it with understanding and not shock.

I stand, forcing her to take a step back, and look down at her. "Put your hands on the desk and spread your legs."

Her breath hitches as I step to the side to give her room. She looks at me as she takes a step forward and places her palms on the desk, stepping one leg out and then the other, as I come to stand behind her.

"Wider."

She steps out again, and I press against her backside, taking one of her breasts in my hand. Keeping the cigar in my other hand, I bend forward and trail it up her leg that's sticking out of the slit. The tightly wrapped cigar scratches up her leg as her breathing increases. I tuck my hand inside the slit in her dress and down over her bare pussy.

"Try not to tighten—cigars are fragile," I growl in her ear.

A nervous giggle escapes her lips, but she stops almost as quickly. "Sorry."

I take the uncut side of the cigar and rub it around her entrance, pushing it in slightly, letting it pulse in and out a few strokes before pulling it back out.

"Oh shit," she pants.

I lean in over her shoulder, running my nose down her neck. "Sweetest pussy I've ever tasted. Now I won't have to miss you."

My hand slips back out of her dress, and I straighten, smoothing my jacket. Sarah's face comes into view over her shoulder, a naughty smile on her lips.

"Is that all, Mr. Sovrano?" she purrs.

"For now." I wink and turn, walking out of her office, leaving her hot and needing with her fingers dug into her desk.

CHAPTER TWENTY-ONE

SARAH

This is unbearable. All night his eyes have been on me as I walked around, silently fucking me with every glance. I can barely concentrate. All I want is to be devoured—long and hard and without mercy.

I arch my back and cross my legs, leaning against the bar, my chin lifting as I wait on the inventory report. My thighs squeeze together for just a small bite of relief. Jesus, Dante's going to kill me with all his sexy.

"Sarah," I hear called out from across the room.

Holding a finger up to the approaching bartender, I turn, my eyes scanning and landing on one of the seating areas tucked in the corner. An internal sigh runs through me when I see Bill waving a hand.

For fuck's sake. I should just let Dante kill him.

I nod and push off the bar, making my way over, glancing to where Dante is standing and talking to Matteo. He doesn't seem to notice me, maybe because the conversation seems serious.

My gaze drifts to the glass he's holding by the top, circling it between his fingers.

As I approach Bill, I see he's sitting by himself, but there are two drinks on the table.

Don't say it, Bill.

"Hello. Two nights in a row. Lucky me."

I smile tightly. "What can I do for you?"

Bill tips his head to the chair. "Sit, Sarah. I ordered you a drink. You look like you've been working hard."

Would you just give up, already?

"Yes, but I am working, so I'll pass on the drink. Thank you though. You should mingle, Bill. There are open couples here tonight and quite a few singles as well," I add, motioning around the room.

My wrist pulls, and my gaze shoots to where I see his finger is tucked just underneath my bracelet, pulling it toward him.

"What's this?" he asks, staring at me.

"That's a bracelet. Please remove your finger from it. Now," I deliver calmly, feeling less than.

"So, what? You like sparkly things. I'll buy whatever you want. Stop teasing me and have a drink. I can make it worth your while," he coaxes arrogantly as his fingers try to crawl up my arm.

"Did you just proposition me?" I reply, stunned as I jerk my arm away, but he grips my wrist in his sweaty palm, holding me in place.

I open my mouth to tell him to go fuck himself and remind him that I will revoke his membership if he doesn't take his hand off me when my voice is quieted by a stronger one.

"I'd keep your hands to yourself if you'd like them to remain attached to your body," Dante growls from behind me.

Bill's hand drops from my arm as he swallows hard. "I apologize. We were just talking. I didn't mean any disrespect."

Well, that was fast.

Dante trails his hand around my back as he crosses in front of me to lower himself into the seat across from Bill.

"Sarah," Dante calls, patting the arm of the chair. I smile and take a step closer, perching to watch the show.

Let's see how you like it, Bill.

Bill's knee begins to jump nervously, and I love it. He's such a slimy bastard. Serves him right to get the shit scared out of him. The thought gives me a small pause as I look to Dante's face...*will he only go as far as scaring him?*

Bill takes an anxious sip of his drink. If he's searching for courage, he's going to need a case of whatever he's drinking.

Bill wipes the side of his mouth with his cocktail napkin, smiling weakly and trying to excuse himself to Dante.

"You can't blame a guy for trying. She's gorgeous. I didn't realize you two were a couple."

"We're more than a couple. She's mine, Bill. And do you know what I do to people who try and steal from me?" Dante leans into me, laying his arm heavily over my stacked legs. "It's not good, Bill."

"Total misunderstanding. She said it was just a bracelet." Dante's hand grips my leg, and I know he's pissed about what Bill just said. Fuck.

Bill's groveling continues, but I can already sense the shift in Dante. He's livid, and Bill is about to get the brunt of his anger.

"It won't ever happen again. I'm just going to go now."

Bill begins to stand, but Dante shakes his head, so he sits back down. *Shit.* Bill's eyes implore Dante to let it go, but I know he won't.

Dante's thumb rubs small circles on my leg through the fabric of my dress as he stares at Bill, deep in thought, as if he's considering all his options.

"As of now, your membership is... something I should've done sooner, but I didn't think you would be this big of a prick... revoked. Don't try and reapply. You're not welcome here, and don't ask for a refund,"

When Dante looks up at me, his smile fades, the irritation he has toward me showing. I open my mouth to tell him I didn't mean to hide the meaning, to diminish it, when we're interrupted.

"Hold on. I don't think so."

Suddenly, Bill is pissed; it's as if a different guy altogether shows up. I can't help the huffed-out laugh that pops from my mouth as I turn to look at Bill.

His head pulls back as if he's angry. "I just paid for next year. That's bullshit. This is going too far," he spits as he jabs the table. "That's a lot of money."

Dante sits up straighter, his voice dropping lower.

"Too far was the second time she told you to leave her alone. By my count, this is the fourth. So, take my generosity and get the fuck out of my club."

A sneer grows on Bill's face. "Generosity? You're a fucking thief. My lawyers are going to have a field day with this." He laughs smugly. "Are you sure you want that headache? At the end of the day, this is all over some cheap pussy—"

Bill doesn't get to finish because Dante bursts over the table, grabbing Bill by the top of the head and smacking his face down with a lightning quick hard knock against the wood table.

He does it again and again, as I scramble to stand, jumping back as the glasses go flying. Liquid sloshes and spills everywhere as the tumblers hit the ground, making a clinking sound before shattering into a million pieces.

I spin around to see Matteo making his way to us quickly, but the look on his face isn't calm like someone coming to stop

Dante; it's more like he's coming to join in. I spin in the other direction and see security ushering guests out—they're working on his behalf as well.

Dante throws Bill back into his seat and slaps his bloody face then wipes his hand on the front of Bill's jacket. "You'll be fine, you fucking prick." Dante sits back into his chair, adjusting his jacket, breath pulling from his body like a bull. "But this time, you remember who the fuck you're speaking to."

Bill sputters and begins to wail about his nose being broken as blood gushes over his face and down his shirt, making his words sound unclear and gurgled.

I start to turn back to the bar to get something to clean up the mess with, but all I hear is "Sit."

Turning back slowly, I take a step forward, Dante's eyes locked on my movements. I sit back in my place on the arm and take a deep breath.

The energy is tenuous. I can feel Dante holding on to his temper, trying to strangle it into submission. This isn't some bar fight or an argument that ends in expletives being hurled around. Fight with Dante and you may not make it to see tomorrow. I need to calm him down before this asshole pays a price too big for my crime.

Before I can reason or think, my hand darts out, bringing my fingers under Dante's chin to turn his head away from Bill and focus on me. Dante's eyes lock with mine, and he stares at me, all manner of anger behind his eyes.

"Punish me," I mouth, knowing why he's really so angry.

He told me I'd be a lifesaver...guess he wasn't joking.

Dante reaches for my hand and brings it to his lips, kissing my palm as Matteo comes to stand on the other side of him, crossing his arms.

"Bill, you're a jerk-off. You deserved that, but I believe in second chances, right, Matteo?"

"Absolutely. You're a saint, Dante," Matteo answers, and it reminds me of the way a cat plays with its food before it kills it.

Please don't kill Bill.

Bill is shaking and trying to negotiate, but his words are lost between his tears. I look down at Dante's face to see him smirking.

He likes Bill's fear. But what's more fucked-up is I like Dante's power.

Dante stands and cracks his neck before buttoning his jacket. "You need to apologize to my girl. Go on, say you're sorry, or you won't see tomorrow."

Bill nods his bleeding face and begins to mumble his words. "Please don't hurt me. I'm sorry. I'm fucking sorry. Okay. Please. I'll say whatever you want."

"Consider the broken nose more of a slap on the wrist," Dante reasons as he takes my hand. "Now, what Matteo is about to do will serve as more of a permanent reminder not to touch those who do not belong to you."

Dante's jaw tenses as he says it.

He nods to Matteo before leading me past the seated area, my heels clicking in the silence. We get more than halfway to the staircase that leads downstairs, and I start to look over my shoulder, but Dante places his hand on my back. "No, Billy."

My head stays forward as I hear a muffled scream come from behind, fading away as we walk down into the silence. The wide hallway is dark, with doors on either side. Behind those doors are fantasy rooms and rooms that cater to those with more particular needs.

My heart is beating out of my chest as we pass each one, trying to discern which one he'd take me to but already knowing deep down.

My fingers reach for my choker, stroking over the bumpy surface as my thoughts weigh heavy on me. I knew what these pieces on my body would mean, but what I didn't anticipate was how much heavier they would feel when I forgot my place.

"I didn't mean to call it a bracelet. I mean, I did, but because I didn't want him to know anything about me, not because I was ashamed," I whisper into the dark.

Dante says nothing as we stop in front of an all-black door, a gold plate fixed in the middle with the inscription *Ego te Absolvo*, which translates into *I absolve you*.

This room is for punishing.

This room is for penance.

Dante takes a deep breath and places a skeleton key into the door, twisting the lock. He pushes the door open and steps aside for me to enter, refusing to look at me.

"What's your word," he breathes as I stand facing the room filled with whips and floggers that line the wall.

"Mercy," I answer, tipping my chin up, intoxicated and drawn into the darkest parts of this man.

"Will you ask for it one day?" he whispers, bringing his lips to my neck and assaulting the flesh.

"Do your worst, Dante." I walk inside the room all the way to the center.

I hear the door lock, but I don't turn around. There's nothing around me as I stand alone, waiting for what he'll do, the pain he'll inflict. My body's begging for it, wetness slick between my legs and my nipples pushing harder against the fabric of my dress.

His footsteps grow louder as he gets closer until I feel his warm breath on me. Dante's fingers find the clasp for my dress, and he unclips it, letting the front fall over like a bib. He dips his finger inside the fabric, cinching it down slowly over my body until it pools at my feet.

He gives me his hand, and I step out, dressed only in my jewels. I feel beautiful.

"You look gorgeous wearing me around you."

Dante dips to pick up my dress and sticks it between my legs, wiping my center as a gasp leaves my mouth. "Your pussy is dripping. Begging to be fucked." He tosses my dress to the couch and steps back. The sound of his belt buckle coming undone makes my eyelids flutter.

"Spread your goddamn legs."

I take a step out, giving myself a wider stance.

"Arms up," he orders.

I lift my arms above my head and hear the quiet buzzing of the hook being lowered from the ceiling. Dante walks in front of me holding the remote and watching the glimmering metal hook descend.

He looks back to my face as the noise halts. Dante grabs my wrists and pulls me up. I push to my tiptoes as he uses my bracelets to connect me to the hook. When he releases me, I lower back to my heels as he licks his lips.

I'm completely helpless, trussed up, nude. And I've never felt more on fire. He steps back to admire his handiwork, running his fingers over my nipples, taking one between his thumb and forefinger, pinching until I groan against the sensation.

The chain rattles above my head. "Be still," he warns, and I tense my body to not move. His hand lowers down my body and traces over the swell of my ass. Goose bumps ignite over my body as I envision him kneading the skin and slapping it.

"You forgot your place tonight. You let him touch you... *You* let him touch what's mine."

I bite my lip, closing my eyes. Hearing those words, the way Dante calls me his. I want to be punished because I'll never forget my goddamn place again. I am his.

Only his.

For as long as he'll have me.

"Who do you belong to?" he growls.

"You."

"Who?" he questions darkly, a little louder.

"You, Dante. I belong to you."

I hear his intake of breath before he walks past me silently to the wall of skinny black sticks, all with differing tops meant for pleasure and pain. Dante pulls a drawer open and pulls out a short-handled black whip.

His fingers wrap around the handle, and his head bows for a moment before he lifts it and looks at me. "You don't know how many times I've thought about this moment."

He shoves the whip handle into his pocket as he undoes the buttons on his shirt, leaving it open to his muscled and inked chest.

He tilts his head as he watches me shift my weight with an amused look as I watch him unbutton his shirt cuffs, rolling each up his forearms.

The veins in his arms protrude as he pulls the whip back out of his pocket, then hangs it next to him while he takes me in. I do the same to him.

He's a beast—shirt open, sleeves rolled, and his belt undone, gripping a leather whip. I could come on the spot.

Dante walks back to me slowly and stops directly in front of me.

"You're going to need this." He pulls the belt from his waist with his free hand.

My lips part, and he places the leather in between my teeth. I bite down to hold it in as he trails his fingers up my arms before walking around me to where I can't see.

"Let's make sure you remember who the fuck you belong to next time."

The first slash bites across my ass, and my entire body jumps as a rush of air leaves my body, hissing against the belt. Another sting on the other side pulls a moan from my lips, but Dante is unrelenting.

The pain is exquisite.

The sting of the leather tendrils that tear against my ass make my clit throb with a wicked ache. My teeth bite down hard as my body jumps over and over with each hit, bringing me up on my toes and back down, the chain clinking and swaying as I do.

My body is writhing against my torment; another slap and I open my mouth with a decadent scream, letting the belt tumble out.

I begin to chant, "I belong to you," against the ragged breaths and grunts Dante is making behind me as he turns my ass red. My hands pull down, making the chains fight back against my desperation to rub my clit as he shows me no mercy.

I hear a thud, but my mind is on a lag, soaked in desire and wanton need. I'm panting as Dante pulls my hands from the hook and dips his shoulder, hauling my body over his shirtless body.

I don't remember him taking it off, but I don't even feel like I'm in my body. He places me down, my back pushed against a wall with a large wooden X. The sensation against my raw ass sends jolts through my body, and I gasp. Dante's fingers work quickly, fastening and buckling my wrists and ankles into thick black leather cuffs.

"Every time you move, that sting on your ass will remind you that you forgot your goddamn place."

The last click at my ankle secures me in.

I'm spread open for his pleasure, my senses heightened, feeling every bit of air that touches all my most intimate places.

Dante reaches between my legs, pinching my swollen clit. "This is mine."

I cry out, the sounds muffled by his mouth covering mine. His tongue pushes into my mouth, tangling with mine as I whimper with every soothing rub he gives.

His kiss is aggressive and unrelenting, and I love it.

He pulls back, our eyes locked as he begins a slow and steady pace with his fingers of constant thrusting inside of my pussy. My pelvis pushes into his hand, our breaths creating a rhythm, building as we stare at each other as I'm finger fucked.

Over and over at the same pace, pushing just hard enough that my body begins grinding so hard that I shudder with each movement.

I can feel the build begin, but as I do, his fingers pull back, forcing my body to chase him, but I'm held to the wood behind me.

Sob-like gasps tumble from my throat, but he smirks, his eyes wild, bringing his fingers to his lips and running his tongue over them.

"Just like fucking honey."

I pull toward him again, but he shakes his head. Dante won't give me what I want until he's ready. Until I behave. I still my body and wait as he watches, my body screaming at me for relief, but his approval is what I'm seeking.

Dante steps back and shoves his finger back inside of me, pushing faster, increasing the pace as I suck in air, my head tipping up. The build comes quicker this time, but like the first time, he pulls his fingers out, stepping back again as I let out a desperate scream.

"Your pussy is so tight. Fuck, you want it so bad. Don't you?" he teases darkly.

"Yes," I moan unabashedly, circling my hips and trying to get closer to his fingers.

He steps up to me, grabbing my center, the tiny hairs pulling against my skin. "You come when I say. Because who do you belong to, Billy?"

My head bows as I take in a breath and look up. I'm overwhelmed by the sensations that I'm drowning in as I stare into his eyes.

"I belong to Dante Sovrano,"

"Good girl."

He keeps me there, bringing me to the edge and then denying me over and over until I feel like I can't take it anymore, but I know I will. I'll take it all.

"Ask for mercy, Billy," he challenges, stepping back again.

I shake my head as my body shakes in a constant state of pleasure.

"Ask for it. Give in," he whispers, running his tongue over my nipple, closing his mouth around it and sucking.

He runs a hand up my arm, and my limbs are detached from the cuffs, one by one. My limp body is carried to the bed, my legs draped over his arms. I'm tossed onto white silk sheets, and Dante grabs my ankle and spins me around, yanking me toward the end of the bed. "Come here."

Before I can process the whirl, his mouth covers my exceedingly teased center. My back arches off the bed violently as I suck in air, grabbing at the sheets. His tongue flicks my clit as he sucks, pressing his hands against my pussy to spread it wider. He's devouring me, dining like it's a five-course meal.

"This is my pussy," he breathes onto my clit.

"Yours. Always yours." I moan.

Every growl and hum from his mouth drags me closer to the threshold, and my fingernails dig into the sheets as I pray for him not to stop. My stomach tightens as my insides begin to curl inside itself from the delicious pursuit of my relief.

But then he's gone.

"I belong to you!" I scream, tears leaking from my closed eyes caused by my frustration.

I bring my fist down onto the bed over and over. I'm there. Ready to say it. Ready to say, "mercy."

Dante's hand circles the back of my neck, pulling me to sitting.

"Wrap," he growls, and I do, realizing he's removed his pants. He swings us around and pushes me against the wall, "Now you come, with me inside of you." His voice drops down to a tender hush. "Because who do you belong to, Sarah?"

I can barely hold back the emotion of what I feel. I can barely handle the emotions he's bathing me in. But we're dripping in it, soaked by our possession, cleansed by our need for one another.

"I belong to you, Dante," I whisper, bringing my eyes to his. "Because I love you."

His long, thick cock thrusts inside me, hard and unapologetic, pressing to the hilt as he lets out a groan.

"More," I beg. "Give me more."

Dante presses his hand to the wall, giving himself leverage, and begins to fuck me hard and fast, his other hand holding my waist. He's pounding into me with so much force it feels like he's pulling me down onto his dick. Like he's fucking himself using my body.

My arms are wrapped tightly around his neck, and we carnally assault each other, climbing toward our climaxes.

Grunts and desperate breaths are the soundtrack that plays for our carnality as my teeth grit, wanting it harder and faster.

"Yes. Please. Dante."

"You're so fucking tight and so wet. I could die inside of you."

A string of "fuck me's" litter the air as Dante's hand slips, and we crush against the wall.

His hand smashes against my face, his thumb in my mouth as we come in unison with a roar.

Dante sits on the couch opposite the bed in our little den of iniquity as I open my eyes from where I was laid to sleep.

"Hi," I whisper and yawn.

"Come here," he directs, his legs stretched out over the coffee table and crossed at the ankle.

He's wearing his slacks again, but no shirt, and it's a fucking wet dream. I push off the bed, bringing my feet to the floor, walking slowly toward him, still only dressed in my jewelry.

He holds a hand up to stop me about five feet in front of him. "Sit," he smirks, motioning to the chair to his right.

I walk over and take a seat, sitting up straight, ankles crossed, watching him pick up the whiskey from the table. He reaches over the top of the couch, rummaging in his suit jacket to pull out his cigar case and flip it open.

He extends it to me, and my brow furrows.

"Light my cigar, Billy."

Reaching in, I pull the singular cigar out. I lean forward and take the lighter from the table and strike it, watching the blaze burn bright. Bringing the cigar to my mouth, Dante gives me a tsk-tsk before it touches my lips.

I look at him bewildered, but he grins.

"You have to wet it. Roll it around your lips, use your tongue."

I do as I'm told, and the sudden tartness makes my eyes

grow wide. He gave me the cigar he put inside of me earlier. His smirk is devilish as he swigs his drink. But I double down.

I run my tongue around the cigar, bringing it between my lips erotically then dragging it out. "Is that wet enough?" I half smile.

Dante rubs his cock and nods.

Giving a few puffs, I draw in the flame and watch as the end burns red. I hand it over, letting my fingers brush his, and smile. Dante takes it from me and places it in his mouth, giving me a wink.

"Now spread your legs. I want to watch while you rub that delicious little pussy. I want to see you come as I drink my whiskey and smoke this cigar that tastes like you."

I don't even hesitate, spreading my legs and giving him exactly what he wants.

"Good girl, Billy,"

Smoke dances from his lips and up toward the heavens, the same direction my eyes are facing as our hedonism takes over.

CHAPTER TWENTY-TWO

DANTE

Laughter and conversations float in the air from where we're seated outside on Dominic's glassed-in patio for Sunday dinner. My arm's slung over the back of Sarah's chair, her ponytail tickling my forearm each time she tips her head back to laugh.

We're spread out around the table. Dom is next to Drew to my right and Luca with Gretchen seated across from us. The table is filled with pasta, bread, and wine, and overhead globe lights set the mood, casting shadows and light where needed.

This is family. And Sarah seems to fit as if she was always meant to be here.

We didn't discuss how we'd act before we came. There wasn't any point to it. I'm not keeping my hands off her, and she doesn't want me to. But since our Thursday night at Church— and her admission of love—we've been holed up at my place, fucking and living in a bubble.

She loves me.

That one piece of truth has burned a hole in my chest. We haven't spoken a word about it, but it's all I can think about.

Sarah smiles at me as I lean in and kiss her forehead. My eyes shift back to the group, who just keeps talking as if nothing's happened.

The funny thing is, I think my brothers saw this coming because there wasn't a shocked face in the room as we walked in. Just a lot of knowing grins and nudges shared between them.

The night is rowdy as my brothers and I toss insults back and forth, drinking too much whiskey and enjoying good food, while the girls seem to suffer us with eye rolls and humor. Sarah's stuck hearing all of it unlike Gretchen and Drew, who leave occasionally to check on the babies.

It makes me think about what Sarah would look like carrying my babies.

"It's strange to think you three just met." She laughs, pulling me from my fantasy. "I would've thought you grew up together if I hadn't known." Sarah smiles as she sips her wine, melting into my touch on the back of her neck.

She looks beautiful tonight. Then again, I can't think of a time in which I don't see her as beautiful. Even when she's yelling at me...actually, that's when I think she's the hottest.

"Yeah, I guess we're all pretty much cut from the same cloth. Then again, our uncle's passing had a way of bringing us closer together," Dominic says coolly, relaxing back in his chair and exchanging a look with Luca.

My foot wasn't the only one on Uncle Giovanni's chest.

Sarah's eyes dart between them, shifting to me. I can see the question. She knows about my part in Gio's demise, but now she suspects they had something to do with his death, too. This girl's too criminally wise. I lean down and kiss her temple, whispering. "For another day, Billy."

She gives a nod, never dropping her happy expression.

"And here I thought we were all brought together because I almost died," Luca complains humorously.

I hate when he jokes about when he was attacked. It was fucking terrible to find out you have a brother only to hear he probably won't make it.

"Come on. You know I hate when you joke about that."

"Look at you, just a big softie," Sarah teases, gently elbowing my hard gut.

I look around the table and nod. "Only for these jerks...and you."

Her eyes stay fixed to mine, and then she inhales deeply, breaking away back to our riveted audience.

"It's a long story, but our uncle Giovanni kept us apart. He lied to our father, God rest his soul, and to us. It wasn't until Gio thought Luca was going to die that he let Dante know about us. But we've made up for lost time. There's no family stronger." Dom asserts holding up his glass.

We all do the same, taking sips for good luck.

"You know, Sarah," Luca pipes up, placing his glass on the table with a stupid grin on his face. "If we knew that all it would take to get you to family dinner was shooting this asshole, I would've hand delivered the gun."

My chest shakes with my laughter as Luca perfectly executes a change of subject. I pull Sarah in closer to me and whisper in her ear, "Here it comes."

Dom joins me laughing, and Drew smacks his stomach. "Quit it." She scolds as he gives her a growl, nipping at her ear.

Gretchen shakes her head at Luca but smiles as she says, "By the looks of you two, that bullet was like some kind of twisted little cupid's arrow."

"You two deserve each other." I smirk, pointing to her and Luca.

Gretchen stands, telling Luca she's going to check on their daughter, Ella, and he brushes a kiss on the top of her hand.

Grinning over at Sarah, whose cheeks are now blushing from the teasing, I wink. "You want me to make them disappear?"

She pats my cheek as she giggles. "Maybe if they don't give me a raise."

"Consider it done, gorgeous." I grin as I lean down and kiss her lips softly.

Her mouth melts into mine, following my lead, and a cacophony produced by "awws" and hollers bring a grin to my lips as I look up.

"I swear to God. I can't introduce you to anyone," I chuckle half-heartedly in complaint.

Sarah hides her face in my chest as she laughs. She's such a badass, but seeing her like this, embarrassed by their easy teasing, makes me want to tell her...

Tell her that I think I've loved her from the minute I danced with her at Luca's wedding, when she basically told me to fuck off, then followed my lead.

"Introduce? We knew her first, dick," Luca calls, grabbing my attention.

I toss a dinner roll in his direction, hoping to smack his face, but he catches it and takes a bite. "Good looking out."

He wags his eyebrows in challenge until his gaze drifts to the door, and I watch his eyes soften. The sound of the French patio door calls the table's attention, and Gretchen steps through with a freshly cleaned Ella.

Ella's wrapped in a towel that has a hood with a penguin on it. She looks ridiculous and adorable.

"I stole her to say good night to everyone before Rose puts her down for the night."

"There's the little love of my life. Come here." I smile,

holding my arms out for the little monster covered in dark curls and blue eyes. "Get over here and let your favorite uncle hold you."

"Favorite? Nah, I win by default. I'm Luca's twin," Dom protests, reaching out for Ella only to be ignored.

I laugh deeply as the little thing tosses her body forward toward my arms. "You need to accept that I'm superior in all ways, little brother."

Luca claps and barks out a laugh, enjoying Dom's torture. Before I came along, Dominic used to love to call himself the big brother because he came first. Tormenting him by calling him little is one of my greatest pleasures.

Sarah laughs softly, and I look to my side at her as I snuggle the wiggly toddler. "Sorry, Billy, but my heart is taken."

Ella's chubby arms wrap around my neck. Her fingers quickly find their spot tracing all the pictures peeking out above my T-shirt on my neck.

"Are you trying to make me swoon to death?" Sarah teases, smiling at me.

"Yeah. Is it working?" I question, wagging my eyebrows before blowing raspberries into Ella's little neck.

Deep belly laughs rock Ella's body, and Sarah laughs again. "Maybe."

Her eyes shine with her joy in this moment.

The conversation is flowing around the table, the others talking about Dom and Drew's new twins as Sarah and I speak quietly.

"It's strange to be here with everyone," she says, hushed, as she rubs Ella's back. "I spent so much time keeping people away, trying to stay ahead of my father, that I didn't realize how much I missed out on."

"Well, now you never have to miss out again," I reassure her as Ella's little head lies on my shoulder, her fingers still trying to grab at the colorful art on my skin.

"Sure. Well, until we find where they are..." she replies absentmindedly, playing with Ella's chubby little fingers.

My head swings to Sarah's. "Hold on, are you still planning to leave? Take off when we find them?"

No fucking way is she saying this to me. After all of this. After the fights, the deals, the fucking...after the I love you.

She pushes her hair behind her ear, avoiding my eyes as she reaches for a crumb on the table. "No...well, yeah. But I could come back...or... I don't know, it's just more complicated now. I feel different, but the circumstance is the same."

My voice stays quiet, but I want to demand, yell, shake the shit out of her.

"It's not the same. These people consider you family, Sarah." I look around and back to her. "You've had more people in your corner than you knew."

Her eyes stay on mine, searching for something. Our fingers touch when I reach to pat Ella's back gently as she stirs, and I see the sadness behind Sarah's eyes.

Sarah's tongue darts out through the seam of her lips before she speaks. "What do you consider me, Dante?"

Everything. Tell her, you idiot.

"You already know that I consider you mine, but don't ask that of me if you're planning to leave because I can't be held responsible for what happens around me if you tear me up."

Sarah stares at me, her mouth opening then closing before opening again. "I..."

"She's falling asleep," Gretchen interrupts, smiling down at us, completely unaware of the moment. Sarah exhales, turning to smile at Gretchen, and nods.

Gretchen smiles down sweetly as Ella reaches up. "Come give Daddy kisses before you pass out, monster."

Gretchen pulls her up, taking Ella around the table to give kisses and hugs to everyone before Luca smothers her with love, then pulls Gretchen down to kiss her too.

"My mommy," Ella whines, hitting at Luca's face, and we all laugh.

"Yes, she is." Luca smiles as Gretchen winks at him and takes Ella inside to give her back to Rose, their nanny.

I turn to finish my conversation with Sarah, but she stands, and my eyes lift to her face as she reaches for my empty glass. "Do you want a refill?"

Conversation tabled.

"I'd love one." My hand absentmindedly finds her hip, giving her ass a tiny pat.

"Anyone else?" she asks as Drew stands up to help her.

The guys shake their heads, and the girls walk inside the house, leaving us alone. The very moment the door closes, the two buffoons in front of me raise their eyebrows.

Luca spreads his arms wide open in a "what the fuck" expression as Dom points a finger at me, nodding his head.

Jesus.

"Everything. Now. Come on." Dom smirks.

"You two are fucking exhausting. I'll give you two questions each, and then we're done with another episode of the fucking Brady Bunch."

My brothers look at each other and nod, each tossing questions at me left and right.

Motherfuckers.

I shake my head and start laughing.

"Quit, dicks. All right. All right," I forfeit as they laugh and drumroll on the table.

I take a deep breath and narrow my eyes, ready to admit something to them I haven't said to her.

"She's a problem," I state frankly.

Their faces grow more serious, the amusement beginning to fade.

"Because you love her," Luca surmises, tapping his finger on the table.

I nod, sitting silent, crossing my arms over my chest.

Dominic angles in toward the table, rubbing his scruff. "And you don't want to bring her in knowing what you know. How this life eats away at you?"

My eyes meet Dom's as he finishes, and I answer, "Yeah. And she's still considering leaving."

Luca reclines back into his chair, bringing his drink to his lips, a smirk fixed on his face.

"I hate to break it to you, Dante, but that girl isn't scared of anything, least of all the shit you bring to the table. She just needs you to give her a reason to stay."

I consider what he's saying. I need to tell her the truth—all of it.

Dominic gives a small laugh and picks his drink up as well. "She was made for you, brother. And what or who is ever going to get through you in order to hurt her?"

I shrug with a bit of arrogance, knowing the answer is nothing. I'll protect her at all costs.

Against anyone. Even herself.

Luca huffs a laugh, tossing his napkin at me. "And if something does manage to make it past you, D, then it has to go through me, Dom, Nico, Vincenzo, fucking Matteo, and Antonio."

Dom nods his head and smacks the table. "What's important to you is important to us, Dante. It goes both ways. This is family. So, love your girl and be done with it."

My eyes travel inside, through the glass, and see her standing at the bar.

"And if she tries to run again?"

"Don't let her," Luca answers with a wink.

I won't.

"You don't suck, you know that?" I chuckle. "You're ugly and dumb as fuck, but you're all right as far as brothers go."

They toss shit at me from the table, and we laugh as the girls walk back outside, staring at us like we've lost it.

CHAPTER TWENTY-THREE

SARAH

I've been watching him all night. Watching the way that he laughs, the way he loves the jokes his brothers make about each other, and all the light that seems to have taken over his face.

He's so different but the same. I feel as if I've seen every side to Dante now. I wonder how many people can say that?

His arm hangs across the back of my chair while he laughs at something Luca's said, and I find myself smiling too. I wish I could crawl into his lap and nuzzle into his neck, wrapped in his arms. Jesus. What's happening to me? He's tamed me, and it only took a week.

Real badass, Sarah.

Right on cue, Dante looks up at me and winks through the glass that separates us.

"Oh, shit, girl. You've got it bad." Gretchen smiles, joining me and Drew at the bar.

I'd planned on getting Dante a refill and a water for myself, but Drew has me parked on a barstool while she makes some disgusting-looking chocolate concoction she wants me to try.

"What?" I counter, looking away from Gretchen's scrutiny.

"Don't 'what' me. It's written all over your face. You've fallen for Dante."

"He's easy to fall for. And I don't like to share my things, so I put that shit on lockdown," I joke with a shrug, hoping humor will stop the inquisition.

Gretchen starts to laugh, and Drew looks at me shocked. My eyes drift outside, and he looks at me, tilting his head and giving me a little nod—his way of asking if I'm good. I reassure him with a wink.

Is it possible to fall harder than love? Because that's where I'm headed.

My face pales as I turn back, seeing the drink Drew just put in front of me. I lower down and take a sniff. Shaking my head, I turn and meet Gretchen's smiling face.

"I am not drinking this. I adore you, Drew, but no, babe." I say wide eyed and politely push the martini glass back toward her.

Gretchen lets out a loud laugh and looks at Drew. "Buddy, it's gross. Stop trying to make that nasty-ass drink. You keep trying to kill someone. Stop it."

Drew purses her lips and points between us.

"Hookers, it's delish...just take a sip."

"You take a sip. I'm not dying today," Gretchen says with a straight face.

Drew rolls her eyes and looks to me.

"No," I answer, dragging out the word, and chuckling at the end.

Drew picks up the glass and brings it to her lips, taking a small dainty sip. Without saying a word, she turns around and empties the contents into the sink as we both erupt into laughter.

"Fine." She grabs a bottle of wine. "But G is right—you are

so hot for Dante, and honestly, I've never seen him so smitten before."

"I swear I thought he was gay." Gretchen smiles, tilting her head to take in the guys' boisterous conversation.

Drew swats her shoulder. "G, that was wishful thinking." Gretchen's head swings back to us.

"True." Gretchen shrugs. "Man on man is hot. But he's never brought a girl here or anywhere for that matter."

Holding out my wineglass for Drew as she wiggles the bottle at me, I look over my shoulder. I can't help the smile that lives inside of me at the thought that I'm the first...and last?

Not if I leave.

"He's definitely not gay." I smirk, taking a sip of my wine.

"I knew it. You had sex at my wedding, didn't you?" Gretchen teases.

"No...it was after." I laugh, and they almost explode.

Questions are lobbied at me left and right. I can barely turn them down before they ask something else.

"I'm not telling details. I'm just saying he's pretty amazing and knows what he's doing. The end. Now stop asking—this is why I don't have friends."

Drew rolls her eyes at me and shakes her head. But Gretchen tilts her head toward me.

"You know, these guys aren't like other men. When they set their sights on something, nothing stands in their way."

"You act as if I don't have a choice," I muse, taking a sip of wine.

Drew leans over the bar, touching her finger against my bracelet, and gives me a knowing wink. "It's cute you pretend you want the choice."

I take another sip of my wine, wondering just how kinky the King brothers are.

Gretchen smiles at me then looks outside at Luca. "Love is

never a choice. It's an affliction that you'll want to die of. And there's no better love than one from a man who wallows in his devotion to you."

We're both pushed into silence at her words. I stare at the rim of my wineglass and think about the word devotion, because I think that's what's after love.

The thing I've been headed toward.

I'm devoted to him, and the idea that I could leave is unimaginable. But then so was the idea that I would spend my life running from my family.

I'll do what I need to in the end because I'm devoted to him, in spite of my love.

When I look up, the girls are watching me, waiting for me to say something, so I go with the truth.

"I love him. There, I said it. But I don't know if he loves me back, and I'm not sure it's enough to weather the storm my life brings," I confess quietly.

Drew comes from around the bar and stands next to me. "If you need someone strong, then you found him. I don't think there's anything Dante can't handle."

Gretchen nods. "Yeah, and he's gone over you—there's nothing that he won't try and handle."

I give her a soft laugh, knowing she recognizes his bull-dozing ways. Taking the empty glass that's Dante's drink, I hand it to a smiling Drew for a refill. "Maybe, but everything is so complicated that it makes me unsure where that leaves us."

Gretchen rolls her eyes at me and takes one of my hands. "There's nothing complicated about your life for him. You two speak the same language, Sarah. He's perfect for you. If he were a baker or an accountant, I'd worry for you two. But he isn't. Get out of his way, and let him love you back."

First, he has to say it.

Drew brings Dante's refilled drink back to me and grins.

"You can ignore us, but don't say we didn't warn you. That man wants you. Nothing will stand in his way, Sarah."

My brow furrows at her words, and I look between her eyes and Gretchen's.

"Not even you," Gretchen warns, grabbing her wine and walking toward the door.

———

The drive back to Dante's is quiet. Our unfinished conversation hangs over our heads like a dark cloud. The rest of the night seemed to go by fine, but I could tell it was on his mind, needling him. He kept staring at me like he was deciding what to do with me.

I reach for his hand, sliding my much smaller one into his palm. Dante closes his around mine, but he keeps his head turned, staring out the passenger window.

"Are we ever going to talk about it?" I whisper to his profile.

"Did you have a good time tonight?" he answers flatly, finally turning his head toward mine.

I guess not.

I nod, hating how off we feel. With my free hand, I unbuckle my seat belt and close the space between us, crawling into his lap. I want to be close to him; we might be sitting inches from one another, but he feels a million miles away.

"Billy," he breathes out, tipping his head back again to look at the ceiling of the car. The way he says my name sounds like regret.

And I know it's my fault. I placed that acid on his tongue.

I don't say anything, choosing to just stay curled in his lap with my head on his shoulder and held close by his strong arms. The entire time I lie on him, I listen to him breathing, the steady rhythm of his heart beating inside his body as his hand trails up and down my back.

How do I walk away from him?

Before I knew him this way, I would've slipped right out of the door and never given it a second thought because leaving was the only choice. It was the only one I could make to protect the people who I've come to love here, but now all I want to do is stay.

If I stay, I put everyone in danger. How do I do that...even in the name of love?

The car slows to a stop, and I drag my head from my Dante pillow and look into his eyes.

"I'm sorry," I whisper, hoping it's accepted for everything I'm planning to do.

His face is serious, not a hint of tenderness, as if he understands everything I mean. I search his deep hazel eyes as his features become hard and removed. Dante's eyes falter, and the man I know, the one I love, disappears.

"There's something you need to know," he says gruffly.

It's the way he says it that tells me that whatever I'm about to hear is going to be hated by my soul.

Dante lifts me off his lap, pushing me into my seat as if he's discarding me. His door is opened, and he steps out, holding his hand out for me to take.

The freezing night air bursts inside the car, so I hand his jacket out to him before putting on my own.

I duck my head and take his hand to join him outside on the sidewalk in front of an older building. My head swings around as I begin to realize that we're a block up from my apartment.

"What's going on?" I question, fear creeping up my spine.

The last time I was here, I saw Christopher.

Dante stares at me with unreadable eyes—ones that feel like they're burning right through me.

"Dante." I squeeze his hand. "What's going on?"

Blinking, he looks away from me, and my stomach begins to fall.

"Come with me," he directs, stalking forward and pulling me inside the concrete building.

I'm immediately ushered up one flight of stairs. The old, dank linoleum cracks under our footsteps as we walk, announcing our presence.

Dante stops in front of an apartment with a tarnished number 4 on the door, and I look down the hall, noticing the old tattered wallpaper and the busted light on the wall. He reaches for the handle, twisting and opening it.

Stepping inside, he motions with his head for me to enter. Everything inside of me says to run. To refuse. And with every look I give him, the angrier he becomes.

"In," he demands, repeating the head jerk.

I hesitate but move, slowly looking up at his face as I pass him. Dante follows me in and shuts the door behind him as I wrap my arms around my center, turning to look at him in the middle of the disheveled pigsty.

"This is where your father and brother were staying. After they called you that night, when they got a look at who you were with...that was all it took. They split."

All the breath leaves my body. They were around the corner...and for how long? The thought makes me physically ill.

"How long were they here? Watching me?"

"We found them two days after you were brought to my home."

"So, you've known where they were all this time? You lied to me."

"I didn't think I had a choice...I was right."

I turn and look around, noticing little things, like the empty pack of menthols on the counter—the brand my brother smokes. The ones he was smoking when he called me the other night.

My eyes jump to the small kitchenette and see the empty bottles of Bushmills cheap Irish whiskey that litter the counter-tops, and I can smell my father's breath on my neck again.

He was always such a sick bastard when he was drunk, loving to knock me around. Come to think of it, he was just as sick when he was sober.

"Why did you bring me here?" I bite out angrily, hating all the emotions brewing inside of me. "If they're gone, what does any of this matter?"

Dante levels a glare at me.

"Because I need you to make up your fucking mind. Tonight, my brother told me to give you a reason to stay. And I kept thinking about what I could say that would be reason enough. Because it's clear that I'm not."

His voice is shredded with contempt when he says it. I can feel all the hurt I'm causing him. And it almost breaks me. This rough, cruel, domineering man is begging for me to need him. To choose him. Because god knows his mother didn't.

No matter which way I turn, my decisions hurt people.

I take a step toward him, ready to beg him not to hurt anymore, but he shakes his head.

"No, don't do that. Don't act like you care. It's funny—I thought if I told you how I feel...but you know how I feel. I know you do. And just now...down in the car, when you said sorry. That's when I saw your lie."

All I can do is shake my head as the lump forms in my throat.

"If you loved me, you could never walk away," he accuses.

My voice answers in a whisper. "If you loved me, you could never let me become a monster."

He laughs and tightens his fists with all the energy and intensity of a caged animal, but I don't stop talking now that my voice has found its way out.

"You're the only reason I want to stay. But think about what that means, Dante. How do you know they won't come back? Try something? I can't risk hurting the people you love, all the same people who I've come to love. But goddammit, all I want to do is turn my back on them because of how I feel about you." Tears prick at my eyes as I will him to hear me. "And that makes me a monster."

Dante laughs menacingly and punches the flimsy Formica countertop. He looks at me, tensing his jaw, rage behind his eyes. "You don't fucking get it. You still don't understand. Look around, Sarah," he roars, opening his arms wide. "You're so fucking afraid of these pricks and what they could do that you don't see that I'm the scariest goddamn monster you know. I'm the fucking nightmare, and I was yours."

His arms drop as his chest heaves in breaths. My hands cover my mouth, holding in all the words I want to argue with, everything I want to hurl at him to prove him wrong, to push back and scream at him.

I hold it all in.

Because it's now, in this moment, that I realize I've withheld the one thing Dante has been needing from me. My submission.

He wants me to turn my back on everything and everyone, to make him my singular focus, and to let him handle the rest because he can. And he will. I'm not alone unless I choose to be. He'd protect everyone for me.

That's his "I love you."

Dante's face is a mask of anger and hurt...and it's the latter that's scary. It makes him cruel. He wants me to hurt because I've ripped out his heart, but I can put it back together.

He walks over to me and takes my ponytail in his hand, letting it weave through his fingers as he looks down at me.

"Maybe you need to be reminded of how cold it is without me."

Oh, my beautifully broken man. He'd try and starve me because I won't let him feed me.

I narrow my eyes and shake my head. "Or *maybe,* I need to remind you who you're speaking to. You won't issue threats to me. Unless you want me to shoot back..." I pat his shoulder and nod, sliding my hand down his arm to his hand, our fingers intertwining. "I'm with you. I choose you, Dante. And I'm sorry that I forgot my place, but you forgot it, too."

His head bows as he exhales a shaky breath.

"It will never be under you, because I belong next to you." He looks at me with regret, and I lock my eyes with his. "Bringing me here, making me come this close to the people who I despise...you will never do that again," I state resolutely, bringing his hand to my lips and pressing a kiss there. "Punish me in our bedroom, but because you love me, you'll never do that in our life."

I can see how much he hates what he just did, but it's no more than what I feel for bringing him to this place. We're both broken in our own fucked-up ways. I want to save him, and he wants to save me, but one of us has to give.

"Do I love you?" he counters, tilting his head.

I hate the hard look on his face, like he can't let himself hope. I've never seen Dante scared of anything; he's unshake-able. But right now, as he looks down at me, it's the fear on his face that makes me hate myself.

"I don't care if it takes you a year to tell me you love me because you'll show me, every day, Dante."

His eyes search mine, his hands gripping my waist and pulling me against him. "Don't you fucking leave. Ever. I won't last. This city won't last...I'll burn it to the ground."

"I want to go home, and I want you to make everything in this room go away. Including the people who were in it," I admit, not caring about the repercussions.

"Il piacere è tutto mio." *My pleasure*, he breathes, crushing his lips to mine and holding me in one arm as he walks us out of my past and into my future.

Chapter Twenty-Four

Dante

The phone buzzes on the nightstand, and I smack my hand down on top of it. I hit the Answer button quickly as to not wake Sarah, who is asleep on my chest.

It's been five days since she asked me to "take care" of her family. And five days since she chose me.

I made her a promise, and I intend to keep it, but planning takes time and that's the one thing we don't have. I can feel it. Wheels are in motion and barreling straight for her, but I don't know what direction it's coming from. And my fear is that I'll be there too late to stop her from taking a hit.

"Hold," I growl into my cell as I untangle her body from mine and walk quietly out to the living room.

I look down at my phone and see it's Antonio calling and bring it to my ear. "Spero che questo ne valga la pena." *This better be good.*

"It is. Good enough for me to call from a burner. Daddy dearest and the piece-of-shit brother were seen having a sit-down with the Irish. Your gut was right. So was hers. They're trying to make friends. These fucking guys are looking to take her, Dante."

"Call our guy. Uccidiamoli. Fateli a pezzi e inviateli agli irlandesi come messaggio. Her family line ends with her." *We kill them. Gut them and send the pieces to the Irish as a message.*

"You need to tell her, Dante. If you ever listen to anything I say, this is it. If you leave her in the dark about what they're planning, it won't play out well."

I hear him, but I'm still deciding whether or not I'll listen.

"The Saints and Sinners party is at Church tonight. Make sure we have extra guys watching there and here at the house. I'll tell her after—she's been looking forward to this, I want her to have a good time."

"I'll call when it's done," he adds.

"Make them hurt, Antonio."

"I'm looking forward to it."

I kill the line and turn around to see Sarah's nude silhouette posed against the doorframe, the jewels catching the moonlight as it shines in through the glass wall in the living room.

"Did I wake you?" I smirk, taking slow strides toward her.

"No, but do you want to keep me awake?" She teases, following the curve of her body up and over her hip.

A growl pulls from my throat as I come to stand in front of her and grip the wood frame.

"Billy, I'm looking forward to wearing you the fuck out."

"Me first."

Sarah drops to her damn knees, tugging my pajama pants with her, my cock springing out and hitting my stomach. Her hand covers the veined flesh and pulls it toward her warm mouth, and I hear her moan as she closes her lips around my cock.

"Fuck." I hiss as she pushes forward until I almost feel her throat. "Swallow me back." I groan, digging my fingers into the doorframe harder.

Her head begins to bob in unison with the figure-eight motion her hand is doing, and it's fucking white-hot bliss. My chin tips up to the ceiling as I push my hips forward, feeling her cheeks suck in around my cock each time she lowers and pulls back.

"That's good. Take it all."

Sarah pulls my cock into her mouth deeper and deeper each time, leaving spit pooling over her hand and onto my dick as she strokes me.

"Goddamn, you give good head," I groan, grinding into her face.

My balls pull up as I feel my climax building, making me want more from her. I reach my hand down, fingers weaving through her hair, and grip hard to hold her in place as I begin to push faster into her mouth.

The sensation tickles at the bottom of my stomach as it builds more and more with each stroke inside her hot fucking mouth.

"Fuck yes," I growl, thrusting harder and faster.

Her eyes pool with tears, but she takes me, all of me, right to the back of her throat.

Seeing her like this, me fucking her mouth as she kneels in front of me, takes me over the edge.

A gentleman would ask. But that's not something I've ever been accused of. Instead, I let go, and it hits me like a Mack truck. I grit out a pained growl as I release into her mouth. Warm cum explodes down her throat as I watch her body undulate from her knees.

She swallows every last drop. And my dirty girl loves every damn minute. I pull back, letting her hair go, my breathing ragged, but she leans in and runs her tongue over my spent cock.

My body jumps, sensitive to the touch, but calms as she does it again, cleaning the glistening cum still on the tip of me.

"Good girl. Lick up every drop, and then I'll reward you," I say, breathless.

Sarah lifts my still-hard cock and slides her tongue under the base of my balls, running it all the way up my cock until she gets to the head. Her mouth closes over the tip and gives a small suck, pulling a groan from my throat, before she lets me glide slowly from between her plump lips.

She sits back on her heels, her hair falling over her shoulder, and looks up at me.

I'm struck by her beauty and completely halted by how I feel about her.

Sarah's so strong and independent, and yet, she chooses to be mine. She's given me such a gift. One I can never repay.

"You've never looked more beautiful," I say reverently. "Because you choose to sit at my feet when you know that I would be the very ground you walked on if you asked."

"I love you, Dante," she answers even though I didn't ask a question.

Her voice is so sincere and raw that before I can think, I'm kneeling down in front of her, making us equal.

Because we are, even when she's on her knees. This woman has taken hold of me, and I'll be damned if I ever allow her to let go.

My hands cradle her face as I speak, our lips almost touching as I press my forehead to hers.

"Love isn't enough. It's not a big enough or a strong enough word. Love is something that people can stop feeling. But what I feel for you, Sarah...it's more. Whatever I've fallen into isn't something I can fall out of. You're inside me. In my veins." I grab her trembling hands and bring them both to my chest. "It beats for you. Only you. So, if I have to settle for the word love, then I'll say it a hundred times a day, so it will measure at least half of what I feel."

She scrambles onto my lap and wraps her arms around my neck, molding our mouths together, causing us to tumble backward.

"I love you," I mumble between kisses as she answers back.

Rolling on top of her, I spread her legs, using my knees to push in between.

I kiss her lips one last time and travel downward, slowly dusting kisses and "I love you's" against her soft skin until it's not my words I hear anymore, but instead, her pleasured screams.

"That's not what you're wearing," I bark from the living room.

Luca chuckles as the girls walk out of my bedroom all wearing slinky "barely there" dresses. But Sarah is pushing the envelope the most in a silk, black stringy number that doesn't hide a goddamn thing.

"Thank you," she says, pleased with herself, turning in a circle as Gretchen and Drew laugh.

I stand from the couch, crossing my arms. "You didn't hear me. You're not wearing that."

Sarah saunters toward me grinning and not at all intimidated.

"See, what I hear you saying is, 'Damn, you look hot.' And I really like that version."

Her hands brush the lapels of my tux, and I stare down at her, trying for an angry glare, but when she winks up at me, I can't stop the side of my mouth tugging up into a grin.

"People are gonna die tonight, Billy. And it'll be your fault."

Her shoulders shake with humor as I grab her waist, smacking her ass before I bend down and kiss her.

"Get a room," Dom yells, and I flip him the bird.

"Go get your coat and whatever dumb sparkly thing you're gonna put your lipstick and nothing else in," I direct as she laughs and walks to get her purse and coat.

Everyone grabs jackets and the essentials before we walk to the elevator. The doors open immediately, and we file in, laughing and chatting, riding down to head to the cars I've arranged to wait in the garage.

I laugh to myself, taking in the group from the mirror of the elevator.

It's fucking domestic.

Doesn't matter that we might be the three most dangerous men in Chicago; right now, we're husbands and boyfriends. My face darkens at the thought.

I lean down to Sarah's ear as we exit the elevator. "I don't want to be your boyfriend."

She coughs, "Excuse me?" as I catch her completely off guard. We round the corner of the hall and walk out toward the garage.

I shake my head, pushing the door open for her. "Not like that. The word...it sounds so..."

"Inadequate?" she supplies as I help her up into our SUV and climb in after her.

"Yeah..." I smirk, biting my bottom lip.

Sarah reaches out and pulls my lip from my teeth. "What would you prefer I call you?"

I take a deep breath and let it out, staring at her. A million words come to mind, but the only one that sticks is the one I won't say. Not yet.

Changing the subject, I peer down at her dress as the car comes to life and rolls forward.

"You do look beautiful, Billy. But I can't decide if you're a saint or a sinner." Sarah crosses her legs, letting her top leg fall from the slit in her dress.

"Oh, I'm a saint—it's you who's a sinner, and I'm really looking forward to all your bad ideas tonight, Mr. Sovrano."

My hand brushes over her leg, pushing my fingers between her thighs to hold it possessively.

"Careful, Billy. I'm searching for a reason to tear that dress off your body."

She wags her eyebrows as we pull out of the garage. With the other cars in front and behind, we head toward Church.

The entire drive is spent with me pawing at her and trying to get her naked before we get there, but I lose the battle. The girl needs to make an entrance, and I'll give her anything she desires, so long as I get what I want later.

Dom's car is already stopped in front of the entrance, and I see him get out and help Drew from the car. The moment our car stops, I do the same with Sarah, and Luca and Gretchen join us moments later.

The door to Church is opened as we walk up. I place my hand on the inside of Sarah's coat, pulling her close to keep her warm as we walk up the steps.

Dom looks back to me from the top of the stairs, saying something offhand, but I don't hear his words because it's the expression on his face that has me looking over my shoulder.

"Cosa?" *What?* I question, shifting back to him after seeing nothing behind me.

He shakes his head, his eyes still scanning the empty sidewalk. "Nothing. I thought I recognized someone."

He turns back and walks inside, but I look over my shoulder again, taking in the empty street, letting my eyes focus on the shadows. Sarah gives my waist a tiny tug, and I walk forward, turning away and focusing back to the inside of Church.

The doors close behind us, and we're instantly transported into New Orleans. Purples and golds line the walls, with accents of green spread around the room. Vibrant music takes over my senses as I'm given beads by a topless blonde.

My brows raise at Sarah. "You thought of everything."

My grin grows as I pull the top of her dress open and peer inside, giving a whistle of approval. She laughs as I wink, letting go of the fabric and putting the multicolored necklaces over her head.

"I had to see the goods to give the beads," I tease.

My hand finds its way to the back of her neck as we walk through the entry and toward the main room. Two shirtless men in devil masks approach us, and Luca laughs. "Jesus Christ."

"Those would be devils," I answer sarcastically. "I'm sure it's hard for you to tell the difference anymore."

The three of us stop and look at each other as the costumed guys greet us.

"What the fuck are we going to have to do to get beads from them?" Dom chimes in, making me and Luca laugh loudly.

We're handed our anonymity for the night in the form of masks from the devils—animal masks for the men and beautiful lace eye masks for the women. Sarah takes her slender piece of black lace and holds it out for me to tie around her head.

I bring the fabric to a close behind her head and tie it in a bow. "All good?"

Bending down, I press a kiss against her neck over her collar. *All fucking mine.*

"Yes, thank you," she says, turning around smiling, her blue eyes even bluer now that they're highlighted by the black on her face.

"Who are you? I don't even recognize you," I tease.

I take my own mask, holding it up to look at it. A half-faced silver wolf looks back at me. Placing it over my face, I pull the tie over my head and adjust it to my face. Angling to Sarah, I growl down toward her.

She laughs and pats my chest. "I picked that one out specifically for you."

I'm gonna hunt you down later, Billy.

I smirk as she turns around and answers something Drew asks her as we make our way to the table that's been reserved for us.

As we walk forward, I grab Dominic's arm and hold him back, taking a moment before I relax. "What was that earlier? Something I need to worry about?"

He shakes me off, smiling. "No. I'm sure it was nothing. Let's have a good time. It's a party."

It's a party...so I throw away my questions and worries as he throws an arm around my shoulder and waves the waiter over.

"Let's drink," he bellows, and the room cheers back.

Champagne is delivered to our table, and we all take glasses, lifting our arms in a toast.

I wrap my other one around Sarah's waist and tug her in close as glasses clink, and we sip the Dom Perignon. Her face lifts to mine as our eyes lock, and I can't let another moment pass before I say what I wanted to before.

But first I want to kiss her.

My hand splays across her back, sealing her against me as my lips melt into hers. I break our kiss, watching as her eyelashes flutter before she focuses on me.

"Earlier...when you asked me what I wanted to be called...." I say, locking our eyes as my chest rises quicker. "Husband. That's what I want."

A shot rings out, screams erupting from every corner, as people scatter from the room. I blink seeing the glass Sarah was holding falling to the ground, her face ashen and blanched by fear.

Everything is in slow motion as I reach for my gun, swinging it to where the sound came from as I shove myself in front of Sarah and rip the mask off my face.

A man in a full-faced venetian mask stands in front of my gun with guards at his side. He places his Glock behind his back and takes a step closer toward me. Beady eyes dart behind the holes in his mask to where Sarah is protected behind me and back to my face.

Lifting the mask from his mouth, his words land like a bomb.

"Get your filthy hands off my fucking wife."

Chapter Twenty-Five

Sarah

ife? What the hell did he just say?

My head swivels to see Dom and Luca standing with Drew and Gretchen, but the room is otherwise empty, filled only with tension that's heightened by silence.

The man across from Dante slowly removes the all-white venetian mask from his face, and my will for survival snaps in two.

"Declan," I breathe out.

I don't feel myself moving or fighting, but I'm doing both. I'm screaming and digging into the ground as I lunge for him again and again, over and around Dante, heaving in gulps of breath each time I empty my lungs with my ferocity.

Dante's arm hooks around my waist and drags me backward, lifting me off the ground as I scream and swing my arms out, hoping to get a piece of Declan.

"I killed you. I killed you."

Declan laughs, jumping back and holding up his hands, as I shriek and claw at Dante, trying to get free. My feet touch the ground, and I hear Dante telling me to calm down, but my eyes scan the room for a weapon. My hands dart to the gun in his hand, but he grabs my wrists.

"Billy, look at me," Dante pushes, but I refuse, craning my neck past him to shoot daggers at Declan.

"How are you alive, you piece of shit. I hate you. I'll kill you again," I scream.

Grabbing the stem of a broken champagne glass from the mess on the table, I charge at him again, only to be pulled back easily by Dante. This time I'm pulled into Dante's arms and held firmly against him, quieting my struggle, forcing me to give-in, and calm down.

Unintentionally forced to acknowledge the ghost standing in front of me.

"This isn't real. Tell me this isn't real," I whisper to myself, dropping the crystal from my hand.

Declan smiles, but it always looked unnatural on his face, one only a mother could love.

No matter how attractive he is outside, he's rotted and twisted on the inside.

"Oh, I assure you, darling girl, I'm real. You've been gone so long, I bet you felt like you were seeing a ghost. We have so much to catch up on. Let me start—I run the O'Bannion crew. It's a real 'rags to riches' story. I'm at the top, but I'm still missing one thing." Declan crosses his arms over his chest, twisting his wedding ring with his thumb. "Care to guess?"

His voice is still as cruel as I remember, and I almost choke on the bile trying to come up from the sound of it. My eyes cut to him, and I wish I could shoot him again.

Dante stills behind me, and I can tell it's sinking in. He understands why I just came undone. He turns me around to look at him, touching my face so gently with the hand that's holding his gun, that I close my eyes, so I can block out everything but his touch and the scratch of the hard metal against my cheek.

"This is the guy? The one they sold you to?" Dante grinds out angrily, his chest heaving as he points the gun back at Declan. "The one you thought you killed."

I nod, unable to even answer. I never want to say the words again.

Dante moves me to stand in front of me, and I clutch the back of his jacket, willing my body to stop trembling from my anger.

"Don't address her, or I'll cut your fucking tongue from your mouth. In fact, you tell me why I shouldn't blow your head off now..."

I feel Dante take a step forward but stop abruptly. I step to the side to see the two guys flanking Declan lift their shirts, exposing the guns they're carrying. Shit.

"There's one reason," Declan answers arrogantly, "and here's another...because then you'd make her a widow, admittedly something she tried to do herself eight years ago when she shot me on our wedding night. Except I didn't die, Sarah, and now I've finally found you."

Declan looks at Dante and grits out cruelly, "I've come for what's mine."

Fuck. My head whips to look at everyone in the room. I did this. This is my fault. I brought this here, but each set of eyes I look into don't reflect anger toward me. No, everyone is glaring at Declan like they want him dead.

I look up and see Dante's jaw tensed, the muscles rippling as he grits his teeth. Taking a deep breath, I slip my hand into his and step up to his side, the other finding its way to my choker. "I've never belonged to you Declan. You can't own what you've never had."

He sneers, and I stand straighter. *Not today, motherfucker.*

"Always such a smart mouth. It should be fun breaking it in," Declan answers.

A rumble in Dante's chest vibrates all the way down his arm as he shakes his head. "I'm gonna make you choke on those words. You may have these assholes with you now," he barks, motioning to the gunmen, "but they won't be there forever. I will though. I'll never stop, and I won't just stop with you...I'm gonna chop down your whole goddamn family tree."

Luca's voice comes from Dante's right. "You aren't taking Sarah. You tell the rest of the Irish we're coming. E taglieremo la testa dal serpente." *And we'll cut the head off the snake.*

A deep laugh pulls from Dante's chest from whatever Luca said, and Declan looks between them, his eyes growing wild with anger.

Declan steps up to Dante's face, smiling wide. "You have forty-eight hours to deliver my bride to me, or you'll get your war."

He barely gets the words out before Dante's head connects with Declan's skull, sending him stumbling backward.

Guns click, two pointing at Dante as his stays on Declan. I squeeze Dante's hand, but Declan begins to laugh from his bent stature, holding up a hand and waving it.

"Put them away. I'm fine. I'm fine."

Dante's quiet rage is so palpable that I'm feeding off it, as if it's being siphoned from him as he lowers his gun. I dig my nails into my leg, watching as Declan stands and wipes a trickle of blood from his busted eyebrow.

"I was warned about your temper. It could take down cities, they said..." Declan laughs again, pulling a handkerchief from his breast pocket. "You definitely live up to it."

Declan's eyes swing to mine as he blots his face. "You always were a survivor, but this time you hid in the lion's den."

His face swings to Luca, as he begins to pace. "You've got

one brother who's so calculating and vicious, and he may have stepped away from the mafia, but nobody would ever dare to question him for fear of what he'd do."

Declan looks at the handkerchief with disgust, seeing his blood, and puts it back to his cut. He walks past me and Dante and points to where Dominic is standing protectively in front of Drew.

"And his twin, or should I say the mob's Priest...that's your real name, right? The one you go by when you take confessions of the men you kill. I have to say...you live up to your reputation the most. It's the eyes—you're dead behind them."

My eyes tip to Dante, who gives nothing away. I've heard rumblings before about what Dom did and still does for his "family," but I didn't give them any weight.

Declan looks back at me, amusement in his eyes. "You didn't know any of this? Even though you're in bed with a man who rivals even my power and viciousness? And I was the monster you ran from?"

I hate his smug grandiose attitude as if he's the better choice.

My voice is cutting and angry as I deliver my words. "These people are my family. They protect those they love. There's nothing but honor in that. You bought and tortured me before you tried to rape me. The only monster in this room is you. And I will watch you burn in hell, Declan. In fact, I kinda hope I get to strike the match."

His face contorts as he straightens his jacket, pulling it in place harshly. "Forty-eight hours. In the meantime, I'm sure you'll all need a motivator, so I left you a gift as a reminder of what we Irish do best."

Declan smiles and turns, pushing his hands into his pockets as he strolls out past the abandoned mask station, tossing his back in. His henchmen follow him, walking straight out of Church.

The closing door echoes through the empty space, and Dante's arms pull me into him as he kisses the top of my head. An exhale releases in a whoosh as I realize I've been holding my breath. Dante shoves his gun into the small of his back and pulls out his phone, turning to Dom.

"Where the fuck is everyone? The security, the extra guys... there better be a fire."

All their phones start to buzz. A crease forms in my brow as the guys look to each other.

Dante answers his phone angrily, "Where the fuck is everyone?"

Whatever is being said immediately silences him, Luca, and Dom. I know it's bad because I watch the life in his eyes dim, making him the scariest person I've ever seen.

This is the gift Declan warned about. I know it.

"What's happened?" I question.

"Jesus Christ, he did it before he walked in here...that's why I didn't see any of the guys when we walked in," Dante growls, gritting his teeth.

Luca brings his fists down on the table as he hangs up his phone. "That motherfucker came in here—knowing. He fucking knew, Dante."

Dante's hand lowers from his ear, and he looks at Dom, where Drew's face is buried into his chest as her shoulders shake. Dom lowers the phone from his ear and shakes his head.

My head shifts to Luca as he puts his arm around Gretchen and holds her close, still visibly angry as he whispers into her ear.

My hands shoot to Dante's face, and I survey his features; it's as if pieces of him are dying, and I don't know how to help him.

"What happened?" I plead. "What did you all just find out?"

His eyes connect to mine, and all I see is fury.

"Declan blew up the apartment. The building's a fucking mess of fire and scrap metal... Sarah, we think Matteo was inside. He was fucking inside."

CHAPTER TWENTY-SIX

DANTE

S he shakes her head and pushes away from me.

"Who can confirm it?" she spits out angrily. "Who can confirm he was inside? I won't treat him like a dead man before I see his body. Find him. Dante...you have to."

I nod my head, holding her cheek in my hand. "I'll find him. It's going to be okay. I'll find him, Billy."

I press a kiss to her forehead, and she melts into me, hugging my waist.

"He's fine. You know Matteo—he's probably off with some girl."

I know she's clinging to that hope because Matteo is close to her. But where she's hopeful, I fear the worst.

Antonio and Vincenzo bust through Church's doors, making Drew let out a gasp, and my head swings in their direction as they stop to look at us.

They look like hell, as if they ran all the way here.

"What the fuck is going down, boss?" Vin rages. "We thought you were still at your place... Jesus, Dante. We all rushed straight there."

"Who the fuck told you to go there because it wasn't me. I was here. By myself...left open to be fucking shot. Declan played us. Who helped him?" I roar.

"Matteo," Antonio states cautiously. "The text came from his phone to all of us."

"Then they took his phone," I shoot out. "Matteo's no rat."

"Agreed," Vin and Antonio say in unison.

Sarah buries her head into my chest as I start giving directions.

"We need to get everyone to the safe houses. The city isn't a good place to be right now."

"I already took care of the kids." Antonio nods to my brothers, and Gretchen lets out a breath, walking straight for him and wrapping her arms around his neck.

"Thank you." She nods, pulling back and rubbing his shoulder.

Nico comes in from the back entry of Church with a few of the guys and interrupts her gratitude. "Boss. What the hell is going down? We've got the cars out back and ready."

I rub Sarah's back and look down at her.

"Go with the girls, Billy. I'll be there soon," I say softly, but she raises her eyebrows and shakes her head. "I don't have time for this shit. You need to park your ass where it's safe."

She grabs my tuxedo jacket and pulls me close to her. "I walked into this family eyes wide open. It's not perfect, but we take care of each other, and that means you, too. You take care of everyone else, but I take care of you. I can't do that burning a hole in the carpet from my pacing in some safe house."

My entire body dips to wrap my arms around her waist, picking her up to level her face to face with mine.

"I love you, Billy. Just give me twenty-four hours. I can't

think straight if I'm worried about you. I need to sort out my next move, and I can't do that with you here."

She plants a kiss on my lips, her hands cradling my face. "Then I'll burn a hole in the carpet, but if you wait longer than twenty-four hours, I'll set the place on fire."

I wink and jut my chin for her to kiss me. She does as she's told, and I pull back, placing her back to her feet.

"I love you," she calls out to me, walking backward.

"It's not enough," I answer back, smiling reassuringly as she turns and takes Nico's arm.

"Take care of my girl."

"With my life." Nico nods and walks them out the way he came in.

My eyes stay fixed on the hall she disappeared into until I know she's gone, feeling the weight that's on my shoulders. Dom comes up beside me and pats my shoulder.

"This is the part you weren't looking forward to. But you'll always have enemies, and they'll always try to hurt you where you're the most vulnerable."

My palms press against the table as I bow, letting my head hang down between my shoulders as I take in a deep breath and let it out.

"Dante," Luca says lowly, pushing a tumbler of amber liquid under my face on the table.

"We need to sit down and plan a war."

I nod from where I'm bowed, taking one last moment, then straightening up.

"First, we find Matteo. If he's alive, we keep him safe. If he's dead, we bury his body, and then we make sure to take twenty of theirs as payment." My head swings to where Antonio and Vincenzo are standing, "Vin, call the doc...have him check the hospitals."

"Done." He pulls his phone from his pocket and walks away.

"Office," I say to my brothers, waving Antonio over to walk with us.

The rest of the night travels by in a blur. More of my men file into Church as the four of us hole up in the office to strategize how to take down the entire Boston crew.

We sit around the desk, me behind it, and listen to Luca as he works out each life we'll take like a puzzle piece for the bigger picture. He's detached and calculating.

But this is always who he is.

Just like when he hugs his wife and child, that's who he is, too.

We're the most dangerous when those two purposes intersect. Declan has threatened those who matter most to us. And now he gets the worst versions of who we are.

Dom pushes some papers out of the way to place his drink down on the desk.

"What I don't get was why the family was doing work for him...his reach far exceeds theirs. They were unneeded. If he wanted her all these years, he could've taken her. I don't buy the 'I just found you' bullshit he was spewing."

I nod. "Yeah. I hear that. He's a sick bastard, that's clear, but there's a bigger reason."

"It's the drugs," Luca pipes in, crossing his arms and sitting against the desk.

Antonio walks to the small bar in the corner and grabs the bottle of scotch. "That makes sense. He's been starving her family. Only allowing them to make enough, so that he keeps them begging him—willing to do whatever he wants."

Dom's eyes grow wider as he connects more dots. "He's giving crumbs. Her family is so desperate for pennies that he's been using them to do his dirty work, dangling the fulfillment of the drug buy-in over their head. But why?"

Luca shakes his head. "Sarah's been a sick hobby until now, probably something to satisfy his cruelty."

I put my hands behind my head, letting out a breath before I speak. "The deal he made for her was behind closed doors. Nobody knew—he couldn't exactly get everyone involved to search for her without raising questions. So, he used her family. The question is what's changed...why now?"

Antonio pours himself a glass and looks up. "From what we pieced together with our guy in Boston, Declan took the crew by blood. He killed anyone who stood in his way during his climb, and we think that his sudden immediate interest in Sarah has more to do with who she's in bed with...he came for her to start a war with us. She's a means to an end."

Motherfucker.

"All this time, she worried she was bringing trouble to our door, but it's us who brought it to hers," I say to myself before speaking louder. "He wants our streets for his filthy drugs. And he knew that if he laid down this ultimatum, I'd push back, and we'd go to war. He could blame me and go unaccountable —not having to answer to the other families in his crew," I add, rapping my knuckles against the desk.

Luca takes a swig of his drink and levels a look at me. "And if our backs are turned in the middle of a war, shit slips through. We know how much he likes to pull that distraction shit. Chicago would be his before we even fought for her."

I let out a small huff as we all sit in silence, letting it sink in. Declan would've had us.

"He's smart," Luca muses. "We just have to be smarter."

My phone buzzes, and I look down to see it's Nico. "Everything okay?"

"Golden. Girls are dropped and protected. She's good, Dante—worried about you, but all good. She left her purse and phone at Church, but the other two have theirs. She wanted me to tell you that."

"Thank you. Get back, you're needed."

"Done."

I hang up and look up at the room. "Girls are good."

Nobody responds, just gives a nod as we get back to business. The more everyone speaks, the more my mind flips through scenarios.

I recline back in my chair, listening to Antonio and Luca debate whether or not to consult with the other families on the Irish side, when a thought begins to form.

"What's in your head, Dante?" Dom questions, tilting his head in to listen but not disrupt the others.

"It's something Luca said when Declan was here...he said we'd cut the head off the snake. Declan's an arrogant cocksucker. He came in here with only two men. How'd he know you two weren't carrying? He cleared everyone with that explosion, but he knew the three of us were together."

Dom rubs his jaw as he answers. "You think he's bought into the idea that he's powerful? That he walked in assuming you'd have to respect him because he's another boss."

I nod, running a hand over my head. "Yes. He's not one of us...he doesn't come from tradition. Declan doesn't know how shit works. Take what Antonio was saying—he bloodied the ladder his entire climb, and that makes him the kind of person who isn't very popular with those he leads, because he isn't really one of them."

Dom tenses, seeing my thoughts before I say them.

"You want to take him first? Bet on that everyone will back down once he's taken care of, but..."

I cut him off, answering honestly, still working through the idea.

"Clipping Declan could mean the kind of war that makes everyone fair game; because if I'm wrong, there'll be no holds barred."

"Are you willing to risk her?" Dom looks at me, waiting for my answer. I can see the worry in his eyes. He's not sure I won't do just that.

It's fair. There was a time when I would have made that move for the sake of my family, but now, she stands protected above all.

"I'm never willing to do that."

Relief and pride.

That's what I see in my brother's eyes.

Luca clears his throat and puts his hand on the desk, propping himself up. "We need to call in the other families, Dante. If we're going to take the Irish down, we need their support. New York, Boston, LA...we need them all."

"Tomorrow," I say, the firmness of my answer in my tone. "The other families will want to know how helping will benefit them. Everyone is selfish, motivated only by their gain.

Loyalty is a distant second. So, I'm going to need to know exactly what jars Declan's got his fingers in." I turn toward Antonio and give him a knowing look. "I'm gonna need to know all the inventory."

He nods and pulls his phone from his pocket to start to get to work. I take in a deep breath and look out at the room, feeling the violence of my thoughts start to pump blood into my veins.

"Not only am I keeping my queen, I'm taking that piece of shit's fucking kingdom too."

Chapter Twenty-Seven

Sarah

My fingers brush through Ella's little curls from where her head lies on my lap as she sleeps. Gretchen stepped away to speak with Luca, and I stayed here to watch the sweet toddler while Drew put the twins down, and I suspect herself, too, since she's been gone for a while.

The door from the bedroom opens as Gretchen walks out with a small frown, making her way to the couch in the living room. The small house we're holed up in can best be described as cozy.

Nico said it was left for Antonio by his grandfather, who preferred the silence of the woods to the clamor of the city.

"Hey," Gretchen whispers, sliding down and lifting Ella's feet to place them on her lap.

"Hey. How's everything going?" I question, keeping my voice low.

"Jesus. I don't know. Luca seems confident, which is reassuring, but I'm worried about you. Not them," she answers, giving me that look she gets.

Gretchen seems to have an uncanny ability to read people right down to the lies they tell themselves.

"Me?" I counter, rolling my eyes.

"Yeah. You," she pushes. "You haven't stopped looking guilty, like you're carrying the weight of the world on your shoulders, since we left...this shit isn't your fault, Sarah. Whatever's happened to Matteo isn't your fault. And I don't trust for a second that you believe that."

I hate her. She makes it impossible not to love her.

My shoulders give a small shrug. "You're right. I feel guilty because I wish I could make it all go away. For all of you. But especially for Dante. Because he'll kill himself to protect everyone so that I don't have to live with the reality that none of this would've happened if not for me."

Gretchen reaches out and touches my shoulder, shaking her head. "No. That's not true. Luca said Declan is using you as a means to an end. He wants to expand whatever he's running into Chicago, and you're the button he's pushed to cause a war. A war that would be the perfect distraction for slipping by the guards, so to speak."

"Jesus Christ," I breathe out. "This is too much."

Gretchen brings her hand back to her head, resting her temple on her fist. "Listen, it's no secret that I wanted my husband out of this game when we married, but that just meant I wanted him out of the day to day...this is about family. You need to trust them. You don't just have Dante, Sarah, you have all of us. You are our family." She smiles, reaching for my hand.

I squeeze her hand back. "Thank you. I know it's not enough, but thank you."

She nods her head, and we lapse back into silence, sitting with Ella lying across us, me stroking her hair and Gretchen rubbing her little feet. My head begins to form an idea I know I can't say aloud, but I'm positive is the rightest thing I've ever thought.

"I'm going to take her to bed now."

Gretchen lifts Ella into her arms, and I give a small wave as she rounds the couch and walks toward one of the three bedrooms in the cabin. She nods to the guys who are sitting at a makeshift table playing cards that were sent with us.

I turn, folding my arms over the brown leather couch and resting my chin on them. "Has anyone heard anything about Matteo?"

My gaze drifts to the small digital clock sitting on a wooden bookcase by one of the burly guards as it blinks and changes to 10:30 p.m.

"Not yet, but they put Vincenzo on it...he'll find him. It's impossible to hide from Vin," one of the guys says as I draw my focus back to them.

"Really? That's what he does? Finds people?" I question, curious to hear more from my chatty Cathy.

"Yeah. It's like his specialty. That's why Dante's family is so powerful—the seven of them together is fucking scary. Nobody in their right mind would fuck with them unless they wanted a war that would destroy everything." He chuckles.

But what he says hits my gut with a thud. A war. Declan wants that. My eyes falter as I push back and turn around to stand. Declan wants to destroy everything. He wants something long and drawn-out...because he'll wear them down, so he can pick them off one by one.

I brush my hair back out of my face and then rest my hands on my heart, willing the emotion not to overwhelm me. Flashes of family dinner pass through my mind like a slideshow.

Gretchen and Luca with Ella. Dominic and Drew with

their twin boys. Matteo smiling when he speaks about the girl he can't have. Antonio reading his damn paper. Vincenzo, Nico. Dante.

Every moment we've spent falling in love and finding our way. All of it would've been for nothing because in the end, we'll have nothing left. Not the people we love, not the memories, and not our future because it will all be replaced with destruction.

But there can't be a war if the terms are settled.

Turning around, I fake a smile and brush my hair over my shoulder. "Guys, I'm going to bed. I'm wiped."

"All right, Sarah," one of the other guys answers as I walk past and into my room.

The door closes softly behind me, and I lock the door as I try and steady my breathing.

Fuck. This is the only way. I need to do this.

My eyes scan the room and lock in on the window, my feet already in motion. I reach for the lock on top, undoing it quietly and pushing the window up.

It's old and heavy and probably hasn't been opened in months. Wincing, I freeze when it makes a squeaky sound, but push again, getting it opened wide.

The cold air billows in, and I shiver. I'm still wearing the outfit I had on at Church. Thankfully, my coat is here in the bedroom. I take quick steps to the bed and tug it on, buttoning it and hoping it'll be enough.

Don't think, just do.

I only make it halfway back to the window when the collar of my jacket snags on my choker. My feet still, and I bring my fingers to my neck.

My chest rises and falls with the regret over what I have to do. I reach back behind my neck with both hands and struggle to undo it until I finally feel a pop and the clasp comes loose, falling open, and my eyes squeeze shut.

"It's just jewelry. It's just a necklace," I whisper to myself, but the lie does nothing to stop the jagged breaths that slip between my lips because it's not just a necklace—it's Dante.

And I just ripped my heart right from his chest.

I take the two steps to the nightstand and place it down, adding my bracelets.

"I'm sorry. I love you," I whisper.

It's crazy to talk to myself, but it's the closest thing to him.

I hurry to the window and stop my mind from going backward. I fling my leg over the side, hoisting myself up and tipping myself over, landing on my bare feet.

The sting from the cold and the rocks on the ground, stab at my feet sending pain shooting up my leg, but I try and block it out because my heels aren't a viable alternative.

Turning, I close the window, so any outside noise or breeze doesn't give me away because I'm going to need as much of a head start as possible.

My feet take a tentative first step on the cold ground, causing more of a chill to run through my body. I'll be lucky not to freeze to death.

Pulling the collar of my jacket tighter around my neck, I take a few more cautious steps, hearing the crackling of leaves and the stabs of hard stone, before I become bolder and move quickly into the cover of the trees.

I saw a road as we came in, so if I can find it in the darkness, I can hitchhike or follow it into a town. I don't slow as I head in the direction I think I should go, praying that the guys in the front of the house don't shoot if they hear a noise.

The house becomes dimmer as I retreat farther into trees, and then I run as fast as I can until I can't make my lungs suck in the cold air anymore, but even then, I still don't stop, opting to walk quickly. The burn on my feet from the frozen ground is becoming painful, but I know the road has to be here. It has to.

Sweat drips down my brow; I've been moving so quickly for so long that I've managed to sweat in single-digit temperatures. But I know I'm close. I know it.

I squint, trying to make out a darker shadow, when my thigh runs smack into something hard.

"Dammit," I breathe out and rub my leg, realizing it's a large broken tree that's lying across the path. I jump up, putting my backside on it, and toss my legs over. As I land, a streak of light passes over me, illuminating my tattered dress.

Headlights.

I gather my dress in my hands quickly, breaking into a full sprint, hearing tires on the road as I get closer. My breath is ragged as the trees begin to thin, and moonlight filters in, helping me to make out more details. My hair blows across my face, and I shake my head to help it move, almost screaming when I see asphalt. I did it.

Throwing caution to the wind, I run faster as I see a car coming from down the road and run directly into the middle of the lane, waving my arms wildly.

Tires screech, and I close my eyes, frozen in place. Peeking one eye open, I see the car pulled to a hard stop about twenty feet away from me. I sprint toward it, breathless and grateful.

"I'm so sorry," I say in my sweetest voice, trying hard to emote a damsel-in-distress feel. "Can you please take me to the nearest town? I need help. Please. It's my boyfriend—he's gone nuts. Please help me."

"Yes, get in, dear!" the old woman rushes out, her husband unlocking the doors.

I climb inside, rattling off a hundred "thank yous" and pull my dress over my feet to warm them.

"Thank goodness we saw you. Are you okay?"

"Yes, thank you so much. You're a lifesaver."

Sinking back into the seat, I look over my shoulder for the last time to say goodbye.

Chapter Twenty-Eight

Dante

Luca walks back inside the office, having just hung up the phone with Gretchen, and rolls his neck. "They're all going to bed. Things are quiet."

I don't answer, but I'm happy to hear it because I haven't stopped thinking about her.

How could I? She's my reason for everything, and I'll be damned if I let this shit go south and destroy the life she deserves to have.

"Nico should've been back by now," I throw out, catching Antonio's attention.

He pulls his phone from his pocket as the office door opens bringing with it, Nico, Vincenzo, and a battered but smiling Matteo.

Thank fucking god.

The room erupts, everyone standing and cheering and throwing out questions all on top of each other that it's impossible to make out what anyone's saying.

I stand from behind the desk and move closer to Matteo, bringing my hand to his cheek and patting it lightly.

"What the fuck happened to you, ya dumb son of a bitch? You had us thinking you were dead."

Matteo winces as Luca pats his shoulder. "Easy. I'm fragile," he complains, and we both take a small step back, making room for him to walk to the chair that's closest.

I motion my head, and Antonio swivels the chair around for Matteo to sit; he makes his way to it slowly, holding his ribs and hissing a breath through his teeth when Nico helps him down.

We all stand and gather around, waiting for him to explain what the hell happened to him tonight.

He looks up at us and takes a breath. "I went to your place to keep an eye out, and a couple of scumbags jumped me out front when I got there. Fucked me up bad and tossed me in a goddamn trunk. I thought they were gonna kill me until I realized they were just leaving me there."

Nico crosses his arms over his chest. "That's how they got his phone; they took it right off him and sent the message to everyone. Vin found it in the trash a couple cars away from where he found Matteo."

Matteo adjusts himself in the chair and groans. "I made a big fucking commotion in that trunk, even though my body was hurting. But nobody was paying attention. I heard the blast, felt it, too. It shook the shit out of the car. Then the sirens started howling, and I knew I had to wait it out."

Vincenzo laughs as he sits back against the desk. "I stopped back by the building, just to look around, and I was standing across the street. Out of the corner of my eye, I see this car rocking and bouncing. I thought to myself, either someone is fucking or someone's trying to get out."

Luca starts to laugh, and I join in while Dom just shakes his head.

"Fuck. That was the longest five hours of my life. But I'm sorry, Dante," Matteo says, a crease forming between his eyes.

I exhale harshly. "No, you are not responsible for this, Matteo. Don't put that on yourself. Did you already see the doc?"

He nods as Vin answers for him.

"Yeah, that's what took us so long. I called Nico for backup, just in case."

"Smart," I agree as I walk back around the desk to my chair and grin at Matteo. "Well, since you're useless," I laugh, "you can ride with me to the house and stay with the girls."

Matteo sits back and closes his eyes, stripped of his regular sarcasm as I continue. "Antonio, fill in Nico and Vin about the plans. Let's wrap this shit up, so I can go see my girl...we all need to sleep and be clear for tomorrow."

"Will do," Antonio answers.

Luca and I wrap up how we plan to reach out to the other families and come to a consensus for what we should offer them for their help.

I stand and grab my jacket and catch the time on the wall— 3:30 a.m. My eyes widen and blink as I try and keep them open. The night's beginning to wear me down.

Each of the men follows my lead and gathers what they brought, and as we head out back to our cars to go our own ways, I look at each of them.

"Thank you for your loyalty and your bravery. The next step we make needs to be made together because we're only our strongest together. So take this time to think it over and make sure you're ready."

My words hit hard. I see it in their faces, and I'm grateful that these men will all be with me to protect our city and to keep the woman I love safe.

I let out an exhausted breath as we pull up to Antonio's cabin and twist my neck, hearing the cracks as I try and wake myself up. Running my hand over my head, I smack Dom's shoulder. "We're here. Get up." He opens one eye and grumbles.

Luca stretches from the front seat next to my driver and rolls his shoulders. "That wasn't enough sleep."

The car crackles over branches and debris and pulls to a stop. I reach for the door, pushing it open and stepping out into the early-morning air.

The other car pulls in behind us with Matteo inside. I stand, buttoning my jackets, and flip up the collar of the heavy trench.

"Fuck, it's cold." A cloud of breath billows out in front of me. I rub my hands together as Matteo slowly climbs from the car to join us.

"You want a piggyback ride?" Luca jokes as Matteo shakes his head and flips him the bird.

"Dick." I smirk as we walk toward the door.

The guys at the front greet us and open the door, stepping aside as I enter. The place is small, but comfort isn't what I care about. It's safety. And nobody knows about it.

Two more of my guys sit at a small gray fold-up table with tired looks in their eyes, but they stand as we walk inside.

"Everything's good, boss. Girls are still asleep. We took shifts, but it's been quiet. I think the babies woke up a few times, but Drew seemed to be fine."

Dom pats the guy's shoulder as he walks past him and points at the door, getting a nod before walking inside.

Luca comes up next to me. "Where's my wife and daughter?" He sounds as tired as I feel.

The guys point to the back room, and Luca wastes no time

making his way to the room. I turn as Matteo walks through the door, the cabin lights making him seem even more bruised than before.

I look back to my soldiers at the table as I shrug off my trench coat and toss it over a chair at the table. "Put Matteo on the couch. And then get some rest. The guys outside can switch with you."

I turn and walk to the only other bedroom that's left. With each step, my body calls for her, needing her close and in my arms. I want to wrap her up, let her legs tangle around me, and sleep like I'm dead.

Reaching the door, I grab the handle, but it doesn't twist. My eyes dart down, needing the visual to make sense of the action.

I try it again, twisting it harder, back and forth, as it rattles in place.

My eyes are fixed on the silver knob as my voice raises, demanding over my shoulder while I jerk the door against the frame.

"Why is this fucking door locked?"

My body spins around, and the men's eyes grow wide. They exchange a look, landing back on me confused.

"We don't know. She said she was going to bed..." one of the men tosses out.

Fuck. Fuck!

Panic sets in as I turn back around and rattle the door with all my strength, calling out her name. "Sarah. Open the door."

My palm pounds against the wood, my voice louder this time. "Sarah! Open the fucking door!"

I push off the handle, shaking my head and my mind begins to split in two. All I want is to get through the goddamn door. Nothing stands between me getting to her. Nothing.

I can't lose you, Billy. You chose me. I won't fucking lose you.

Pain ignites against my skin as my shoulder connects with brute force against the door, and a loud crack sounds through the oak, splintering the wood, leaving jagged edges and frays.

Her name pulls from my throat as I take a step back and charge the door again, splitting it open. The hinged part flies open, bouncing off the wall, and back into my hand that's up to stop it.

There's commotion behind me, but I'm focused on what's in front of me.

"What the fuck is going on?" I hear Dom yell almost on top of Luca's voice booming through the space.

"What the fuck is happening?"

I stand silent inside my room, letting my eyes take in the unmade bed...the high heels on the floor, and the window that's still cracked at the very bottom.

Because closing it completely from the outside is near impossible.

It's as if I can't catch my breath as I look around. I know this all means something, but my mind won't let me think it. I can't know this because I told her...

I told her she could never leave...

My eyes drift around the room until I see it. I see her goodbye because it doesn't matter that I already knew she left by the other pieces of the puzzle. It's the diamond choker and bracelets on the nightstand that hold my attention, paralyzing my breath.

I take a step backward, feeling the rage settle itself inside my bones, guiding me toward what I'll do next. I turn to my brothers, hollowed and emptied of my heart.

"She's left. Sarah's gone."

My vision goes black, giving in to the comfort of my haze of fury as my fist busts straight through the wall next to me.

Chapter Twenty-Nine

Sarah

Pushing the heavy door open, the smell of stale beer and cigarettes attack my senses. My sneakered feet make a squeak on the floor as I step on whatever sticky shit hasn't been cleaned off the floor of this crappy bar, but I pull my hoodie down over my face and walk inside.

I stole my new ensemble right out of a suitcase being unloaded from a bus that came from Chicago, and then I stole a car and headed right for Boston. By the time the people in the overnight parking figured out their car was missing, I'd be long gone.

I want to feel guilty, but I don't.

It took fifteen hours, and I drove it straight because I knew if I stopped and stood still, Dante would get to me. But now my body is surviving on adrenaline and Red Bull, leaving me jittery and unsettled.

It could've been worse. Dante could have stopped me. Thank god I still have survival skills—if you can call theft and hot-wiring a car "skills."

My eyes scan the room looking for the man I'm here for.

This bar is the kind that serves as a feeder for anyone who wants in with someone like Declan. It's a hot spot for wannabes and losers.

A guy sitting at the bar takes a drag of his cigarette as he speaks loudly about his latest fight. He's throwing money at the bartender, buying drinks, while his arm hangs lazily over a woman who looks as if she's fifty and still hoping for her prince.

I make my way over to where he's speaking too loud for the story he's telling and take a seat on the stool two down, raising a finger to the bartender and pointing to the whiskey on the shelf.

"And then I told him...you better fucking apologize because my boss isn't someone you want coming for ya."

The man's breath gets caught in his throat as he laughs, making him cough like someone who smokes three packs a day.

He clears his throat, wiping the back of his dirty hand over his mouth, before reaching to the cigarette that's rested among another fifty in an ashtray. Putting the smoke to his lips, he takes another drag.

"Because Declan Murphy is a man of his word..."

"Bullshit," I say aloud, interrupting him, pulling the shot of whiskey toward me. He coughs again, and I hear the stool move and feet shuffle. "Did you just say bullshit?" I don't answer, opting to nod instead.

"Who says I don't work for Declan? You better watch your big mouth before I break it."

I slam my shot down on the counter, letting the burn run down my throat, and bring my hands to my hood and pull it back, locking eyes with him.

"Hi, Dad. Been a long time."

He stabs his cigarette into the ashtray vigorously, a sneer spreading across his face.

"Call your fake boss. Tell him I'm here and that I'd like to come home now. Go on," I coax, motioning to the old shitty phone on the bar top.

I stand and pick up the second shot the bartender puts in front of me. "I'll be over there in the booth. Let me know when it's time."

Walking away, I hear my dad on the phone with my brother, and my eyes stay focused ahead when I hear, "We just hit the lotto."

I push into the booth and set the whiskey on the table and let my head fall back against the torn, cracked faux leather that's on the seat, closing my eyes.

It's almost over.

My peace is interrupted by the smell of my father as he joins me. "When they come for you, you're going to tell them we found you."

"Yep," I answer, unsurprised by his opportunism. I was actually banking on it.

I open my eyes as the smoke from his newly lit cigarette infiltrates my nose. I level a glare at him and pick up my forgotten shot and throw it back.

I place it back on the table and lock eyes with him, noticing the deep lines and worn skin on his face. I wish I felt something for him or had one good memory. But I don't.

He might as well be a stranger to me.

"Did you ever love me? Not love what I could do for you... but like the love a parent has for a child."

"No," he answers frankly, giving a shrug.

"I'm glad." I nod. "I'll never have to mourn. So I guess, thanks for that."

His mouth opens to say something fucked up but shuts immediately as he holds his smoke in between his teeth and scrambles from the booth to stand.

He looks downright afraid. I glance around to see similar expressions, and I know my ride's here. Pushing from the booth, I stand and turn around to see two men in dark suits standing at the door.

Without speaking, I start toward the men, and my father calls from behind, "Don't forget what I said, Sarah."

I give him the middle finger as I walk straight out the opened door, letting it close behind me. My eyes squint, trying to adjust to the dimming light of the late afternoon because I was in complete darkness.

A car door opens, and one of the men behind me grunts, "In." I climb in, immediately relieved that I'm alone. No Declan in sight.

The suits climb in on either side of me as the driver gets in and starts the car. My body is squished, even in the back of the SUV, because I'm being swallowed up by the two gargantuan men.

The tires kick up rocks as the car peels out of the parking lot, darting into traffic quickly and causing me to ram into the suit next to me.

"Jesus. Is that necessary...are you trying to kill us?" I shoot out, gripping the seat between my legs to right myself.

A strong hand connects with my mouth as my head shoots backward, the metallic taste of blood filling my mouth. My hands shoot to my face to where the pain stabs at me.

"Keep your mouth shut, bitch."

Tears spring to my eyes as my mouth throbs. I wipe my hand over my lip, seeing crimson on my fingertips. I should keep my mouth shut. I should listen. I should.

"Is your boss going to like it when you bring him damaged goods?" I challenge.

Suit number one grabs my hair, pulling my head back with such ferocity I'm sure he's pulled the strands out of my scalp.

Suit number two comes close to my face, his eyes filled with his enjoyment as a pained whimper catches in my mouth.

"Your husband told us we could have as much fun as we wanted with you...but today's your lucky day because dirty, filthy whores aren't our type. Maybe after he cleans you up, we can show you what we specialize in?"

A sharp hit to my stomach forces a scream from my mouth as I'm released to double over in pain. I stay like that, bent over myself and quiet, hugging my legs, wishing that I'd fall asleep, wake up, and realize this was all just a nightmare.

The bolt on the door sounds as the locks are removed from the outside. I scramble to my feet off the old, pissed-on mattress that's in the room. Pulling my zip up around my body tighter,

I cross my arms, preparing for who's coming in.

Declan walks through the door, smiling like the arrogant prick he is.

"You've looked better," he greets, leaning his head in, sniffing, and recoiling as if I'm disgusting. "I'm surprised to see you here. I trust you're comfortable."

"Sure, as much as anyone can be when they're beaten and thrown in a fucking dungeon."

He rolls his eyes. "That's a bit dramatic—there's a mattress. And from what I heard, you're to blame for the beating you got. Seems your smart mouth keeps getting you in trouble."

The look in his eyes makes me nervous. He isn't leveling me with anger—it's excitement. Declan wants to hurt me, and he's waiting for me to give him a reason.

"You're right. Let's start again. I'm here, cooperating, and ready to behave," I lie.

Declan is a dead man walking, and I'm just playing him at his own game.

He walks toward me, pushing a hand into his pants pocket. "Mmmm. I don't know.

You're a sneaky one. You managed to evade your father for eight years, but he catches you now?

Where'd he grab you at?"

"A bar. The exchange was made there. You should be celebrating. You've won. They discarded me, treated me like a piece of trash. You were right. They are the monsters." I keep my eyes on his, saying each word with more conviction than the next.

It's the best con job I've ever pulled, but Declan tilts his head, his lips pulling up in the corners. He's trying to seem friendly, but the disbelief in his eyes remains.

"You could prove it to me. Show me how committed you are to being here," he offers.

The tiny hairs on the back of my neck stand on end, fear creeping over me.

"By?" I swallow nervously.

"Drop to your knees and crawl to me." He grins as he squats down and claps his hands as if he's calling a dog.

I stand, staring at him and seeing him for the small man he is. He wants my humiliation like we're playing some sick game. But he won't get it. Because while he plays his games with me, I know the Devil is coming for his soul.

I drop down slowly to my knees and place my palms on the floor, closing my eyes and stilling my breath.

"Come on. Come here," he calls whistling to me like I'm an animal. "And when you get here, you can swallow my cock."

My head snaps to his, and I push back to my feet, standing up angrily. My nostrils flare as the breath rips in and out of my lungs. I'll never let him touch me.

"Go fuck yourself. Get out of my hovel. I'd rather die in here than ever be in the same room with you again."

I spit on the rank carpet toward him and watch the mask he tries to wear drop from his face. I've fallen right into his plan.

A deep guttural cry erupts from Declan as he charges me, his fist connecting with my face. The first hit is the only thing I feel. After that, my mind goes numb as the blackness takes over.

CHAPTER THIRTY

DANTE

The plane touches down on the private Boston airstrip, and I'm already standing as we taxi in. The moment I saw the empty room, I knew. I knew she'd come here.

Not everyone was as convinced, but there's no changing my mind. I know exactly why she did this. There's no war if Declan gets her.

But she knows I'll come for her. She fucking knows that I'll kill everyone in my way to make sure I take back what's mine.

And that's exactly what I'm going to do because this was the move I couldn't make. I could never risk her, even if it meant a swift end to the problem.

So, she did it for me.

My beautiful, loving girl did it for me.

I run my hand over my face, trying to restrain the energy coursing through my veins.

"Call Matteo, check in with him and the girls," I direct to Vincenzo.

He nods, getting straight to task, and my head swings to Antonio. "Check in with our guy here, see if he has eyes on her yet. I want to know exactly where she is because getting her back is the number one priority...clipping Declan is just icing on the cake."

"I still can't believe she did this," Dom growls as he stares out the small cabin window.

Luca stands up next to me, holding a hand on the seat to steady himself.

"I can. She's smart and a damn force of nature. She's bought us time using his own method against him. Declan will be too caught up in her torment to pay attention to what we're doing. So, we need to make sure her efforts count. When we meet with the Irish council tonight, we need to make sure they're on board with taking Declan down."

"And we'll do that, whether it's by reason or force," Dom adds darkly.

I smack the ceiling of the plane hard twice, angry at the images that are pushing to the front of my head. "I'll kill every single person who's touched her."

Antonio stands as the plane rocks to a complete stop. "We all need to stay level. So that we play this smart."

I look over my shoulder as he gives me a nod, and I understand what he's saying. I'm only getting one shot at this, and I can't let my feelings rule my decisions. Not if I want Declan's demise to fall into place.

The sound of metal connecting to the door means the stairs are rolled. I pick up my small black duffle and adjust the Glock on my back as the door is opened. I duck my head, taking each step to the bottom, waiting as my brothers join me.

Three men begin walking toward us and away from at least ten Black Range Rovers.

"The Boston family. Carlo and Lou Scorleone," Nico says to Luca as he nods.

"Let's go," I direct as Luca and Dom join me on each side to close the distance and greet them.

I pick out Lou and Carlo right away, but it's the guy in between them I don't know.

"You recognize him?" I say to my brothers, who both shake their heads.

I undo the button on my jacket for easier access. I don't want to shoot someone out in the open, but if I have to, I will.

"Ciao," Lou greets, but the stranger pushes forward.

"The Sovrano brothers, it's a real pleasure." He extends his hand, but I ignore it. "I'm sorry, where are my manners. I'm Connor O'Bannion."

"What the fuck," I roar. I take a step back, reaching for my piece, and pull it on him.

Luca and Dom both hold their guns at Carlo and Lou, jaws tensed and ready to follow my lead.

"No, Dante. Lui è con noi. Per favore. Per favore." *No, Dante. He's with us. Please.*

Please. Carlo and Lou yell over each other, holding up their hands.

My Glock points at Connor's forehead as I take an angry step toward him. "Why the fuck are you here? You get one answer. Make it count."

Connor is calm, adorned with a wide smile as my gun hovers inches from him.

"We have a mutual enemy, and I'm here to offer my help. Lou was gracious enough to call me and let me come. My father was always friendly with the Italians, and in that spirit, I'd like to help Luca and Dominic with the council meeting tonight."

"How'd you know about our meeting with the Irish council? Lou and Carlo didn't know," Luca pushes.

"I'm not the only one who wants things in our family to

return back to the old ways. This crew was named after my family, and Declan isn't one of us. He's a low-life who gunned his way to the top, killing good men like my father to run a family he should've never been accepted into. An O'Bannion has always run this crew, and I intend to see that happen again...with your help of course."

I stare at him, looking into his eyes. He's angry, and I believe him. Dropping my gun to my side, my brothers do the same.

"You want Declan dead?" I question.

"I do," Connor answers. "I can't touch him, but you can."

"Are you prepared to make sure your council is on board? Because we're not really asking. You need to understand that."

He gives a curt nod and looks back at me. "So, do we have a deal here? May I tag along?"

"You have a few hours tops to get a consensus before news gets out that Declan's dead. My brothers will be with you; they can let me know you did the job. Because, Connor, if you can't run your crew, they will."

I look at Carlo and Lou, jerking my head for them to follow as I leave Luca and Dominic to handle the diplomatic negotiations.

We approach the cars, and I see Nico, Antonio, and Vincenzo approaching with our bags.

"How many men do I have?" I bark, taking my duffle from Nico.

"As many as you want, Capo. Whatever we need to do, we're at your disposal," Carlo answers, pointing to the cars for the guys to take.

Lou pulls my door open, and I duck inside, throwing my bag next to me. "I'll make it worth your while. You can rest assured after today that the Sovranos will take care of the Scorleones."

They exchange an appreciative look and nod. "We'll take you to a spot about a mile outside Declan's place, and you can give everyone direction, then we can go in," Lou offers.

"Let's roll," I agree, before he shuts my door, the two of them climbing in the front of the car and bringing it to life.

The cars pull out in succession, one right after the other, each ready for what's ahead.

There's a calm that happens in moments of extreme violence. It's almost as if your mind needs to slow down so that it can detach from the adrenaline and emotion that's clouding your judgment and causing a person to make an irreversible choice.

But that doesn't happen for me. I'm present, void of the filter that stops normal people from killing. Because these deaths are just. Necessary. And a goddamn forgone conclusion.

"How do you want us to enter, Dante? His gate is guarded, and I fear it's too heavy to take the car through," Carlo offers as he pulls on his black leather gloves.

"I've got the guard. I'll handle the door, boss," Antonio says coolly, checking his gun.

"Then we're ready. Whatever happens, she gets pulled from that fucking house. I don't care if I'm lying dead on the ground. You get her out of that house and take care of her like she's my fucking widow. Am I understood?"

"Understood" is answered back to me from around the room.

Antonio, Vincenzo, and Nico walk past me, each giving my shoulder a pat as they do. I take a deep breath and follow them, heading outside to the cars. Antonio jumps into the lead car, pulling out first. The rest of us check our guns again before climbing into our cars to roll out in darkness.

It's a ten-minute drive, tops, but it feels like a damn hour. The car is silent, only the whispers of death spoken into our ears, preparing us for what we're about to do.

"How are we going to know if Antonio got to the guard?" Carlo questions as he slows the car, turning off the headlights. The elaborate iron gates come into view, and I know my girl is behind them.

I'm coming, Billy.

My head pushes toward the window as we wait anxiously for a sign that Antonio's done his job.

"Maybe he got caught?" Lou worries, but I shake my head, a cruel anticipation playing across my face as I watch the gates come to life, opening slowly.

We pull in covertly past the guard station, Antonio's face coming into view as he unscrews his silencer. Behind him a man is lying at his feet with a single shot blackening his forehead.

"Go," I bark out, and the car peels out, rushing the front entry. We barrel out, men pouring out from every ride. Before we give them too much time to prepare, I charge the front door, lifting my foot and kicking it the fuck in.

Melee erupts, clicks come from every direction. But I'm undeterred, knowing that for every one of his men, I have five.

"Bring me Declan," I thunder, my voice echoing through the room as I walk to the middle of the vaulted entry flanked by staircases.

When nobody moves, I stalk over to the first motherfucker I see and pull my trigger, executing him where he stands. His body crumbles to the floor as I turn in a circle, my arms spread wide.

"Bring me Declan or everyone dies. Look around—you're outnumbered," I yell, enjoying the indecision and fear on the assholes' faces.

His slimy fucking voice comes from behind me, and I spin, locking eyes with him.

"Don't you mean Sarah?" Declan counters.

He walks toward me, stopping about three feet away, and tilts his head. "I have to give it to you—using her was a good distraction. It's something I would have done. Maybe we're more alike than we realize."

Declan's eyes scan the room, and I see his mind start spinning. He's outnumbered.

"I'm here for my girl. Bring her out, and maybe I'll let you die quickly," I counter.

He takes a step backward with a smug look, as if he has the upper hand. "That's a great idea. We should ask her...she would know how alike we are since she's had both of us inside her."

My finger taps against the trigger of my gun as I stare at him. "I told you I'd make you choke on every word. I'm here to do just that."

Declan lifts his hand, snapping his fingers, and two men in suits come into view behind him, each tugging on one of her arms, shuffling her forward.

"Dante," she breathes out, and my heart drops.

She's battered. Barely recognizable. Covered in bruises and cuts. Her breathing is so shallow like it's hard to inhale, probably because of broken ribs, and I feel as if I'm on fire. Like all the wounds on her body are on mine.

But it's the dog leash around her neck that shifts something inside of me. Fracturing my reason and my logic.

No,no,no,no,no. He put her on a leash...on a goddamn leash.

My gun begins to tap against my temple as my chest heaves. Rage courses through me, giving life to each of my darkest thoughts. I'm gonna make him suffer. I'll make them all fucking suffer.

I drop my gun back to my side, staring at her face, letting all the marks burn their way into my memory as Declan says what will be his last words.

"Now, maybe you'd like to negotiate. Be smart, or she gets to feel real pain."

My eyes shift back to him, a calm possessing my body. I have one singular objective.

He dies.

I cut the head off the fucking snake and then chop up the body.

I rush toward him, my teeth gritting so hard they may break, and his eyes grow wide as I press the tip of my gun against his forehead. "I'm gonna gut you so slow for every goddamn mark you've put on her."

I grab the back of his head and press the barrel harder into his skin until I hear her scream out in pain. My eyes shoot up as I throw Declan back to see one of the suits who's holding her is biting her cheek as her face contorts in pain while she struggles.

My voice roars in a thunderous clap as the guy Antonio is holding his gun toward falls to the ground, from the bullet in his head. Antonio pivots towards the suits, and charges them, pointing his gun to lead the direction.

I catch something out of the corner of my eye, and my head swings to Declan, who's wracked with panic as he starts to bolt. My mind goes silent as bullet after bullet pierces Declan's chest, throwing his body back in quick jerks as he falls to the ground.

The men holding Sarah are frozen in place, but begin to tug her backward as I turn to face them. My gun swings in their direction, empty clicks sounding through the room as I close the distance.

"Nobody can help you now, not even God himself, because I'm not only taking your lives, I'm gonna keep your fucking souls."

Antonio grabs the suit on her right by the head and tosses him back, pulling a screaming Sarah away from her biter as he does.

Gunshots begin to ring out around the room, creating a fervor. I launch onto the asshole who hurt her, ramming the butt of my gun down onto his face as I fall into a haze. My voice explodes out of my body as a guttural cry rips from my throat.

"You don't ever touch her. You don't ever fucking touch her!"

I hear his teeth crack as I pound his soft flesh into a mangled, bloody, deformed version of a face. I grab the sides of his head and pick it up, knocking it back onto the tiled surface, feeling the crack in his skull begin to give more and more.

Hands grab at me, pulling me back onto my ass, dragging me away as I try and get back to beat his lifeless body. I'm crazed, alive through death, unable to pull myself out.

Warm arms wrap around my neck, and a body presses against me. Her voice fills my ear.

"You came. I love you. It's done. Dante, it's done. I love you. Thank you."

My hands scramble up her back, pulling her in closer as we sit in the middle of the floor locked in our embrace. My heart beats slower as she pulls me from the darkness I was sheathed in, allowing the devil inside of me to do his work.

Sarah pushes back to look at me, her eyes glistening as tears stream down her face, making streaks through a smudge of blood on her cheek.

My lips find hers, and I breathe her in before breaking our kiss. "You knew I'd come. There's no version of us where I don't show."

"I know."

She wraps her arms around me, and we don't speak as I

push off the ground, refusing to put her down. I stand, glaring around the room at the death and destruction, taking stock of my soldiers.

"Burn it to the ground," I direct to Antonio, pulling Sarah even closer to me.

She buries her face into my neck as I walk us out.

"Don't look back, Billy. It was all a nightmare, and you'll never have to be afraid again."

Chapter Thirty-One

Sarah

I shoot up from the bed, gasping. My limbs are a sweaty, tangled mess gathered up in the sheets of the bed. With fear still pulsing through my veins, my hand reaches for my throat to calm myself, to remind me where I am. As my fingers skim the delicate necklace I demanded was given back to me the minute we arrived back in Chicago, I close my eyes. "I'm okay. It's over."

My breaths come out slow and long, and I wipe my hair from my forehead and steady my pulse, glancing around the room, wondering where Dante has gone. He hasn't left me alone for the entire day we've been back.

Pushing to the edge of the bed, I place my feet on the floor, looking over my shoulder when I hear his deep laugh come from the living room of our hotel suite.

My shoulders fall thinking about Dante's apartment. Everything was destroyed, burned to ash. I'm just thankful nobody was hurt. Most of the damage was contained to his apartment, but we're still homeless. But we have Matteo. I've never been happier to see my friend.

I wiggle my toes on the carpet before I stand, walking to the chair and pulling on the luxurious hotel robe, tying it in the front. I follow the voices out of the door and see Dante with his men—Nico, Vincenzo, Matteo, and Antonio—all sitting on and around the couches.

They look happy. It's strange to think that the men most fear have become the ones I'm the happiest to surround myself with.

Dante looks over to me tenderly, and I can see that my bruises still bother him. He would bring those bastards back to life just to kill them again for what was done to me.

"Sorry, I didn't mean to interrupt your meeting. I just couldn't sleep..." *Alone. I couldn't sleep without you.*

Dante opens an arm, inviting me onto his lap. "You are never interrupting anything. Come sit."

I pad over, the guys giving me nods and grins as I walk by. I return the smiles, even though it hurts, and crawl into Dante's arms, pulling my legs up. He closes his arms around me and kisses the top of my head.

"Are you okay?"

I nod and put my head onto his shoulder as Antonio gives me a reassuring wink.

"How'd Luca and Dom fare with the council?" Matteo questions, looking almost as battered as I am.

My bottom lip pops out in a small pout as I look at him, and he grins, motioning between us, mouthing, "Twins." I reach for my face as if horrified, and he touches his ribs, wincing when he starts to laugh.

Dante rubs his hand down my back as he speaks.

"Turns out that the Irish crew was more than happy to give their blessing. Declan didn't make any friends with the way he came into power. As a show of their gratitude for what we did, the Irish are working a gun deal with our Boston family. It should be pretty sizeable and beneficial to all involved. And Connor O'Bannion is back in his rightful place, and he knows he owes me a favor should I ever call one in."

My head tips up as my eyes grow wide. Dante doesn't talk business in front of me.

"Should I go?" I whisper.

He looks down at me, shaking his head. "Why would you do that, Billy?"

My eyes shift around the room and back to Dante. "Because...you're talking about business...I'm not..."

Dante looks out at the men. "Anybody object to Sarah being here?"

Antonio pipes up from across the couch, pulling my attention his way, "Come on, Sarah, you're one of us. You put that shit in blood the minute you took a beating for us."

My brows narrow in as I sit up, trying to understand him. I look back at Dante, who runs his thumb over my sore cheek.

Nico leans forward. "Yeah, and even though I think it was stupid for you to go it alone, what you did, that was stand-up."

I can't say anything. I've been practically alone my entire life, raised by men who hated me, ignored me, disregarded me, and used me for what they could gain.

But as I look around the room, listening to what they're saying, I realize this is the first time I've felt like I belong somewhere. Not just with Dante but with his family too.

"You're a part of us now, and forever, Billy. You're a made woman." Dante teases pulling a smile to my lips.

My fingers roll the belt from the robe around my fingers. "Can I ask a question?" Dante nods.

"What happened to my father and brother? Did you guys go after them or just come for me?"

Vincenzo squats down by the couch, his hands curving

around the arm. He has the kindest eyes, but I know what he's going to say won't be that.

"I took care of it, Sarah. The official cause of death will be a heroin overdose, but it was in no way that easy. I made sure it lasted hours and hours. I wanted them to beg and go unheard. But I thought it was fitting for them to go out by the thing they were so desperate to possess."

My hand darts out and cradles his cheek. "Thank you."

It takes everything inside of me not to cry. Although, these tears wouldn't be sad ones, they'd be joyful, but I won't ever shed another tear about my past or the demons that haunted me.

He pats my hand as he stands, letting it fall back to Dante's chest. I turn to the group and pat my cheeks, taking a steadying breath.

"This doesn't mean I like any of you." I laugh lightly. "But thank you will never be enough."

Dante pulls me back into his chest as we all sit in silence for a moment. His voice vibrates against my shoulder as he fills the space. "I have a question. What if we didn't come? What would you have done?"

Without so much as a pause, I answer, "I would've killed Declan myself and then come home."

I hear a rush of breath, and then Matteo laughs. "You better marry her, or I will."

Dante's chest shakes as he laughs, and it makes me think back to the last words he said to me before all hell broke loose.

My chin tips up, taking in his scruffy cheek. "You still not wanting to be my boyfriend?"

His mouth pulls at the ends into a smile as he twists his head to the side, connecting with my eyes.

"You wanna be called wifey?" he croons, pulling his bottom lip between his teeth.

"Is that a proposal?"

We sit staring at each other, the room noticeably silent. His face is unreadable, as always, but it doesn't matter because I know he feels what I do. There is no place I'd rather be than right by his side for eternity.

Dante breaks our connection and looks out at the room.

"Someone go wake up a fucking judge."

———

Two hours later, I'm standing in a long oversized white T-shirt that belongs to Dante in the middle of the hotel suite surrounded by my new family.

A barely awake city judge, still in his pajamas, looks between us, pausing before he starts.

"We'll have to fudge the date on the official paperwork for after you're declared a widow..." The judge's eyes shift to Dante's smiling face.

"Oh, he's dead, Judge...news just travels slow."

The judge's brow shows his discomfort with the admission, but he can't do anything even if he wanted to. But I'm not sure he would anyway. After I explained his initial worry away, telling him I looked like this by my former husband, it's amazing how understanding even the most law-abiding man became.

"Okay, well," the judge says, adjusting the Bible in his hand. "Let's begin. Sarah, do you..."

My hand shoots out to Dante's chest. "No," I blurt out as Dante looks at me with raised brows.

I giggle and shake my head, waving to the room. "That's not what I meant." Clearing my throat, I add, "Seraphina. My real first name is Seraphina."

The room erupts in laughter and claps as I give a tiny shrug to Dante's amused face. He leans down, kissing my lips softly then pulls back to look at me. "Goddamn, Billy, you keep things interesting."

We look at the judge as he begins our wedding ceremony.

"Do you Seraphina O'Malley take Dante Sovrano to be your husband, to have and to hold from this day forward—"

"Yes," I breathe out excitedly, cutting off the judge, who lets out a small laugh and turns to Dante.

"Dante?"

"Abso-fucking-lutely," he agrees grabbing my waist and pulling me toward him to plant the deepest kiss against my lips.

Our tongues swirl as my arms raise and wrap around his neck as he bends over me, kissing me senseless amongst the cheers and applause. The judge yells over everyone in order to be heard.

"By the power vested in me by the state of Illinois, I now pronounce you man and wife. You can keep kissing your bride."

Dante laughs into my mouth and lets his hand walk down my body, then dips his shoulder, hauling me up and over as I squeal.

He stands and the cheers erupt again. "Now get the fuck out. I got work to do."

I can't even look up as he walks us into the bedroom because my cheeks are on fire.

The bedroom door closes behind us, and he sets me to my feet, grabbing the ends of my T-shirt and lifting it slowly over my head.

"I'm going to bury myself inside you until neither of us can remember our names." "Yes, please."

Dante's fingertips skim over my body, starting at my hips and making their way up the dip of my waist. He moves tenderly past my sore but unbroken ribs, brushing over the swells of my breasts to lay flat on my chest, then running up and over my shoulders to cradle my neck. His thumbs come under my chin to tip my head back, locking our eyes.

"You don't have to be gentle with me, Dante. I won't break."

His head drops as his tongue runs across my top lip before caressing and kissing his way to my ear.

"I want to take my time, savor every moan, feel your body ignite around my cock. Tonight, I want it slow because I want to memorize every moment the first time I fuck my wife."

My hands grip his hard biceps as his lips start their torturous assault of my neck, his mouth and tongue against my skin. Sighs push through my partially opened mouth as my head moves with the movement of his kiss on my neck.

"That feels so good it should be illegal."

"I plan on murdering your pussy, so that's fair." He smiles into my throat.

A moan escapes my lips as our hands roam and brush over each other, exploring and blazing a trail of heat wherever we touch.

"You will tell me if I hurt you. Do you understand?"

"I will," I breathe, "But I want you...the way I like you best. Rough."

I can see Dante considering my words before he grabs my thighs and lifts. Hoisting me up, I wrap my legs around his waist as he walks us toward the bed.

He nips at my collarbone, and I run my hand over his shaved head, letting my head fall back. His knee dips down on the bed as he lays me back, crawling over top, nestling between my spread legs.

"Are you going to make love to me, Dante?" I taunt, feeling his fingers dig lightly into my hips as he presses his hard cock against my center.

"I'll do whatever the fuck I please. Don't forget your place, Billy."

My entire body comes alive, begging, desperate to be fucked. Even with a soft touch, his words are wielded like a threat. There's no way this man could ever be fucking gentle. It's not in his DNA.

He doesn't answer in words; instead, he growls into my breast as he pulls my nipple into his mouth, sucking hard and flicking it with his tongue.

"Dante," I moan, writhing under him.

Dante sits up between my thighs, looking menacing, just how I like him.

"You're gonna get fucked, Billy."

My heads nods enthusiastically in response, every nerve ending standing at attention.

"Careful what you wish for."

He stands, his massive body looming over me, as his words are spoken without a hint of negotiation.

"Roll over."

I let out a tiny breath, swallowing, before I twist my body over slowly to lay flat on my stomach.

Silence surrounds us until I peek over my shoulder just as a strong hand slaps directly across my ass, leaving a delicious sting and heating me up.

"Fuck. Thank you" I whisper into the comforter.

"Don't thank me yet," he warns, his voice filled with the gravel that makes him so fucking sexy. "Scoot to the edge, slowly. And press your clit against the bed as you do it."

My entire body shudders as I drag myself down the bed, pressing my pelvis forward, feeling the friction. As my legs drop off the bed, I use my hands to push me down until my feet solidly touch the floor.

"Spread 'em."

I take tiny steps out, my legs spreading wide, open for him to do whatever he wants to me.

"What's your word?"

"Mercy."

The word comes out in a rush as I feel his fingers push inside of my pussy, bucking me forward.

"Hold still," he demands, pressing my lower back to the bed as he pumps his fingers inside of me, owning me. "You're so fucking tight and wet."

My breath comes out in pants, my fingers gripping the blanket, bunching it into my palms from the sweet crime of seduction his fingers are committing.

I hear the zipper of his slacks open, and I close my eyes. Biting my lip, the sweet anticipation of him assails my pussy, making me wet.

He presses against my entrance, teasing it, circling the head of his cock. It's a welcomed torture. Pushing up to my tiptoes, I try and move backward to get closer, needing him inside me.

My wetness slicks the head of his cock as he pushes in the smallest measure, pulling back only to repeat the motion over and over.

"Beg for it," he grits out cruelly, and I fucking melt.

"Fuck me."

"Not enough," he scolds, gripping my ass and squeezing the muscle hard.

"Fuck me. Destroy me. Ruin me," I chant like a prayer.

His cock thrusts inside of me, halting my breath. Dante's hand weaves through my hair, pulling my head back as his other digs into my hip bone, unleashing an onslaught of merciless fucking. Primitive, animalistic fucking.

Dante pounds into me from behind in full control of my body as I hold on, savoring the erotic scene with absolute pleasure.

His hard cock fills me to the hilt until my moans and gasp becomes screams, begging to come. Begging him not to stop.

The tingle starts in my toes, working its way up as I begin to feel every muscle in my body begin to tense and freeze, taking me into my bliss.

"Dante!" I thunder as I hear him groan, releasing inside me.

We're frozen, connected to one another and unable to move as the rhythm of our panting beats against the silence of the room.

My fingers uncurl, feeling stiff from the blanket I gripped for dear life as my breathing slows. His fingers massage through my hair, and I rest my head on the bed.

I can't speak as he lies over me, kissing my shoulders, still inside of me.

"Tell me."

His voice is tender as he asks, still brushing my body with reverent kisses. Swallowing, I open my eyes and lick my lips.

"I'm more than okay, and I love you."

His lips kiss the soft spot right behind my ear.

"I love you isn't enough because you'll always be my everything, Mrs. Sovrano."

"Then I guess we'll just have to devote ourselves to finding a new word because you'll always be mine, too."

Epilogue

Dante, One Week Later

"*Scusami.*" *Excuse me.*

The tailor interrupts me and my brothers, holding up another fitted tuxedo shirt for me to try on. I've been here for an hour being fitted for my goddamn wedding tuxedo. The things I do for this woman.

I shrug off the previous shirt I'd tried but couldn't button.

"You're so swole," Luca teases like the asshole he is.

"Who the fuck says that?" Dom chimes in as he adjusts his bow tie.

"Shut it, dick." I laugh, rolling my eyes at Luca. "He's just jealous because I can kick his ass... Need a reminder?"

Luca grumbles, undoing his collar. "Fucking monkey suits. I've never enjoyed them."

I nod my agreement as our tailor, Sal, helps me into my shirt. I push my arm through the sleeve, but Sal stops, looking at me with concern. I pull my brows together, confused by his abrupt halt.

"Sal. Why are we stopping?" I ask over my shoulder.

"I apologize, signore. I didn't want to hurt you."

His old eyes drop down to where the nasty scar from my first and only gunshot wound mars my arm.

"It's fine, old man. Your eyes are tired. That's an old wound." I frown, the memory flitting through my mind.

He laughs and continues to help me on with my shirt, and my brothers look at me solemnly, knowing that I didn't just lose some skin and blood that day.

"If you don't mind me asking..." Sal coaxes, his curiosity getting the better of him.

"It's a gunshot wound," I answer, staring ahead as I fasten the buttons up my chest.

The surprise on his face is evident by his wide eyes. "I hope they paid for that, Mr. Sovrano. Who would be stupid enough to shoot you?"

My face grows serious at the thought.

"My late wife."

"Oh, I'm sorry. Excuse me for a moment," the old man says softly as he walks away to answer a ringing phone.

Luca doubles over laughing, and Dom spreads his arms, smiling at me like I'm crazy.

"What?" I bark, turning toward them.

Dom throws a shiny black dress shoe in my direction. "You dumb fuck. You said my late wife."

I lift my leg, dodging the loafer, and shrug. "And? She is fucking late—she was supposed to be here twenty minutes ago to approve these damn outfits. I don't even know why she's making us do this again. The first time was perfect."

Luca shakes his head, still laughing. "You've been speaking Italian too much—you said it like she's dead not tardy, dick."

I look at him and then start to laugh a deep rumble, just as she walks through the door. My laughter doubles as the tailor gives Sarah a sad nod as she walks by.

Sarah looks at me confused, and Luca almost falls off the bench he's sitting on from laughing too hard.

"What's so funny?" she questions with light in her eyes.

"Nothing, Billy." I deflect and reach for her just as she gets close enough. "Just a translation issue. Come here."

My lips slip between hers as I pull her close and kiss her deep.

Sarah pushes against my chest and breaks our kiss, smiling before she opens her eyes.

"You look handsome."

My hands travel down to her ass and squeeze. "You look edible. Let's do the honeymoon right now." I look over my shoulder at my brothers and grin. "Get out."

She rolls her eyes and slaps at my chest. "Technically, we're already married, so..." She shrugs.

My eyes lock with hers. "I'll give you anything you want. Tomorrow, I'll stand up in that damn church and give you the wedding you've always dreamed of. Then I'm going to take you away and make sure I give you the one thing you've always deserved."

"What's that?" she questions sweetly.

"Your own family." I wink, rubbing a hand over her stomach, watching the happiness explode on her face.

Sarah, Christmas Day

"Keep your eyes closed," I snap as Dante tries to pull my hands from covering his face as I ride piggyback toward our new dining room.

The house was my Christmas present along with the first family dinner we had last night on Christmas Eve.

"Just a little closer. A little closer." Dante tilts his head, trying to bite at my hand, and I giggle. "Okay, stop."

I let my hands fall as he lowers me to the ground. The moment my feet hit the floor, I run out in front of him and spread my arms in a "ta-da" motion.

"What is this...what did you do, Billy?" he asks, taking in the twenty small white boxes all over the table.

I can barely hold back my excitement as I explain. "I was struggling to figure out what to get you for Christmas."

Walking to the table, I start to open the lids. "And then it hit me. I know it isn't your birthday, but..."

"Oh shit, Billy..."

Dante is grinning ear to ear as he takes a step forward, peeks inside one of the boxes, and sees white frosting with "Happy Birthday" written in delicious swoops.

"Are you happy?" I whisper, wrapping my arms around his waist.

He stares down at me with so much love in his eyes that if I'm never any happier than I am in this moment, my life will be perfect.

"Happy isn't enough to describe what I feel." His thumb brushes my hair to tuck behind my ear and his eyes falter, "You've given me more than I deserve and more than a man like me has a right to ask for. But Billy..." Dante bows his head, closing his eyes and stands silent unable to finish his sentence.

The moment is too much for him because I give him the one thing he's always needed.

Unconditional love. Squeezing him tighter, I press a kiss onto his chest and step back.

"Which do you want to try first?"

Dante looks up at me, happiness on his face. He jabs a

finger into the cake, scooping a chunk of frosting and holding it up to his mouth. But pauses, shifting his eyes down my body.

He takes his free hand and bunches the side of my dress pulling it up until my center is exposed and brings his cake-covered finger to my pussy, slathering it across my clit, grinning as he does it.

"I want to start here and work my way over your whole body with every fucking flavor, Billy."

Thank you for reading Dante and Sarah's fiery love story. If you loved this, then you'll be obsessed with Calder and Sutton!

Click here to read JUST LIKE HEAVEN!
He's a criminal—an abomination.
We're wrong in every way.
If only I could've convinced my heart.

His lips whispered promises of all the stars in the sky.
I dreamt of a love that would last forever.
We were gorgeously young and desperate for one another.

But we were star-crossed.
Fate had decided our course.
Leaving us to cling to each other as we crumbled to ash.

His need became possession.
My innocence turned jaded.
Our families declared war.
All that remained was hate.

But Calder was raised by wolves. The rules didn't apply.

I was his until he said otherwise—for better or for worse.

Our love story's bathed in crimson and drenched in bullets. *Because sometimes, Romeo comes with tattoos, guns, and a taste for blood.*

Click here to read JUST LIKE HEAVEN!

THE HOLIDATES SERIES

THE SCANDALOUS SERIES

THE STARCROSSED SERIES

THE KING BROTHERS SERIES

ACKNOWLEDGMENTS

I've never been so excited to put out a book. This one was special for me. The entire process turned me upside down but in the end. I truly believe it made me better. These two lived inside my head, fighting and loving non-stop. My fingers couldn't type fast enough to keep up sometimes...not every book speaks to you and this one sang. It was incredible and they will always be some of my favorites.

There are so many people to thank for this. It takes a village to give life to a book!

To my Team—you keep it real, and you keep it amazing. Thank you for continually taking a chance on me. It means everything. Jen, Michelle and Annette, Gretchen, Sandra, Rebecca, Sarah P., Sarah. Camila, Grazie! Hai davvero portato le parole all vita per me!

To my Posse—There are no words I could use that would describe the appreciation I feel for you loyalty, your faith, and your support. I am privileged you chose to be on this team, and I love you all so much!

Every single damn blogger that held it down for me, I see you. I'm so grateful to you for taking a chance on me.

And to THE READERS!!! Seriously, you guys rocked my world, you shared my cover and blurb and excerpts and everything. But mostly you shared in my excitement and hope. I love you for that.

You read. I'll write.

ABOUT THE AUTHOR

 #1 Amazon and USA TODAY Bestselling Author, Trilina Pucci, loves cupcakes and bourbon.

When she isn't writing steamy love stories, she can be found devouring Netflix with her husband, Anthony, and their three kiddos. Pucci's journey into writing started impulsively. She wanted to check off a box on her bucket list, but what began as wish fulfillment has become incredibly fulfilling. Now she can't see her life without her characters, her readers, and this amazing indie community.

She's known for being a trope-defier, writing outside the box and creating fictional worlds her readers never want to leave. With every book and each character, she's committed to writing book boyfriends worth binging and smut worth savoring.

Connect with Trilina and stay up to date.

Depraved

2019 © Trilina Pucci Books LLC

Cover Design: Kate Farlow

Editing/Proofing: My Brother's Editor, One Love Editing, All Encompassing Books

Printed in the United States of America ISBN-13: 978-1081056704

Printed in Great Britain
by Amazon

44028760R00165